IN MY TUDOR ERA

IN MY TUDOR ERA

A NOVEL

KATE BROMLEY

An Imprint of HarperCollinsPublishers

Without limiting the exclusive rights of any author, contributor, or the publisher of this publication, any unauthorized use of this publication to train generative artificial intelligence (AI) technologies is expressly prohibited. HarperCollins also exercise their rights under Article 4(3) of the Digital Single Market Directive 2019/790 and expressly reserve this publication from the text and data mining exception.

This is a work of fiction. References to real people, events, establishments, organizations, or locales are intended only to provide a sense of authenticity and are used fictitiously. All other characters, and all incidents and dialogue, are drawn from the author's imagination and are not to be construed as real.

IN MY TUDOR ERA. Copyright © 2025 by Kate Bromley. All rights reserved. Printed in the United States of America. No part of this book may be used or reproduced in any manner whatsoever without written permission except in the case of brief quotations embodied in critical articles and reviews. For information, address HarperCollins Publishers, 195 Broadway, New York, NY 10007. In Europe, HarperCollins Publishers, Macken House, 39/40 Mayor Street Upper, Dublin 1, D01 C9W8, Ireland.

HarperCollins books may be purchased for educational, business, or sales promotional use. For information, please email the Special Markets Department at SPsales@harpercollins.com.

Avon, Avon & logo, and Avon Books & logo are registered trademarks of HarperCollins Publishers in the United States of America and other countries.

hc.com

FIRST EDITION

Interior text design by Diahann Sturge-Campbell

Library of Congress Cataloging-in-Publication Data has been applied for.

ISBN 978-0-06-344404-1

$PrintCode

For Laura Schreiber, my phenomenal editor who made this book possible. I couldn't have taken this magical journey without you.

Chapter One

"Zoe, you know that I love you and support your life choices, but please don't meet up with this person."

My best friend gasps. She only saw Rupert's picture ten seconds ago, but her heartbreak is palpable. "Why? He looks like a poet who works in finance. He has a tortured past and a trust fund. And he's six-five!" She rams her phone into my face, and I barely manage to dodge it.

"There's no shot he's six-five, and that statement has so many red flags, I don't know which to tackle first." I push the phone away, careful not to swipe anything on her freshly opened dating app. "His facial hair is aggressive, and not in a good way."

"A man with a mustache isn't for the weak."

"He looks like all your exes," I tell her. "You're reaching for the past."

Zoe groans at my assessment. "Will you pull your psych degree out of your vag for one minute and embrace the opportunities in front of us?"

I look around as requested. We're in a dark, dank hallway of Hampton Court Palace. It's raining outside, and barely any better inside. The only people in our vicinity are an elderly tour group, and every one of them has a wet cough.

"Which opportunities are you referring to? We're in a museum on a Tuesday. We're also the only people in here who can use the stairs without assistance."

"You know what I mean," Zoe counters. "We're in England.

We're twenty-four. We're on a much-needed girls' trip and you'd rather be back in the room crocheting instead of meeting people and having fun."

Okay, this is where I draw the line.

"That is offensive," I retort. "I don't crochet, I embroider. And I happen to be at a critical point in my needlework."

Zoe shakes her head like a woman in mourning. "When you say shit like that, I swear a cold breeze washes over me. I can feel the wrinkles of despair taking shape on your tits." Zoe was a creative writing major. She has a way with words.

"That's a stunning visual. On that note, me and my sad, saggy tits are continuing on with the tour."

I make my way farther down the hall, discreetly adjusting the passport carry-case that I've been wearing under my shirt for the past eight days. It's more or less unisex lingerie for international travel documents, and I regret nothing.

Zoe catches up to me a second later, linking her arm through mine. "Lily, stop. I'm not trying to nag you. I just want you to take a break. You've studied and worked nonstop for the past seven years."

"I *am* taking a break," I assure her, glancing around until my gaze lands on an ornate painting. "And I'm having fun. Look, a portrait of a rich guy in a ruffled flea collar, and he has a mustache. Do you think he could join us tonight instead?"

"Depends on the age gap you're looking for," she replies, waggling her eyebrows.

I walked right into that one. "You are a troubled woman."

"I know," she says, giving my arm a squeeze. "I like that about me."

She nudges my side with her hip, and I can't hide my smile. Zoe is the spicy queso to my chips. She's a fearless, filter-less human chihuahua who will bite the kneecaps off anyone who dares to wrong me. In other words, she's the light of my life.

"Compromise. I'll tell Rupert to bring a friend and we'll all meet up at a pub. If they suck, we'll ditch them." I give her a semi-intrigued look and she goes on. "I just want you to put yourself out there again."

I take a deep breath, and Zoe makes her please-say-yes sad face, which she knows I can't resist. "Fine," I eventually answer. "But only because I'm touch starved and even a cordial handshake would sexually sustain me for the next six months."

"Yes!" Zoe cheers. "I'm going to make sure you have the best handshake of your life tonight!" I chuckle at her elation as we stop walking. "Now, I'm going to the chapel to beg forgiveness for the sins we're *definitely not* committing tonight." She unweaves her arm from mine, granting herself free rein to thrust her hips in her favorite dry-humping gesture.

"Should you really be doing that outside a place of worship?"

"Probably not. Learn some fun facts for me." She nudges her chin toward the headphones that are weaved around my neck, just above my fiery red hair.

I dutifully reposition the headset over my ears. "No. I refuse."

"See you in ten!" She disappears past a pair of thick wooden doors, and I turn to focus on the vast corridor in front of me. Heavy green curtains dangle down the tall, paneled walls. They're decorated with a delicate floral pattern, but it reminds me more of subtle snakeskin, seeming more sneaky than regal. Centuries-old artwork is framed over the fabric, varying in scale from massive to miniature. The cathedral windows lined opposite the paintings are my favorite. Speckled with the still-falling rain, they're gorgeously melancholy, and I have the insatiable urge to don my comfiest wool sweater and fill a journal with prose of female rage.

Alas, the palace closes at five thirty.

Stepping forward, I press play to resume my paused audio tour, and the steady British narrator picks up where she left off.

You are now entering the Haunted Gallery of Hampton Court Palace. In 1541, Catherine Howard, Henry VIII's fifth queen, learned that she was to be charged with adultery, a crime punishable by death. Legend has it that Catherine, terrified and desperate, broke free from her rooms and ran along the processional route in the hope of finding Henry in the Chapel. Just before Catherine reached the door, she was seized by guards, who dragged her away, struggling and screaming. If the king did hear her frantic pleas, they went unanswered.

I stop to stand in front of what seems to be a royal family portrait. Henry is sitting front and center, looking puffed-up, pale and constipated in his over-the-top kingly garb. If this is how he looked with Tudor-era airbrushing, then God knows what he looked like in real life.

Catherine was eventually beheaded at the Tower of London along with her suspected lovers, Thomas Culpepper and Francis Dereham. Her body remains entombed in the Chapel within the Tower walls. Many believe that Catherine's ghost can be seen running through this very gallery, wailing for mercy as she tries to reach the king. Catherine was Henry VIII's youngest queen. He was fifty at the time of her death and went on to marry again.

"Asshat," I mumble, switching off the recording and finding the king's likeness even grosser than I did ten seconds ago. A dependable theme in history is that there's a surplus of powerful perverts, and they always seem to be men. Thank goodness we no longer have that worry in modern times. Ha.

It's thoughts like these that've led to my current romantic dry spell. I tried to date, I really did. Especially last year. I approached my search for love like I would a psychosocial experiment—with curiosity, openness, and objectivity. Even when going for my PhD took everything out of me, I went on a date every other Saturday for six months, meeting up with potentially murderous Tinder dabblers and partaking in less perilous, though more embarrassing, singles' pickleball and game nights. Scientifically, my findings were a failed experiment. Non-scientifically, they were a dumpster fire. The DMs I received in the process were unadulterated nightmare fuel. If I had a dollar for every angry boner pic that sprung forth from my inbox like a haunted jack-in-the-box, I could buy this castle.

So, when Zoe suggested a girls' trip as a mental reset, it didn't take much to get me on board. She's a devout Anglophile who had her heart set on the windswept shores of England, and I was more than happy to hop the Atlantic with her. We've visited all the main tourist attractions, and today's visit to Hampton Court Palace is our last palatial hurrah. We're flying back into LAX in two days.

Reaching the end of the hall, I'm reading through a Haunted Gallery informational placard when I start to hear music playing. It's soft but insistent, leading me to look down at the audio device I'm holding. The screen still says it's paused. I pull the headphones off, but the music keeps playing, growing louder and louder. The melodic instrumentals have an underlying harshness to them. The beat is jittery. I can decipher an organ, a horn, and the sharp pull of strings. Maybe this is how they announce the palace is closing? I tilt my gaze up, trying to find the speaker system, but see nothing but the white painted ceiling.

"Excuse me," I say to a woman who's folding up a paper map a few feet away. "Do you know what that music is for?"

Her eyes are confused as she looks back at me. "What music, dear?"

"Sorry. Never mind." She walks past me as the music kicks up with a pulsing drumbeat. My ears start to thrum. Loud noises have always been overpowering for me, and as I feel the familiar tightening in my rib cage, a sweet, soft voice begins to sing.

"Pastime with good company, I love and shall
until I die. Grudge who lust but none deny,
so God be pleased thus live will I . . ."

The music surges, and I feel a slicing pain behind my eyes.

"Does no one hear that?" I lift my hands to my ears, trying to block out the screeching sound. I think I'm yelling, but I can't be sure. Whipping around to look for help, the few other visitors in the hall are either admiring the art or talking among themselves. No one has heard me. It's like they don't see me at all. The voice sings again, sounding so close that I start to wonder if it's coming from inside my own head.

"The best ensue, the worst eschew, my mind shall be.
Virtue to use, vice to refuse, thus shall I use me."

The lyrics fade into a high-pitched hum, and my chest constricts. I can't catch my breath. I'm slipping into a panic. I try to think of the calming techniques I recommend to my patients during their episodes, but all rational thought feels out of reach. The only word in my consciousness is "chapel." I need to get to the chapel. I don't know why, but I know that I do.

My life depends on it.

I take off in a run, and I don't stop. My thighs are burning, my heart is pounding, but I'm almost to the chapel doors. They're closed now. Weren't they open before? Everything else is muddled, but I can see the doors clearly. The chips in the dark wood. The rusted iron of the hinges. I reach my clammy hands out to push against them—they're so cold that they burn, and before I can force them open, everything goes dark.

"Catherine..."

This voice sounds far away. It's not Zoe's. Or the one I heard singing. This one is deep and steady. Pulling me back to break the surface even though I want to stay where I am.

"Can you hear me?"

I blink my eyes open as the world slowly comes into focus. I'm lying down with my back to the floor, and the first thing I see is a pair of soft green eyes. Mossy green with a ring of blue around the edges. I take in the bigger picture, finding that the eyes belong to man with a well-defined chin and wavy chestnut hair. He seems my age, no more than mid-twenties. His facial features are almost perfect except for his nose. It's crooked at the base, seeming forced back into place. He must have been in a fight or two. "Are you well?" he asks through a crisp British accent. He slips a hand under my back, helping me to sit up.

"I don't know," I answer. A wave of dizziness flares behind

my forehead as I take a deep breath. He smells like honey and smoke as he stays crouched down beside me, looking me over with a scrutinizing gaze. I notice that he's wearing a Renaissance costume. It's a cross between a male ballet dancer and a lacrosse player, and if I'm honest, it kind of works.

I look down and see that I'm in a costume too, and from Party City this dress is not. I can tell from the tension against my rib cage that I'm corseted in. I lift my arms, and my pale blue sleeves have intricate silver detailing and are heavy at the wrists. Judging from the weight against my lap, I must be wearing multiple skirts.

"Why am I dressed like this?" I ask the man. "Where is Zoe?"

The young man is puzzled, sitting back a little on his heels. "I don't know who that is. Shall I fetch one of the other ladies-in-waiting? Or a physician?"

I shake my head, twisting around to take in my surroundings. I think I'm still in the Haunted Gallery of Hampton Court Palace, but all the tourists are gone, including Zoe. The art and decor are different—still historic but newer. Less preserved, somehow. Maybe I'm in a back employee area. So many rooms were roped off and locked as Zoe and I walked around this afternoon. When I look forward, I see the chapel doors—the same ones I touched before I fell.

There's a pit in my stomach as I push myself up to a standing position, feeling the full bulkiness of my garb. I sway on my feet and the young man quickly stands as he reaches out to steady me. He has a hockey player's build and is tall enough that the top of my head barely reaches his chin. We're closer than I thought. His cheeks warm, though his expression stays composed, as he takes a step back.

"My apologies, Lady Catherine."

"My name is Lily," I tell him. "Did Zoe sign us up for an immersive experience or something? Because if she did, I'm not into it."

"Not into what?" he asks.

"Not into whatever this is." I end up raising my voice a bit, and I realize that I'm *also* speaking in a British accent. Not just out loud, but in my inner voice, too. Sweet Jesus. Whatever head injury I sustained must have been catastrophic. I keep my neck straight just to be safe.

"I think I need a CT scan. Can you help me get out of here? And do you know where my cell phone is?"

"What's a cell phone?"

I take a short, jagged breath. "Okay, I appreciate your commitment to the bit, but I need you to break character and tell me what the fuck is happening right now." The man just stares at me with his mouth slightly open and I try to remain calm. "What's your name? Or your character's name. Whichever."

He pauses before offering me a quick bow. "Lord Gainsford, at your service." Then he adds, "But I prefer Simon. I met you when you first arrived at the palace."

"Of course you did." I kick my squared-toe shoe at my ninety-pound skirt. "Listen, Simon, I need to get back to my hotel and then probably go to a hospital. I'm being held against my will, and if you don't let me go, you're facilitating a crime."

Simon furrows his brows and looks around before turning back to me, genuine concern softening his defined features. "Are you sure you are well, Lady Catherine? You don't seem yourself."

Anger creeps up my spine in a prickly burn. If I don't get the truth soon, I am going to fight someone. "You know what?

Never mind. I'll figure it out on my own." I walk off frustrated, growing even more frustrated when I sense Simon keeping pace behind me.

"It feels wrong to leave you in such a state," he says, his words floating over my shoulder.

"I'm fine!" I bark back. "Seriously, please go."

I walk faster, nearing the end of the hall when I pass an elaborate oval mirror fastened along the corridor. I catch my reflection out of the corner of my eye, and when I do, I stop walking. I also stop breathing. I retrace my steps and face the mirror fully. I stare and I stare, and it feels like the universe is closing in around me as I move close to the glass. My reflection isn't me. The girl looking back at me is slightly younger than I am. She's short and lithe, with a heart-shaped face and blue almond eyes. She's the college version of Sabrina Carpenter and is so naturally beautiful that it's almost upsetting.

I lean forward to get a better look. Simon stays at a fair distance behind me. His reflection is just as it should be.

"Why am I the only one who looks different in this mirror?" I ask quietly.

He says nothing, and I start to make little motions with my face. I raise my eyebrows. I scrunch my nose. Prettier-not-me matches every move.

I pull the veiled headband thing that I'm wearing off my head, running my fingers through the wavy hair that, according to the mirror, is sandy brown and at least a foot longer than mine. Dizziness surges again in my skull. My glorious Sadie Sink hair is my best feature. I've never dyed it. I never would. But I must have. I pull the unfamiliar locks between my fingers and look down, seeing and feeling them firsthand.

My hands aren't the same either. These hands are small and delicate and in no way look like they've been kissed by the California sun for twenty-four years. Every memorable trace of me is gone—along with my sanity.

I can't be another person. I'm having a psychotic episode induced by my fall. I suffered a traumatic brain injury. That would explain the hallucinations and my illogical English accent. But if that were the case, I doubt that I'd be aware of my psychosis. And Zoe would be here.

I slap myself in the face, and mirror-me does the same. "Wake up, Lily! Wake up right now." Switching gears, I start pinching myself anywhere I can reach. My cheeks, my arms, my new hands. My skin is blotched and red when I move on to my chest.

"Forgive me for asking, but is there a reason why you're tweaking your nipples?"

I glare at Simon, who is now standing beside me, looking like he's trying not to laugh. "Dude, get out of here! You're zero help whatsoever."

He clears his throat as he averts his gaze. "My apologies. I'll leave you."

I feel a flash of guilt as I look back to the mirror, watching as he turns and walks off. I'm still watching a half second later when his reflection freezes mid-stride.

"His Majesty, the king!"

We both hear the echoing voice. Simon immediately moves to the outskirts of the corridor. I focus back on my reflection and touch my cheeks. My hallucinations are so real. So petrifyingly real.

"Did you not hear? The king comes." I only just catch his tense words as Simon appears beside me again. The king comes?

Comes where? On what? "Turn about and curtsy," he says, grasping my wrist and pulling me back from the mirror. He's so much bigger than me that it takes minimal effort on his part. I glance up and catch a flicker in his eyes – impatience tempered by the urge to protect. He stations me a few feet to his left as the double doors burst open at the end of the hall. My eyeline snaps to the sound, just in time to watch the ostentatious arrival of a wall of a man. An older, bearded wall of a man.

He walks with authority and a pained limp. The laces of his red and gold costume are wide across his chest, and his massive sleeves are trimmed with fur. He moves through the space like he owns it. Judging by the entourage of ten-plus people trailing behind him, maybe he does.

He's close now, and I can't tear my eyes away. This is the king? Or the person they cast to play the king? Personally, I would have gone in a different direction. The "king" is right in front of me now. He looks to be in his fifties or sixties. His eyes seem younger, maybe due to the boyish smile he's casting down on me.

"Catherine, my darling." His voice is friendly as he reaches for my hand and places a kiss to my knuckles. "I know I promised that we would go out riding this morning, but there is an urgent meeting of the privy council. I shall see you for dinner this evening in my chambers and will think of nothing but you until then."

He gives my hand a tender stroke and walks off before I can register what the hell just happened. Looking down the hall after him, I inch closer to Simon.

"Who was that?" I ask in a hushed tone.

He looks back at me with real worry in his eyes. "I should think you know him well."

"Pretend that I don't."

Simon observes me for a second before he replies, "That was Henry VIII, Supreme Head of the Church of England."

He's so sincere. I can tell that he believes what he's saying, and it makes my head hurt. I watch the departing group continue to move down the corridor when "Henry" turns at the last moment, giving me another doting smile before he disappears through a set of doors.

"I must go," Simon says, now walking backward and following in the direction of the entourage, clearly an attendant of the "king's" meeting. "I wish you a swift recovery, Lady Catherine."

He gives me a careful look as he leaves, and just like that, I'm alone. A suffocating silence settles in the air, spurring me into action. I need to leave, too. I need to leave *now*. I power walk like a fiend, moving though endless halls and stairwells as fear tightens its grip on my throat.

Sweat is beading down my neck when I finally find a door leading out. The glaring sun hits my face and it's a complete contrast from the gray skies and rain that Zoe and I walked through no more than an hour ago.

There's a flurry of activity in the stone yard I find myself in, with hundreds of people dressed in different variations of old-fashioned clothing. This can't be a historical reenactment. There's a guy openly peeing beside a horse trough, and the signature scent in the air is inflamed body odor. I mix in with the crowd, getting bumped and jostled as I waddle along in my hoopskirt from hell. When I see a woman my age walking near a hay cart, I instinctively reach out and touch the sleeve of her simple brown dress. She stops to face me, and I try not to be intimidated by her epic stare down.

"I'm so sorry to bother you, but can you tell me where we are?"

The woman takes in my disgruntled hair and flushed face. She crosses her arms across the laces of her dress with an amused grin. "Well, you've seen better days, haven't you, love? We're outside the palace, aren't we?"

I nod my head and glance behind me, taking in a view of the palace from the outside. Then I turn all the way around. The exterior is different. There's no white stone that I saw with Zoe—only red bricks now. It's also more compact. Fortresslike. Something to fear as well as admire. This isn't the Hampton Court Palace I walked into this afternoon.

A nauseous wave comes over me as I turn back to the woman. "And by any chance, could you tell me what year it is?"

I have to actively push down the urge to hyperventilate as I wait for her answer. She seems unsure whether she wants to reply at all when she finally says, "It's the year of our Lord, 1540." I breathe noticeably harder at her response, and the woman whips her arm up to cover her mouth. "You better not have the sweat!" she wails. "First time I talk to you rich lot and now I'm off to die for it!" She marches away with her mouth still covered. A man dressed in purple finery with a greasy goatee walks past me next, and I step in front of him to block his path.

"Excuse me, what year is it?"

He barely gives me eye contact, only puts his hands up and pivots around me. "No, no. I don't speak to women. It's a personal choice. Please respect it." He continues on his way, and the crowd keeps moving, living their busy lives around me—their busy Tudor-era lives.

No. This can't be real. I can't be back in time. I just can't.

But I think I am.

Okay, I need to focus on leaving this place; then I can figure everything out. I spot an exit in the distance, across the yard and through a short tunnel. I could go on foot, but it's so hard to move in these clothes and I don't know where I'm going. There has to be another way.

Looking to my right, I see a saddled horse tied to a railing. The last time I rode, I was five and wore a sweat-marinated helmet provided by the petting zoo. But if I'm going to go a substantial distance, it's my only option. I nervously approach the animal, and the closer I get, the more I realize that horses are the size of dragons. I can only hope that it will trample me to death quickly, but as I place a hand on its coarse white hair, something strange happens—I innately know that I can ride this horse. It's an inexplicable feeling I have in my gut, so loud and brazenly clear. Giving in to the sensation, I grip the saddle and hoist myself up like I've done so hundreds of times.

When I sit astride the horse, my skirt bunches up, revealing the stockings covering my ankles and calves. A collective hush falls over the crowd as countless heads turn to look at me. The women are shocked. The men seem hungry. Time to go.

I bring my salacious legs down at the horse's sides with a firm kick, and we shoot off like a bullet through the yard. Adrenaline explodes in my chest as I sit deep in the saddle, aligning my body with the horse's spine as I laugh instead of scream. Riding a horse at full tilt is a freedom I've never tasted before. The sound of hooves smashing against the stone beneath us echoes in my ears as we erupt through and out of the tunnel leading beyond the palace walls.

I'm still equestrienne drunk when we mellow our pace a few minutes later. I bring the horse to a gradual stop on the dirt road we're on as I take in my new surroundings. There are grassy fields and trees as far as the eye can see. No electrical poles. No signs of technology. The impossible truth of where I am sets into my bones and sends a chill through me. I'm still deciding my next move when I notice a speck on the road in the distance. I shade my eyes as it gets closer and takes shape, revealing itself to be a horse and rider. In almost any other situation, I'd choose the bear rather than flag down an unknown man, but in this moment, I have to risk it.

The approaching horse slows as it nears, and I'm able to see the man astride it. He looks a little older than me, with tousled pitch-black hair that's just short of his shoulders. His plain Tudor clothes are marred with dust, and his handsome but tired face mirrors my suspicion. He squints into the sun to get a good look at me. A split second later, his hard expression shifts to unguarded recognition.

"Catherine?" he asks, almost in disbelief. I don't answer, and he instantly urges his horse forward, right next to mine. "Have I changed so much that you no longer recognize me?" His voice is inviting, almost magnetic—giving the impression that I *should* know him. "Or has the Dowager Duchess finally convinced you to hate the sight of Francis Dereham?"

Francis Dereham.

I know that name. Why do I know that name?

I focus inward to find the connection. I've always had a good memory, and my mind zips back to the audio tour I was listening to this afternoon. The narrator was talking about one of Henry VIII's queens. One that he killed. She was executed with her lovers—one of whom was Francis Dereham.

I meet his hopeful gaze and take a breath, fidgeting with the reins in my clammy palms.

"What year is it?" I ask him.

"It's 1540," he answers.

I stagger in the saddle. This is actually happening, then. "And what's my name?" I ask a few seconds later.

He doesn't hesitate. "Who could ever forget Catherine Howard?"

A sickly buzzing fills my ears. I'm back in time. I'm really, *really* back in time—that or I'm in a hospital bed somewhere, dying from a brain bleed as I stay trapped inside a fever dream.

The voice. This all happened after that voice sang to me in the haunted gallery. My logical mind knows that it's impossible. People don't get thrown back in time. But somehow I'm here, and according to everyone, I'm Catherine Howard. *Catherine Howard.* Her name flashes through my head next. I was listening to her miserable tale on my audio tour. Catherine Howard is the girl who marries the king and gets her head cut off.

Holy shit, they're going to cut my head off!

"Catherine, are you all right?"

I shoot eye daggers at him as only a yet-to-be-beheaded woman can. "Do I look all right to you?!"

He sits up in his saddle, his shoulders tensing nervously. "I suppose you seem a trifle vexed."

"That's putting it lightly. It was great to reconnect with you, Francis, but I have to go."

I kick the sides of my horse and he surges forward, leaving Francis and his horse in the dust as we go full throttle. I see an opening in a thicket of trees to the left and steer us into it. I need to come up with a plan, and I want off this open road.

Sharp branches slice at my cheeks as we race through the leaves. I can barely see two feet in front of me, and when I eventually can, I spot the fallen tree that's directly in our path. It's too steep to jump. I'll never make it. I pull hard on the reins, and the horse bucks up with a pained cry. I lose my seat and go tumbling backward through the air. It feels like I'm in slow motion as my body collides with the uneven ground. Only one thought occurs to me before I black out: I am royally fucked.

Chapter Two

I hear singing again. Or chanting. It could be chanting.

Whatever the musical mode, I let my muscles relax as I snuggle deeper into my blanket, basking in the sleepy realization that I'm home in bed. I keep my eyes closed and pull the blankets up higher, running my hands over the surface and feeling the rich velvet beneath my fingers. I freeze mid-stroke when I remember that my blanket at home is a down comforter and is definitely not made of velvet.

Just then, the bed slumps, and I slant toward the weight that's now resting on the mattress beside me.

"Catherine? Can you hear me? The whole court is talking about your accident. The king has ordered every mass at Hampton Court to be said for your recovery. You're missing out on all the fun."

God damn it.

I creak my eyes open, and a freckled young woman is smiling down at me. She eagerly grabs my wrist and lays her fingers flat against my pulse as her eyes sharpen in concentration. A few seconds later, she drops my hand back to the mattress.

"I knew you were awake," she says with friendly impatience. "Your heart has been steady for hours, and your eyes twitch when I let the light in. Observe."

She hops up from the bed, moving to the windows and whipping the curtains open. I shield myself from the sun like a freshly turned vampire, which makes her chuckle.

"Are you a doctor?" I ask as she moves back to my side.

The girl plops onto the bed. "Your wit is still intact. That's a good sign." She turns to a man in a page boy outfit whom I didn't notice by the door. "Tell the king that Lady Catherine is awake. Tell Mistress Marshall as well."

He opens the door and scurries from the room, and the girl shifts forward to slide a hand under the small of my back. "Sit up slowly now. No brash movements."

I do as instructed, and as I become vertical, I see a small platoon of older women standing in the corner. The chanting culprits have been unmasked. The main one in front is slinging incense from a metal ball and chain as the rest remain focused on the prayer they're reciting—or the spell they're casting. One of the two.

"Do they have to stay?" I ask the girl.

She quirks her lips as she turns away from me to face them. "Ladies! Ladies!" The group pauses their religious rigors as my not-doctor gets up to speak to them. "Thank you for all you have done today. As you can see, our prayers were answered. The king will know of your pious victory."

They look between themselves as the girl gingerly ushers them from the room. She closes the door and leans back against the sturdy wood.

"I'm surprised you had me send them off," she says. "You usually revel in being the center of attention."

There's no bitterness in her voice, only warm amusement, and I get the sense that I can trust her. I sit up against the pillows behind me, fully observing her. Judging from her face, I'd guess she's a few years younger than me. Maybe the same age as I apparently am now. Auburn hair peeks out from under the front of her veiled headpiece, and her long rust-colored dress makes her look like a mix between Maid Marian and the young nun from *Sister Act*.

"You must know me pretty well," I tell her.

She shrugs. "I know you well enough. I'm very observant, and you're quite forthcoming with your thoughts." She moves toward me again, this time opting to sit in the wooden chair beside the bed. "Now tell me, what on earth possessed you to ride out alone? When that man carried you back, Mistress Marshall nearly fell into fits. You know that old crone hates us."

"Who's Mistress Marshall?" I ask. Then, for good measure, "And just to clarify, what's your name?"

The girl leans forward with a discerning gaze, moving her finger in front of my face and tracking my eye movements. "Perhaps your fall did more damage than I thought. My name is Bessie Stanley, and I've been your friend since we arrived at the palace six months ago." Surprise alights her face a second later. "Wait, are you with child, Catherine? Get your legs up and we'll have a look." She eagerly stands, and I pin the blankets to my waist like a roller-coaster lap bar.

"I'm not pregnant," I assure her.

"How can you be sure? I have no doubt that the king would be pleased if you were."

I reactively grimace. The king seems nice enough at the moment, but the thought of him being my baby daddy is pretty fucking sinister.

"I'm sure because I haven't done *that* in over a year."

Bessie rolls her eyes, giving me a "sure, Jan," kind of look. "Of course you haven't," she says. "Is your memory really altered, Catherine, or are you playacting?"

I slide my hips back as I sit up taller on the mattress, trying to gauge how I should approach this. I need to be smart. I need to use everything I can to my advantage.

"Things just feel fuzzy," I decide to say. "It must be from the accident. Maybe that's why I don't seem like myself."

Before Bessie can respond, my bedroom door swings open, revealing the entrance of a severe woman in a gray dress with a mean downturn to her mouth. Her headpiece isn't rounded like ours. It's pointy like a roof, and she says nothing as she stops to stand in the center of the room.

Bessie's gaze lowers. "Good afternoon, Mistress Marshall."

The woman scowls at her in return before focusing on me. "You're awake."

I carefully nod, and Bessie steps closer to my side. "She is, thankfully. I'm sure you're relieved, as are we all."

If "relieved" means unleashing violent hellfire from her eyes, then yes, this lady is very relieved.

"And tell me, Catherine Howard, just what were you doing outside the palace walls?"

I turn to Bessie, and she nudges her chin for me to answer. "I don't remember exactly," I hear myself reply.

Before I can say more, Bessie shoves my head back into the pillow. "Her fall seems to have addled her mind, Mistress Marshall. These things sometimes happen after such an injury."

The woman takes a step closer. "In that case, let me remind you that I am the mistress of the maids and any dishonor you bring to yourself, you also bring unto me."

"I'm sure the malady is only temporary," Bessie says. "No doubt Catherine will be back to her captivating self in an hour, and she is so very grateful for your concern."

"So grateful," I echo. "Very grateful."

The woman pauses before turning to Bessie. "If she is recovered, the king will want an audience with her. See to it that she reaches him without incident."

"Yes, Mistress Marshall," Bessie replies.

With a final stare and a slow exit, Mistress Murder leaves the room, closing the door behind her with a *thud*.

Bessie and I let out a collective breath. I'm not someone who's easily intimidated, but I might have just peed a little.

"Well, that was fun," Bessie muses. "Worry not, Catherine. Once we are married, she won't be able to lord over us anymore. We'll be ladies of the court, and she will remain just as she is. Then I'll tell her what I think of her."

"Will you really?" I ask skeptically.

Bessie takes a beat. "No. I would cut off a toe rather than look her in the eyes." A second later she claps her hands together and flings back my blanket. "All right. You heard the woman. The king doesn't like to be kept waiting. I'll fetch a maid to assist you."

My mouth is open to respond, but the door has already shut behind her. Alone with my thoughts and the after-smell of scary lady and incense, I twist to lower my feet to the floor. I get up slowly, thankful that I don't feel dizzy as I begin to walk the length of the room. I think best when I'm moving, and right now, I need a game plan.

I need to get home. That's my number one priority. My only priority. No—I also need to fit in, avoid suspicion, and not get my head cut off from my body. I need to accomplish all these things, but if I'm going to accomplish any of them, then I need to understand the rules. Knowledge is power, always.

I pause by the window, watching as the sun begins to set. My hand twitches. I want to check my phone to see the time. I want to look up everything I can about Catherine Howard so I can figure out what to do. What *not* to do. If I learn from her mistakes, then I can do better, and I can get out of here with my head intact. I need to be calm. I need to be strategic. And I *need* to get back to the Haunted Gallery.

My white nightgown brushes the bed as I continue to pace, and a soft knock sounds at my door. A no-nonsense-looking woman in a simple dress enters, telling me that she's here to dress me. I don't know which of us is less excited.

Thirty minutes later, I'm sewn into what feels like an inflexible scuba suit on top and multiple parkas on the bottom. The dress itself is beautiful, emerald green with touches of gold. I try to carry it gracefully, but I'm pretty sure I look like Bigfoot who just got spotted in the wild. I stay at Bessie's side as we make our way to the king's rooms, and I feel jumpier with every matching step we take.

"What do you think about my relationship with the king?" I prompt her. I want to ask for specific details. How did it begin? How far has it gone? But open-ended questions and active listening will enable me to learn the most.

Bessie looks at me with an inquisitive upturn to her eyebrow before glancing forward. "It's an honor, of course. The king adores you, and you have certainly benefited from his attention."

I stay quiet, hoping she'll want to fill the silence. A second later, she does.

"I know you said that you know what you're doing, but do you truly, Catherine? Being the king's favorite is thrilling, to be sure, but four queens have already sat on the throne, only to be plucked back off again in some way or another."

Well, I'm glad old Catherine knew what she was doing, because I sure as hell don't. We stop at a pair of heavily armed doors, and Bessie studies them before turning back to me. "I'm sure you're right, though. What you have with the king is different."

Famous last words.

A knock comes from inside the room, and one of the four guards swings a door open.

"I will visit you later," Bessie whispers. "Have fun."

She touches her arm to mine and leaves the same way we came. As she does, a group of men exit the king's rooms, all in fancy Tudor attire. They greet me with cordial nods as they file past. Only the last one stops, and he's the only one I recognize.

I look up to meet his warm green eyes just before he gives me a little bow. "Simon?"

He stands up tall. His gaze lingers on mine as a shadow of a smile crosses his face. "Lady Catherine. I'm glad to see you well."

I give an awkward *Downton Abbey* curtsy in response before straightening back up, tugging on the cuff of my sleeve as I do. "As well as one can be, given the circumstances."

Simon rests his hands behind his back, and I can't help but notice how broad his arms are as they jut out to the side, even through the thick shirt he's wearing. "What are the circumstances?" he asks.

Oh, you know. I'm in the wrong era. I'm in the wrong body. I'm the next historical bachelorette who's going to be murdered in a crime of passion.

"It's just been a long day," I opt to answer.

Simon's mouth pulls in a way that says he doesn't entirely believe me. "And are you restored to your usual self?" His gaze is calm, but I also see the underlying curiosity. Whatever I said to him this morning was un-Catherine-like enough for him to notice. I need to keep a close watch on him, which shouldn't be too hard since I have yet to peel my eyes away from him.

"I was . . . confused. From my fall. Sorry if I seemed off. And for yelling at you."

"Don't be sorry," he says. "I rather enjoyed it." I angle my head at his response. I don't hate the thought of his enjoying our interaction, but I also can't focus on that now. Simon ducks his chin, like he's trying to hide the laughter pulling at his lips as a silence falls between us. "What I meant was, I liked talking to you. That's all."

His admission catches me in a way I wish it didn't. Our eyes hold until he glances back into the king's rooms, and his posture stiffens as he turns his gaze back to mine. "I should get on," he says. But he doesn't get on. He stays rooted in place, drawing me into the stillness with a look that's charged with something I don't quite understand. My breath slows. I'm wondering if I should step closer or back when he suddenly gives me a small nod, like he's regaining control, and bows. "Good evening, Lady Catherine."

He straightens and walks past me. I'm determined not to say anything but can't help the uneven "Bye, Simon" that slips out of my mouth when he's a few feet away.

He looks back at me over his shoulder with the faintest curve of his lips and my stomach instinctively tightens. As he disappears down an adjoining corridor, I have to mentally shake myself to remember the very real danger that I'm now in. Still, no one in this murder castle should have such a devastating smile.

With Simon out of view, I turn back to the doors but make no move to step forward. Several seconds pass, and the guard holding the door open gives me a confused get-in-there look. I take a bracing breath and walk inside. I'm entering the lion's den, but at least I know that I am. I wonder if Henry's other lady loves knew what they were walking into.

As I cross the threshold, my step falters when I take in the candlelit room. I was expecting a medieval sex dungeon, but this feels more homey than anything else. A breeze sweeps through the lavish stone space from the casement windows, and the logs snapping in the fireplace serve as a soundtrack. A dining table is set on the far side of the room, and a smaller round table is on the side where I'm standing. Two high-backed wooden chairs are positioned across from each other, and sitting in the one facing me is the king. When his eyes meet mine, he smiles like he means it.

"Catherine. Praise God you're well." He stands to greet me, wearing a thick velvet brocade of red and silver. It has huge padded sleeves, and he's sporting thickly tailored britches. I notice that his beard is on the thinner side as he takes my hand in both of his, once again kissing my knuckles as he steers me toward the small table.

"Come. Sit, my sweet, and tell me how you are." I ease into my chair as he slides into the one across from me. "Would you like something to eat? Perhaps some wine? Just tell me what your heart desires and it will be yours. I care for nothing so much as your happiness."

His attentive blue eyes stay on mine as I swivel to the left, trying to sit comfortably. "Thank you. I'm fine for now."

"Of course," he says, sitting back in his own chair. "Shall we play cards as we usually do? Or would you rather we just talk?"

There's an almost physical twist of temptation in my gut. The psychologist in me is frothing at the mouth to have a talk therapy session with Henry VIII. The papers I could write! The case studies that could be developed! But I shake the urge off. To him, I'm Catherine. And talking is a two-way street. If I sound like me, he'll get suspicious. And what I need now is to fly under the royal radar.

"Let's play cards," I answer.

Henry smirks and scoops up the deck that's set on the table. "My competitive girl. It brings me such joy to see you recovered. When I was told of your injury, the fear nearly overpowered me."

His relaxed shoulders and calm demeanor don't align with the body language of an overly stressed person.

I nudge my chair closer to the table. "I'm sorry I scared you."

He holds the deck in one hand and reaches out to me with the other. "Never apologize, Catherine. Not to me. To me, you are all perfection."

Intense flattery. I make a mental note of it as Henry begins to shuffle the cards. I really hope whatever game he usually plays with Catherine is in my repertoire, but something tells me that Go Fish wasn't super popular in sixteenth-century England.

"Can I ask you something?" I venture, unable to resist.

"Anything, my heart."

I sift through a catalog of questions, looking for the most telling one. I go with "What is your favorite memory of me?"

Henry leans back in his chair with contented ease. "The night

I first laid eyes you. You were dancing in the great hall. Many were there, but it was as though a light was shining down on you. You were the living embodiment of everything pure and beautiful. I fell in love with you in that very moment."

Henry's voice has a dreaminess to it, like he's reliving the memory in his mind's eye.

"Had we spoken at that point?" I ask.

Henry flashes me a knowing grin. "I didn't have to hear you speak to know your soul. Our love transcends mere words."

Idealization without knowing. Catherine is his fantasy. It's not who she is that he loves; it's who he wants to her to be. Who he's decided she is.

"Your accident made me realize something," Henry goes on to say. "Life is precious, Catherine. Everything can change in an instant, and my greatest desire is to live my life with you at my side."

Oh, shit.

"I want you with me always. As a wife, as a companion, and as the queen of England."

I swear to God, I almost laugh. This love-bombing bastard couldn't give me ten minutes before shackling me to Catherine's predetermined fate. I shouldn't be surprised, yet somehow I am, and I try to look pleasantly speechless as I figure out how to answer.

"It's decided, then," Henry says, his voice chipper. "We will be married in two days' time. I have already given the order, and preparations are underway."

It seems an answer isn't necessary. My "king" has happily decided, and I am now engaged. My mind takes off running in a million directions, but I take a breath to center myself.

Henry is still all smiles as he begins to shuffle the cards. "Now, sweet Catherine, shall we play? I have a new game I wish to teach you."

I smile back at him because I know something he doesn't. I am *not* Catherine Howard. I am Lily Whitaker. I am going to survive this, and him, and I am going to get back home no matter what it takes.

I lean in, resting my elbows on the surface of the table. "Deal me in."

Chapter Three

"Remind me again why we are doing this?"

Bessie groans as I pull her along through the dark corridor. The candle she's holding is half melted away and does little to help me as I look for any sign of the Haunted Gallery.

"Because there are holes in my memory," I remind her. "You promised to reteach me the layout of the palace."

She plants her feet, dragging me to a stop for the millionth time. "We have already walked for over an hour. And why are we doing this in the dead of night?"

I may have omitted the fact I'm trying to pinpoint the exact location of where I magically time traveled almost five hundred years into the past. Something tells me she wouldn't receive it well.

"I'm embarrassed," I say instead. "I don't want people to know that I've forgotten things after my accident. It'll make me look weak."

Bessie bumps my shoulder as she leans into my side. "Of course, one can't appear weak when they're about to be *Her Royal Highness, the Queen of England.*"

She bats her eyelashes at me, and I resume walking. "I knew I shouldn't have told you."

"I would have found out in two days whether you told me or not," she points out. "The whole *world* is going to know of the king's new bride. We just won't tell anyone that your mind is on the lighter side of the scales these days."

My gaze lingers on a baroque tapestry as we round a corner, leading into a hall that is full of windows. Familiar windows. I gasp and grab Bessie's arm, yanking her back to my side.

"Wait," I whisper. "I know this hallway!" Moonlight filters into the silent space, and I quickly look across from the windows to see the doors. Those godforsaken chapel doors that I touched right before I got sent back here. This is where I was in the future! "That's the chapel, isn't it?" My voice is vibrating with nerves and hope as Bessie holds the candle up higher.

"Yes, it's the king's chapel."

I'm here! I'm in the Haunted Gallery! Elation fills my rib cage and bubbles outward. I bounce on my toes as Bessie lethargically begins walking toward the doors.

"We aren't going to pray, are we?" she asks. "I will if you want to, but you should know that I have already prayed on seven separate occasions today."

The only thing I'm praying for is that I can get the *fuck* out of here!

"No," I tell her, gripping her arm to slow her advance. "Just wait here for a second."

She does as I ask, and I take a tentative step forward into the hall on my own. I close my eyes, hoping to feel something—a tingle, a visceral rumbling, anything that could pull me home. But all I sense is my own frenzied desperation to teleport. Opening my eyes back up, I commit to the plan of action I decided on before we got here.

Sprinting.

I take off in a mad dash down the hall with Bessie's astonished voice trailing behind me. I run with frantic purpose and determination, storming the gallery like a too-excited extra in a *Braveheart* battle sequence. This has to work! It has to!

But it doesn't.

I come to a skidding stop in front of the closed chapel doors, my skirts whooshing all around me. And I'm still here.

I'm panting and disappointed, but I'm not giving up. I hike my dress up and walk back to Bessie, whose horrified expression somewhat softens the blow of my initial defeat.

"What madness is this, Catherine?" she asks. "What if someone sees you?"

I move to her side and face down the hall again. "It's hard to explain. I'm going to do it a few more times."

"A few more times?" she chokes. "Catherine, why . . ."

I'm running at full speed again before her words reach me. This hallway is the key to my getting home. It has to be.

A half hour later, I'm bent over at the waist, bracing my hands just above my wobbling knees. "What number is that?" I wheeze out.

Bessie is sitting on the floor with her back leaning against the paneled wall. She doesn't bother to open her overtired eyes before answering me. "Twenty-two."

I'm sweating profusely when I straighten back up. Determined to solider on, I trudge forward to stand directly in front of the chapel doors. I place my hands on the varnished wood, then rest my forehead against it. I close my eyes and imagine myself in the right time. Back with Zoe. Back to that cloudy, rainy day. Back to when things made sense. I want to be there so badly I can almost taste it.

Please. Please. Please.

I open my eyes painstakingly slow. I look at the door. I look down at the floor-length dress I'm still wearing, watching as the moon's rays paint striations of light along the creases. Maybe if I slam my head into the door, it'll work. If a blood sacrifice is necessary to open the time portal, I'll do it in a hot second.

Bessie stretches her arms up from her spot on the floor, letting out a bellowing yawn. "You know, I've read that an injurious fall can cause more dire effects than memory deterioration, but bearing witness to someone descending into insanity is quite another thing entirely."

I push off from the unhelpful doors and walk over in her direction, fanning myself with my hand as I go. After the hallway half-marathon I just ran, it feels like I'm burning from the inside out. "Can you hum some music for me?" I ask when I'm standing just before her feet.

Bessie doesn't even look surprised as she glances up at me. "And what would you have me hum?"

I try to remember the song the girl was singing in the Haunted Gallery. Or maybe it was in my head. I try to remember, but the tune is just out of reach. My memory is good, but it's not *that* good. I'm seriously considering calling it a night when I think I start to hear something—it's faint and muffled, but it's there. Music.

I whip around in the direction of the sound before turning back to Bessie. "Do you hear that?"

She leans to the side to glance around me. "Who would be playing music at this hour?"

She hears it, too! I'm not imagining it! Whirling around, I follow the eerily familiar melody and am once again in front of the chapel. The music is coming from beyond the doors.

I square my shoulders. Maybe this is it. I'm going to open the doors and be sent home. Please, baby Jesus, let this be it! The doors creak as I push them forward. I freeze and hope, then hope some more.

Bessie arrives at my side, speaking in a hushed tone. "Are we going in?"

I suck in a breath at her question. I've just been the victim of a musical bait and switch, and I'm still fucking here!

I want to scream and cry and rip out my no longer red hair, but I opt to walk into the chapel instead. I never made it inside in the future. Looking at it now, it's a decadent mix of wood and stone. It's narrow but substantial. Turning my gaze up to the ceiling, wooden inlays of dark blue are speckled with hand-painted golden stars. It's a splash of color in a world I've found so muted up until now, and the air catches a bit in my throat.

The still-playing music draws me back, and Bessie and I keep walking on the black-and-white marble floor until we find the source. Tucked into the far corner of the room is a group of five musicians. They mostly seem to be in their twenties, and no one has noticed us yet thanks to the blond player in front who's facing them and holding their attention. He's on the shorter side, and judging from his posture, he might be playing a ukulele.

The notes of the song start to fade, ending in a soft finale. I'm about to clap, but the player in front quickly addresses the group.

"Right," he says. "I don't want to single anyone out, but, William, if you ever play like that again, I will plant a spell book in your sleeping nook and accuse you of witchcraft."

Oh damn.

William, a lanky redhead with a shy but handsome face, takes an indifferent step forward. "Just so we're clear, Bartholomew, you do realize that it was *you* who was incredibly flat on that G and not me, don't you?"

The cutthroat bandleader sighs. "I know. I'm sorry. I'm blaming you to mask my shame. Let's play it again, shall we?"

It's the redhead, William, who notices us first. His eyes go a little wide in surprise as he points in our direction. The leader turns, and the rest of the group looks at us in varying levels of shock.

"Hello," I say with an awkward wave.

No one responds until Bartholomew elbows the musician next to him. "Bow, you sods. It's the future queen." Their surprise gives way to nerves as they all bow in quick procession.

I wave my hands in front of me—a knee-jerk reaction to the royal protocol. "Bows really aren't necessary. I'm very informal. My friend Bessie and I were just going for a late-night walk, and we heard you playing."

Bartholomew goes pale. "I am so sorry, my lady. Please don't kill us."

I voraciously shake my head. "No, no. We're definitely not here to kill you. I'm just wondering . . . that song you were playing—what was it?"

William steps forward, nervously clearing his throat. "You mean 'Pastime with Good Company'?"

"Yes, that one!" Then toning it down, "I forgot the name somehow."

"The king composed that song," Bartholomew says. "He's a very accomplished musician."

I smile politely. "I know. He's a marvel, isn't he? Anyhoo, I was wondering if you all would be able to help me with a project I have going on in the hallway."

The musicians look among themselves. Bessie goes to leave, but I catch her hand before she can escape.

Ten minutes later, I'm running back and forth through the hallway with the accompaniment of a full band.

"How much longer do you plan to keep at this?" Bessie asks. She's standing beside William as the group continues to play, her arms crossed over her chest.

I slow jog over, pausing a short distance away from them. "How many have I done so far?"

Bessie shakes her head, refusing to answer. A confused Bartholomew speaks up instead. "A fair bit, my lady."

I'll do one more. One last push. This could be it.

I do a final dash down the hall. My lungs are on fire as I hurl myself against the chapel doors. "Come on, you bitches," I whisper against the heavy panels. I'm so out of breath that I don't immediately notice when the music stops behind me. I turn around to see the musicians and Bessie peering over at me with uncertain sympathy.

It's time to close up shop. For tonight, at least. I make my way over to everyone, holding my hair up in a ponytail to air out my overheating neck. "I'm glad we were able to do this," I say, still out of breath. "I needed to do something to clear my head."

Bartholomew hesitantly looks at his group before directing his gaze back at me. "If you're looking for a distraction, my lady, we're on our way to a gathering in the servants' hall. You could join us. We're celebrating your upcoming wedding, so you'd be the guest of honor."

The guest of honor. That would usually be a nightmare for me, but now I'm not so sure. If I go back to my room and ruminate on how I'm stuck here, I'll start to spiral. Then I'll panic. And I'll inevitably learn nothing.

If I go to the party, I can see things. I can pick up information. I can meet a group of people at the palace that the real Catherine Howard never had access to—or chose not to have access to. Tonight's hallway fail has painfully proven that I may not be getting out of here anytime soon. If that's the case, then I need allies. Connections. And I won't connect with anyone by going back to my room.

I turn my gaze to Bessie. "I sort of feel like we should go."

She looks at me like I've lost my goddamned mind. "You think we should go?" she echoes disbelievingly.

"I mean, they're celebrating my wedding... It feels rude not to."

Bessie closes her eyes and takes a breath. "Let me make sure I understand you. You think that you and I should go to a party in the servants' hall, even though we're unchaperoned, we do not have Mistress Marshall's permission, and you're marrying the king of England in one and a half days?"

"Correct."

Bessie shrugs. "All right, let's be off, then." I may have broken her mentally. Hopefully it's not irreparable.

I smile at Bartholomew as I pivot around to face him. "Lead the way."

The group is flabbergasted but excited as they turn to exit though a side door. Bessie and I follow along, moving with the crowd as we head down a narrow passageway. The space eventually opens up, and when it does, the leader moves to my side.

"If I may be so bold as to formally introduce myself, I am Bartholomew Dover. I've been a musician here at the palace for the past five years, and I've been a fan of your work since you arrived."

"My work?" I ask.

William looks at us over his shoulder, his cheeks blushing. "Bartholomew is looking for a rich older husband, too."

"Aren't we all," Bessie muses.

Bartholomew smirks and offers her his arm. "I like you," he says. Bessie happily accepts, and William falls into step beside us, still not seeming entirely comfortable.

"Out of curiosity," I ask him, "what's the word around the servants' hall as far as I'm concerned? Do most of them like me, or do half of them like me? What's the vibe?"

William and Bartholomew exchange a glance before William answers. "Everyone thinks you're very pretty."

"That's nice. And what do they think of me as a person?"

Bartholomew picks up my hand and pats it. "They think you're very pretty."

I nod at his implication. "Got it."

Bessie and Bartholomew walk ahead. I see that we're nearing a door, and I stop William as we approach it. "Before we go in, I'm thinking that for tonight, I'd rather not make a big spectacle about me being here. I want to blend in, if that's all right."

"Of course," William replies. "I also prefer to blend in. It's the one of the few things I do well."

My expression softens at his words, but the moment shatters a second later when Bartholomew kicks open the door. "Behold! The future queen, Catherine Howard!"

William turns to me, his face coloring with an apology. "Bartholomew is a great friend once you get to know him."

I give a resigned nod. "I love him already."

Putting my game face on, I enter the midsize hall that's filled to the brim with people. The bewildered but intrigued occupants drink from wooden cups as they sit or stand around two long tables. Everyone is dressed in toned-down Tudor attire. The women either have their hair down or tucked back in small cloth bonnets, and the men are dressed in unadorned shades of brown or black.

Music is playing and grows louder when some of the musicians we came with join the solo flute player in the back. William and Bartholomew stay close to Bessie and me as we mingle deeper into the boisterous crowd.

I'm mentally gearing up to launch into networking mode when someone catches my eye along the side wall.

Simon.

He's dressed more informally than usual. His black britches are tucked into his plain boots and his white undershirt sleeves are visible under a velvet vest. I can see his build like I haven't before. The expanse of his chest. The solid outline of his shoulders. A restless kind of tension ripples through me and I'm moving toward him before I realize it. His subtle smile is instantaneous when he sees me approaching. The closer we get, the more pronounced our height difference is, and I keep my tone confident when I stand before him.

"Hello, Simon."

"Good evening, Lady Catherine." He offers me more of a head nod than a bow, which I'm grateful for.

"I keep bumping into you."

He looks between us with did-I-just-bump-into-you confusion. "No, I don't mean physically. I'm just surprised to see you here."

"Are you? Because I'm not surprised to see you here at all." My chin tucks in a bit. "Really?"

He takes a sip from his wooden cup and laughs quietly as he drinks. "Of course not. Your being here makes no sense whatsoever." I nod, biting back a laugh as he goes on, "So then, what brings Catherine Howard to the servants' hall?"

I glance around the room before I return my eyes to him. "I... was in the mood for a change. What are *you* doing here?"

"One of my grooms brought me. Charlie and I grew up together on my family's estate and he came to court with me. He's enamored with a kitchen maid and invited me along for courage. I owe him a debt for helping me with training."

"Training?" I ask.

Simon takes another swig of his drink. "I'll be riding in the joust tomorrow."

"The joust? Like on a horse and holding a..." I break off midsentence, instead switching to a poking gesture.

"A lance?" he asks, amusement present in his deep, gravelly voice.

"Yes, a lance. Obviously." His gaze is skeptical as he continues to look at me, prompting me to ask, "So you enjoy jousting? It sounds exciting."

"It's what I'm good at," he says.

"Sure, but do you enjoy it?"

He thinks on it, his expression touched with quiet humor. "You know, I don't believe anyone's ever asked me that before."

"Oh no? It seems worth asking."

Simon pauses. "I'm accustomed to it. The king is pleased when I win. As is my father."

I don't reply right away, but when I do, I say, "You still didn't answer my question."

He stays quiet another second before his cheeks pull back in a self-deprecating smile. The fact that I was the one who caused it sends a soft heat curling in my chest.

"I like to compete," Simon eventually answers. "But I don't like it when the horses get injured. I've always preferred the company of animals to people."

"Do you still?" I ask him.

His eyes catch mine, unflinching and bold despite his uncertainty. "My opinion might be changing."

Just then, a pair of partiers push past us, stumbling along the way. Simon puts his hand on my waist and urges me closer to the wall, facing his back to the crowd so that if anyone gets pushed again, it will be him. I look up at his tall frame as I adjust to our now very close proximity.

"I'm an animal person, too," I tell him, with an involuntary uptick to my breathing. "When I was young, we had three dogs, seven fish, and a rabbit named Bea who didn't like me at first, but then I grew on her after I brought her chopped-up apple pieces every day at four in the afternoon. Little-known fact: rabbits thrive on routine, and if you integrate yourself into their daily schedules, they'll start to look for you." I stop for air, and Simon seems oddly pleased. "Is that too much information?"

He shakes his head. "Not at all. I want to hear more about you and Bea."

I let out a short laugh as I lean back into the wall. "I'm not sure I believe that."

"You should," he replies. I can tell that he means what he says, and I don't know how to respond to it. A few seconds pass until he speaks again. "May I ask you something?"

"Are you looking for more rabbit tips? Because if you are, you've come to the right place."

Another smile. Another warm feeling in my stomach. And other places. "Not at the moment," he tells me, taking a breath before he goes on. "Yesterday, when I came upon you in the hall . . . when we stood, you told me your name was Lily. Why was that?"

Shit.

I immediately tense up. The collar of my dress feels itchy. When I first spoke to Simon in the hall yesterday, I thought I was in the midst of an involuntary cosplay session. I wasn't careful with my words, and now I have to clean up my verbal mess.

"It's an old nickname," I say, probably too quickly. "I love lilies, so that's what some people called me. When I hit my head, it must have brought the memory back."

My heart freezes. It's a desperate explanation, but hopefully it's believable. A faint smile pulls at Simon's lips as the glint in his eyes tells me that he knows I'm leaving something out. I'm almost expecting him to confront me about it, but all he says is "It's a pretty name."

I can barely hide my sigh of relief. Simon watches me, his eyes still searching. I want to know what he sees.

"What are you thinking?" I ask him.

His gaze eases as he pivots slightly, opening my view up to the rest of the party. "I'm thinking that you're very different from who I thought you were."

My breath catches at his words. I shouldn't be happy. If I'm different, then I'm not doing a good enough job at being Catherine. But I also can't fight the satisfaction I feel at his potentially seeing or sensing me and not her. At least a little bit.

"You're different, too," I say, attempting to cover my tracks. "I'm actually glad you brought it up because now I don't have to feel bad when I tell you that you also seem extremely different."

Simon smiles as he takes another drink. "Am I? In what way?"

"I think it's the hair. Your hair is much browner today, and it has a shine to it. It's very healthy, though. Good for you."

He quietly chuckles at my obvious lie. "A sweet face and a jesting wit. The first, you're famous for. The second is a surprise."

His assertion matches what Bartholomew and William implied, that people see Catherine's beauty before all else—if they even see anything else at all.

"Maybe I always had a jesting wit but chose to keep it a secret." My tone is teasing but also defensive.

"It would seem so," Simon answers. Then he drops his voice a little. "Is this our first secret, then?"

For some reason, my eyes shift to his hand where he's holding his cup. It's calloused, probably from all the training he mentioned, but still inviting. Like it's equally capable of eliciting good screams and bad screams. Bad ones for his competitors. Good ones for . . . not me. Definitely not me.

"I guess it is," I tell him. I turn my eyes up and promptly deem his hands a visual no-fly zone.

His shoulders tilt back toward me, turning enough that I can feel how close we are, and I lean into the sensation. "Should we keep another?" he asks.

My own hand fidgets along the material of my dress as my brain buzzes in uncertain anticipation. I'm about to answer when Bessie suddenly arrives beside me, clearing her throat with the subtlety of someone who is violently choking to death, prompting Simon and I to break apart to a more formal distance.

"Am I interrupting?" she says once she's simmered down.

I twist my body to face her, turning Simon's and my quiet exchange into a group circle. "You're not interrupting at all. Simon, have you met Bessie?"

"I have," he says with a courteous bow. "It's a pleasure to see you this evening."

Bessie curtsies and glances between us with a coy glint in her eyes. "I didn't realize you two were so closely acquainted."

Really, Bessie?

"We're not closely acquainted," I clarify. "He just helped me yesterday when I fainted in the hall."

Bessie's gaze goes from teasing to alert. "You fainted in the hall? When did you faint in the hall?"

"Sometime in the morning. I don't remember the specifics. Long story short—I fainted, and Simon helped me."

"Well, we're very lucky *Simon* was there." She says his name like it's scandalous, and the silent weirdness that falls between us afterward is palpable. Bartholomew arrives a few seconds later.

"I have drinks," he cheerfully announces, handing a cup to me and then Bessie.

"Great. Is this wine?" I take a big gulp before he can nod, and holy freaking hell, the sticky sweetness goes down like a punch to the throat.

"Oh, wow," I cough out. "There is a lot of honey in there. Like, a very intense amount of honey."

Bessie takes a sip without issue. "It tastes as it always does to me."

"Yeah, me too," I agree, biting down my inner agony. "It just went down the wrong pipe."

A heavy silence consumes our circle, and Simon is the first to act. "The hour is late," he says, placing his cup on a nearby table. "I should be on my way."

"Indeed, rest up for the tournament," Bartholomew says. "I have two pence on your victory."

Simon looks down at the floor before glancing up again. "I thank you. I'll do what I can."

"But winning isn't everything," I decide to throw in, even as Bartholomew gives me a glare. "I'm just saying, if Simon doesn't love jousting, there's no pressure. Bird-watching is a respectable hobby, too."

Bessie and Bartholomew are both confused, but Simon just looks at me, his eyes smiling. "I'll keep that in mind," he replies.

Our glances brush before he bows, saying, "Good evening," and walking away.

Bessie calls out after him, "Good evening to you, *Simon*."

He disappears into the crowd, and I shoot Bessie a scowl. "Was that really necessary?"

"You tell me," she counters. "You were the one using the full force of your appeal on Simon Gainsford."

"I was not."

She barks out a laugh. "Of course you were! Your eyes were sparkling, and you smiled whimsically. Did she not smile whimsically, Bartholomew?"

Our new friend playfully squints his eyes in mock thought. "I may have noticed a touch of whimsy from my angle. And her eyes do seem to be less sparkling now than they were when Lord Gainsford was here and we weren't." He turns to face me. "Is it because I don't joust?"

"Medically speaking, her pupils may still be dilated from her head injury."

Bartholomew turns to Bessie with unfettered excitement. "Are you a healer?"

She shrugs. "Of sorts."

"Would you take a look at my cousin? He broke his leg, and the pointy bone is pushing out through his thigh skin."

"How long has he been in such a state?" she asks.

"Just a month or so." My horrified eyes shoot to Bessie, but she isn't alarmed. "He's down the hall, if you'll follow me."

Bessie hands me her cup. "We'll be back shortly."

They walk off together, leaving me with two drinks and no company. Maneuvering through the crowd, I lean in between an opening of people to place our drinks down on the table. Everyone sends me barely furtive glances as I move along the frame of the room, and it's hard to observe others when you're the main attraction. I think about speaking to a group of younger women, but they flinch uncomfortably when I start to approach. The last thing I want is to bother anyone in their downtime, so I switch gears and exit out the door Bessie and Bartholomew went through.

Finding myself in a somewhat deserted corridor, I take my time as I pass several rooms. I'm halfway down the hall when I pass an open door, and my curiosity gets the better of me as I glance inside.

If I was filming the pilot episode for *Hoarders of Hampton Court Palace*, this would be a solid place to start. I step inside the room, and my eyes don't know where to land first. Even with the clutter, it's still appealing. It reminds me of an antique shop—chaotic chic. There are hundreds of books stacked and shelved and discarded piles of papers in every direction. The walls are splattered with dark tapestries and slightly damaged paintings. I'm taken aback by a humongous set of stag antlers mounted above the dwindling fire when I hear the voice behind me.

"I won that in a bet."

I gasp and lurch back toward the sudden sound. A smiling man in his mid-thirties is looking up at the trophy animal. There's an air of mischief inlaid in his edged face. His eyes are sharp, so dark they're almost black, and his brown hair is cut short and a little uneven. He shouldn't be handsome, but somehow he is.

"The earl who lost it tried to steal it back, but I'm very good at hiding things."

His playful gaze lands on mine, and I can only hope that he's not planning on hiding my dead body next.

"I'm sorry. I was just going." I'm fumbling toward the door when his unbothered voice reaches me again.

"No need to rush off. I know that you're lost."

I pivot to look back at him. "That's really nice of you, but I'll head out this way. I remember where the party is." Even when faced with the possibility of murder, I'm still inclined to be polite.

He holds up a hand like he's trying to calm me down. "You misunderstand. I know that you're *lost* lost. Here . . . in time."

My heart stops mid-beat. My throat goes dry. "Have we met before?"

"Have you and I met?" he asks. "No. Have I met the person whose body you're now inhabiting? Yes, I have."

Well, fuck.

He takes in my blank, stunned stare and gestures to the two chairs near the fireplace. "Let's have a drink."

"Okay," I answer unsteadily. Not because I want a drink, per se, but because I have the sneaking suspicion that in a few seconds, I'm really going to need one.

Chapter Four

"How do you know that I'm not the real Catherine?"

The man looks at me with grave intensity. "Because I was the one who summoned you here." I take an uneven breath, but he quickly chuckles, his mouth curving warmly. "I speak in jest. People never perceive me as teasing, but I am actually a very humorous person."

He walks closer, and his charcoal gray clothes give the impression that they were expensive once but aren't anymore. He has heavy bags under his eyes, and patchy facial hair covers his neck and cheeks. He might be hungover. Or functionally tipsy.

"So, you didn't summon me?" I ask.

He shakes his head as he then makes his way to an open cupboard. "I did not. To tell you the truth, I have no idea what brought you here." He begins rifling through a row of bottles, and I give another quick glance around the room. There's a loud squawking sound, and I notice an angry-looking raven caged in the corner.

"How did you know I'm not the real Catherine, then?"

He turns back around, holding two wooden cannisters. "I have very good intuition. Wine or ale?"

"Wine," I answer. He nods and puts one of the cannisters back on the shelf, grabbing two silver cups afterward. I take a step toward him. "If you don't mind me asking, who are you?"

He kicks the cupboard shut behind him as he turns to face

me. "My apologies. I don't often have guests anymore. I'm Matthias. Personal astrologer to the king."

"An astrologer?"

He moves toward a small rectangular table in the center of the room. "I'm also a skilled weaver. I come from a weaving family. I would have stayed with them, but my father said I scared the customers. Ha! Can you imagine?"

I do everything I can to keep my face neutral. "No, I can't imagine that at all." He sets the cups down and begins pouring the wine. "So, when you say you're an astrologer, would that be a code word for something else?"

"Code?" he asks, glancing over at me in question.

"Like, are you a sorcerer or something?"

He slams the wine cannister down onto the table, and I flinch against its bellowing echo.

"Sorcery is a crime punishable by death." His eyes are deadly serious until they shift back to untroubled nonchalance. "No, I'm merely a man who hears things and sees things from a mist in my head." He sits down, taking a sip from his cup and gesturing for me to join him. I carefully approach and take my place across from him.

"Now tell me, not Catherine Howard, are you sure you didn't conjure up some sorcery of your own to send yourself here?"

He takes another sip, and I hold my cup to occupy my nervous hands.

"I definitely didn't send myself here," I tell him. "My friend and I were on a tour of the palace when I thought I fainted, and somehow I woke up like this."

"Fascinating." He leans in a bit over the table. "How does it feel to be walking around in there? It must be strange to be a spirit in someone else's body. Does it tickle?"

I sit back in my chair, realizing how grateful I am to actually be talking about this with someone. "It feels strange, but more mentally strange than physically. I'm trying not to overanalyze everything, but that's challenging considering the field I work in."

"You work in the fields in the future?"

I take a sip of wine then instantly regret it. "No, I'm going to be a psychologist. I'll help people understand how their brain, thoughts, and emotions work together to improve their mental health. I'll also—"

"You study the brain?" he interjects eagerly. "Do mine! Do you need to make an incision to see it, or can you just tap my head and it opens up?" He leans down all the way over the table, offering his skull to me without hesitation.

"What I mean is, I help people work through issues they may be struggling with by talking with them and understanding the root of the problem."

Matthias sits back up to look at me. "That's a bit of a letdown."

"Sorry," I answer.

He shakes off his disappointment and takes another sip of wine. "It's fine. And now you're set to marry the king. Exciting." His smile says that he's genuinely excited for me, and my mouth sets in a grim line.

"I wouldn't call it exciting. I'm going to do everything in my power to not let it happen."

Matthias sets his cup down. "How do you mean?"

"I mean, I can't marry him. The king is old and has no clue who I am, and he kills all his queens."

"Ah, spoiler alert," he says, pointing to me with a grin.

"How do you even know what that means?"

"The mist told me," he answers. "Back to what we were talking about. You have to marry the king." I laugh at his assertion, and he laughs as well for a few seconds before he stops. "No, but you really do."

The humor of the situation dies in my chest, sending a chill through my body. But I'm not scared. Now I'm pissed. "My free will says I don't have to marry him."

Matthias's face twists in uncomfortable sympathy. "Free will isn't really a thing here. The only will is the king's will."

I think the fuck not.

"That's too bad, because it's not happening."

"Your marriage has to happen," he says. "Did Catherine Howard marry the king in your time?"

"Yes."

"Then you have to marry him now. Not now, exactly, but in two days, as planned." Frustration courses through me, forcing me to stand. My chair scratches across the floor as I push off from the table. "If you don't marry him," Matthias says, "you risk irreparably damaging the timeline."

"What timeline?" I snap back.

"The timeline of history!"

I pace the room, but the repetitive motion doesn't soothe me. He can't just pin this on me. I let everything I know about the Tudors flutter through my brain, clawing for a solution.

"No," I tell him. "Everyone who takes the throne after Henry dies has already been born. So there isn't a definite reason why I have to marry him. It won't affect the timeline."

Matthias winces in indecision as he squirms around in his

chair. "I know I shouldn't let you tell me, but I'm so curious. Go on, then, who gets the crown in the future?"

Angry bird attacks his cage in the corner as I answer. "I don't know the specific order, but I do know that his daughter is Queen Elizabeth, and she stays queen for a long time. She takes England into a golden age."

"Oh, bad luck for you," Matthias says.

"How so?"

He pushes his chair back from the table as well, though he doesn't stand. "Well, if Elizabeth becomes queen, then that must mean Henry doesn't have any more sons. And I guess little Edward won't be with us for long. Poor dear. Good riddance to Mary, though."

"Okay," I reply. "And what does that have to do with me?"

"Well, what if you don't marry him, and then the king marries someone he otherwise didn't? They could have sons together who are wretched, and then they would precede Elizabeth in the line of succession. *They* would rule and not her. It could erase the golden age you mentioned and send us all spiraling into a war-torn, scorched-earth scenario. Wars that never happened could come about. Great people who lived might never have been born."

I stop pacing. "You have no concrete proof that that will happen."

"It might."

"It might not."

"But are you willing to risk it?" he asks. He stands up slowly, and his gaze is compassionate but determined. "I'm sure you have a family in the future. This is the only real way to ensure that they'll still exist when you get back."

His words knock the wind out of me—more brutal than a

gut punch. This is some fucked-up historical blackmail. Since I've been here, I've kept the memories of my mom and grandma tucked away in a neat little box. I've carefully compartmentalized them, because if I let my thoughts linger there for too long, I'll disappear into a nothingness of missing them.

We were a trio. We *are* a trio. The three Whitaker women. My grandma was a high school science teacher, and my mom is an English lit professor. We lived, and they still live, in a small Spanish-styled bungalow on a dead-end street. Our lawn is perpetually shabby, so much so that some kids in our neighborhood called it the witches' house.

I love it with every fiber of my being.

The thought of their not existing in the future is unfathomable. The world wouldn't spin without them. They're too real a light force. Too strong a glow. Matthias has to be wrong.

But what if he isn't? What if I change history and they disappear? What if someone I don't know—that someone else loved—disappears because of me?

This can't be the only way forward, but right now, it feels like it might be.

I grit my teeth and scrunch my eyes closed before walking back toward Matthias. "If I'm to go through with this, I need to know for a fact that you are going to help me get back home."

He gazes back at me in bewilderment. "How should I know how to do that?"

"Ask the mist!" I yell. "You're the one saying I have to marry Henry the freaking VIII for the sake of the future universe, so yeah, you better be planning to help me."

Matthias nods. "That's a good point. Yes, I will help you to get back home, but I need some time."

"How much time?"

"A week."

"A week?!" I fume, dropping back down into my chair. "The king could kill me in a week!"

"I'm sure he won't kill you in a week." Matthias pauses as he pours himself more wine. "Mostly sure." He stays silent for a few seconds before shaking the thought off. "I wouldn't be worried. Henry can be very charming when he wants to be. He's well studied. He speaks multiple languages. He's good at cards. Did you know he's an accomplished musician?"

I attempt to skewer him alive with my retinas.

"I need a week to research," he goes on. "I have access to some very rare, somewhat forbidden texts, thanks to my astrologer privilege. Let me look them over and see what I find."

I think of my mom and grandma again, and breathing hurts. Blinking stings. "I just want to go home.

"I know you do," Matthias says quietly. He takes a beat, then lays his hand on the table with forced optimism. "Let's look ahead now. For the time being, your best course of action is to keep your head down and try not to attract too much notice."

I give him a sardonic glance. "I'm going to be the queen in less than two days."

"That's unfortunate. New plan: become the most famous woman in England while also not attracting too much notice. Come back to see me in a week and I'll let you know what I've found. And try to have some fun while you're here."

"Fun?" I ask as he pulls me up to a standing position.

"It's possible." He's leading me to the door now. "You can make friends. You can read. Maybe you'll learn to embroider."

"I know how to embroider," I tell him as he gently shoves me into the hallway. "It's a passion of mine."

"There you go! Who knows, in a week's time, maybe you'll change your mind and want to stay."

The mist in his head must have told him I'm considering stabbing him, because he quickly steps farther back into his room. "Or maybe not. See you in a week!" He slams the door shut in my face, and I'm left standing alone in the dimly lit hallway.

I should get back to the party. I need to blur this grim reality, and that stank-ass wine is calling my name. My *real* name.

An hour later, Bessie has finished up with Bartholomew's cousin's leg and has dropped me off just outside my door. Unfortunately, I'm still sober. I tried to drink more wine, but my esophagus told me to fuck off. I'm sure I'll learn to love it.

I grip the iron latch and push the door with my shoulder, wondering how I'm going to Houdini out of this dress, when I find a young woman in the center of the room. She's spinning in a circle as she pets the fur wrap she's wearing, seeming lost in a daydream.

I close the door behind me, and the sound of the latch falling sends her now-panicked eyes straight to mine.

"Forgive me!" she cries out, flinging the fur off her shoulders. "Forgive me, my lady! I shouldn't have done it!"

She starts backing away from me, and I immediately go into de-escalation mode. "It's all right," I tell her, lowering my tone of voice and maintaining eye contact. "Take a breath. Everything is all right."

She drops to her knees on the hard stone floor, grabbing for the fur and holding it up to me. "I was waiting to undress you for the night and the king sent it. I was only going to touch it, but it was so soft, and it felt so good. Oh God, I couldn't help myself!" She drops the fur back to the floor and buries her face in her hands.

I walk to her slowly and bring myself to her eye level. "It makes sense that you're frightened right now, but I promise you that it's fine."

Her face is flushed, and her jaw is tense. Her breathing is dangerously shallow. "They're going to toss me out of the palace," she yelps. "I have nowhere to go. I'll die of shame! Please, my lady! Please!"

I take her shaking hand in mine and look around the bedroom. My gaze lands on the washbasin and cloth on a side table, and I rush over to reach them. I douse the cloth in the ice-cold water before I squat back down in front of her as she gasps for breath. The last thing I see is her startled stare before I push the cloth onto her eyes like a pie to the face.

"You're having a very strong reaction right now and that is absolutely fine." I make sure to keep my voice clear and steady. The cold cloth on her skin should trigger her mammalian diving reflex. It will slow her heart rate and activate the parasympathetic nervous system. "This feeling won't last forever and I'm right here with you. Can you take five deep breaths with me?"

It takes a second, but she nods from underneath the cloth.

"Perfect," I tell her. "Let's go nice and slow." Five deep, matched breaths later, I slowly peel the cloth from off the girl's face. "How do you feel?" I ask.

Her inhales seem regulated. Her expressive eyes are looking at me instead of darting around the room. "Much better. Thank you, my lady."

The muscles in my back untense as I smile in response. "You're welcome. What's your name?"

"Cecily," she answers. Her plain white bonnet has slipped back a little, revealing her thick brown hair. She has a lean, athletic build, and her cheekbones are so prominent that I have no doubt she would take the contouring world by storm in the future.

"I truly am sorry, my lady," she continues. "I just thought you'd be staying in the king's room tonight, as you do sometimes. But I still shouldn't have done it."

Instead of focusing on the fact that I'm the king's sometimes overnight guest, which is bleak as hell, I opt to stand up and help Cecily to do the same.

"I don't mind you trying it on at all. Honestly, you can have it if you want. Let's just sit for a minute." I lead her over to the chair Bessie occupied this morning, and I sit on the edge of my bed to face her. "How long have you lived in the palace?" I ask.

Cecily seems uncomfortable in the chair but doesn't argue. "All my life. My mother worked in the kitchens, and I was born there. It's a great honor to work as a maid, my lady."

"Please, call me Lil—call me Catherine." My suggestion is so outrageous that she doesn't catch my slipup.

"I couldn't do that!" she answers.

"You can. Please."

She pauses for several seconds. "Catherine," she eventually says, "I can't thank you enough for your kindness. Whatever I can do to repay you, just name it."

I smile faintly and look down at my lap. For the last five minutes, I got to do what I love. I probably feel more indebted to Cecily than she does to me.

"Maybe you could just visit me once in a while," I tell her. "I haven't been feeling myself lately, and talking to someone familiar might help me fill in some of the gaps I still have."

"Of course, my lady. *Catherine*," she amends. "This morning I heard talk of your fall. I'd be glad to visit with you anytime you wish." She shoots up from her chair then, moving to an inner wall across from the crackling fireplace. "I have a flair for shadow puppetry, if you're ever in need of entertainment."

She casts a wildly realistic bunny rabbit hopping across the wall, and Cecily has one hundred percent just found her target demographic.

"Well, that's a hard yes," I immediately reply, much to her to delight. "Can you do people, too?"

"People are what I do best."

I carefully nod in response, tucking my legs to sit crisscross on the bed. "In that case, what do you know about Henry VIII?"

Cecily's smile turns sly. "Oh, I know quite a lot about him." She curves and twists her agile hands, depicting the silhouette of my future husband in the flickering light. "Where would you like me to start?"

Chapter Five

*H**i, guys! So many of you have been begging me to do a wake-up-with-me video, and today, I'm finally going for it.*

First things first, as soon as I wake up on my half-goose-feather, half-straw mattress, I open my eyes, stretch, and, of course, double-check that I'm still in the wrong time period. Yep. Still here! That or I'm continuing on my slow-burn descent into madness. Either one.

After checking that task off, I get out of bed and squat over my favorite pee bucket. To answer your question, yes, I do have two different options. I'm bougie like that.

Next up, I pour out some unfiltered water from my very chic pitcher and wash my face and armpits. I go ahead and forgo putting on any of the creams that I do not have.

There's a knock on my door and Cecily has arrived to dress me. Her official job title is a maid, but she's actually my bestie and personal stylist. She also knows all the dirt on everyone in the palace. She serves the tea, and it's piping hot.

Then it's time for a fit check. Staying on trend is super important to me, so I obviously wear multiple skirts and tops. Because what fun is it to mask my body odor with perfume if I'm not layered up like a beleaguered football player on the reg?

For my first layer, I go with my colonial nightgown from the night before that also works double duty as my chemise. I love a night-to-day look. Did I mention that the women don't wear undies? I don't even know if they exist here. Naughty, naughty.

Then we go with my first skirt. Then a harder skirt. Then a decorative skirt. We then move on to the upper half of my outfit, where I'm laced and pinned within an inch of my life.

Fun hair accessories follow. A veiled headband is my weapon of choice today and goes over the thin little bonnet covering my hair. It's giving Little House on the Prairie meets Renaissance Faire, and it's a slay.

I'm going to leave things here for now. Thank you so much for tuning in. Let me know in the comments what you want to see next, and don't forget to like and subscribe!

"Did you see that, Catherine? His arm was almost knocked clean off on that one!"

I snap out of my fever-like daydream as I turn toward Henry's jubilant voice. This isn't the first time I've used fictional vlogging as a coping mechanism, but it's certainly the most bizarre scenario to date. I'm employing it now to block out the particularly brutal nature of the tournament we're attending. Even from our seats in the royal box, I can smell the sweat and blood.

The tournament is serving as a kind of pre-wedding party before the big sha-bam tomorrow, and Henry is barely able to keep still beside me as he watches the jousting. He's elated as the riders attempt to bludgeon each other to death on horseback, and I have to say, given my well-established *Knight's Tale* fetish, I thought I would like this excursion more than I do. But as it turns out, jousting is a bloody business and isn't my brand of foreplay in the least.

"Does this please you, my sweet?" Henry leans in so I can hear him above the cheering crowd.

"It's really something," I answer.

"I only wish that you could have seen me when I rode in the joust. It was many years ago, but there wasn't a man in England who could unseat me. No king competed as I did." He speaks to me with a nostalgic tenor. The memories of his glory days clearly still affect him.

I can work with that.

"What was it that you liked about jousting?" I ask. "How did it make you feel?"

His eyes are glued to the action in front of us. "It made me feel invincible. Just as you do now."

He flashes me a quick smirk, and the math is mathing. Henry isn't just chasing Catherine; he's chasing how he feels when he's with her. To him, Catherine could be acting as a mirror, allowing him to see everything he still wants to see in himself—someone desirable, energetic, full of possibilities.

"What was it about the joust that you loved, though? Was it the thrill? The sense of competition? What made it special for you?"

He thinks on it for longer than I expect before turning to me with a hesitant openness. My curiosity is piqued, and he knows it. "It set me apart," he says with a shadow of a smile. "There were other kings in the world, but I was brave. Strong. Unbeatable. I was given my kingdom by God and birthright, but I could have taken it if I wanted to. And with every tournament I won and every man I unhorsed—I proved it. To everyone, and to myself."

I nod at his explanation. To him, jousting was a form of validation. It reinforced his kingly image. A monarch's ego is a beast that needs constant feeding, and this is an ideal stage for that.

"Tell me what you—"

My attempt to dig deeper is cut off when Henry's attention is caught by someone entering the royal box. "Ah, Thomas, my boy! There you are."

A young man in an impeccably tailored outfit bows in front of us. "Good morning, Your Majesty. Lady Catherine."

He briefly blocks Henry's view, prompting the king to nudge him over in my direction. The young man squeezes into a small open spot on the bench beside me, and I glance back at Bessie, who's sitting in the row just behind us.

"Thomas Culpepper," she stealthily whispers into my ear. "The two of you used to be quite close."

"How close?" I ask.

She tips her head noncommittally. "I wasn't present in the room."

Well, that's an ominous statement.

I turn back around to face the celebrated bloodshed on the jousting grounds, just as warning bells begin to sound in my head. Thomas Culpepper. I remember the name. That's the name of the second suspected lover of Catherine Howard—my other beheading buddy.

"And how is our future queen on this fine day?"

I glance over at him at his question, wondering if now is the right time to tell him that we share a future death day. The first thing I notice is that he's absurdly good-looking. His coiffed brown hair is spattered with natural streaks of gold, and his roguish blue eyes are actively trying to seduce my soul. Build wise, he's strong enough to carry me to safety, but I can walk, thank you. Face wise, he's an AI-generated photo of a Disney prince.

"I'm fine," I tell him, inching over in the opposite direction.

"Aren't you going to ask me how I am?" At close range, he has the voice and charisma of Henry Cavill. He's not my type, but I can understand why Catherine was ready to risk it all.

"How are you?" I decide to ask.

He shakes his head. "Not well, at the moment. A woman who is very important to me is getting married tomorrow, and I fear I'm rather jealous and heartsick."

The audacity! It's flattering, but still . . .

"I hear doctors use leeches therapeutically around here. Maybe you should give it a go."

They're dragging a half-dead body off the grounds, but Thomas doesn't notice. "Have I done something to upset you, Catherine?" he asks. Then quietly, "You haven't written to me in several days."

We just took a hard left turn out of flirty banter, and I whip around to face him. "Listen, friend. Trust me on this one, you're barking up the wrong tree."

"I'm what?" My words of caution confuse him, but he gets the hint and walks off as Henry excitedly grips my hand, calling my attention back to the tournament.

"Here now, Catherine. Here's our champion. Come on, Gainsford!"

My eyes shoot to the pitch. The king's shouts roar in my ears as a knot grips my stomach. It takes a few seconds, but I find Simon entering the jousting area on horseback. He's in full armor, save for his helmet, and he's looking across the field at his opponent in calm readiness.

My pulse thuds in my ears and I stand without meaning to.

"Whoa, whoa, whoa. Can we call pause? Can we think this through for a minute?"

Bessie pushes me back into my chair by the shoulder. "You cannot pause the joust."

I watch as Simon is handed a lance as tall as a regulation basketball hoop. He turns to the royal box and holds it up in salute before facing his opponent again. He's sliding his helmet on when I anxiously tap Henry's arm.

"Should he really be doing this? I mean, couldn't he die?"

"He'll be fine," Henry says, taking a gulp of wine and leaning forward for a better view. "Gainsford is a sturdy lad."

"But what if . . ."

Before I can say anything else, the flag is waved. Simon erupts from his side of the field, barreling forward full force on his dapple gray as he lowers his lance and takes aim. My heart is hammering hard in my chest as I clench my eyes shut, waiting for the sound of impact.

A crash echoes through the air. The crowd cheers so loud, it's almost deafening.

I slowly peel my eyes open, looking for Simon and any signs of life. I find him steering his horse back around the pitch, still in one piece. His lance is gone, and his opponent is being helped to his feet by three attendants. I slump back in relief, my spine hitting the engraved back of the chair.

Henry is clapping merrily beside me as Simon urges his horse in our direction. He stops in front of us and pulls off his helmet. His hair is matted down with sweat, and a nasty cut is red and swollen just under his eye. He steals a glance in my direction before looking to the king.

"Well done, Gainsford. I had every faith in you." Henry leans toward me now, speaking into my ear. "You may give him your favor, my love."

Excusez-moi?

I look to Bessie for clarification. "The handkerchief you're holding," she whispers, nudging her head toward Simon. "Give it to him."

Right. Obviously. Because all I would give him is my handkerchief.

I dutifully stand and make my way to the wooden divider surrounding the box. Simon is a few feet below, squinting his eyes into the sun as he gazes up at me. My dress suddenly feels a notch tighter than usual. Full armor is . . . not a bad look on him.

"You're bleeding," I blurt out, not sure of what else to say.

"It's from an earlier match. It doesn't hurt." I doubt he would tell me if it did.

"You should still have it looked at. It could get infected."

He nods his head before turning it back up to me. "I will, my lady." This guy just molly wopped a dude off a horse with a wooden plank and now he's calling me "my lady." A quiet tremor winds through my belly, forcing me to partially recant what I thought about jousting not being my kind of foreplay.

Bessie clears her throat behind me, spurring me into action as I drop my handkerchief over the edge. Simon catches it as it falls, holding the dainty material in his hand before he safely stows it away in the armor at his wrist.

"Thank you, my lady," he says. He turns his horse, and I can't stop myself from calling his attention back.

"It was an impressive win," I tell him, "even if it wasn't birdwatching."

Sunlight catches his faint smile as he meets my gaze. "I couldn't let Bartholomew lose that two pence." I suppress my smirk as I dutifully go back to my seat at Henry's side, and he sits forward again to speak.

"Once you've cleaned yourself up, Gainsford, I have need of your assistance. It's an urgent task on behalf of my beautiful bride." The king takes my hand and kisses it. The ick it inspires is strong, but I don't show it.

"Yes, Your Majesty." Simon bows his head and rides off towards a cluster of tents.

Henry turns to me, his expression stuck between amusement and regret. "I would that I could ride in your honor—that you could see me do so. But I'm afraid those times are over."

I force my attention away from Simon's retreating form and focus back on Henry. Maybe if the king had a physical outlet of his own, he wouldn't be chasing the fountain of youth through "love." He seems able enough to ride a horse. Why shouldn't he get out there again?

"They don't have to be over," I tell him. "There must be other things you could do besides jousting to feel fulfilled."

His features brighten with the hopefulness of a bridegroom. "You're right, of course. My happiest days are still ahead."

My stomach sinks.

He kisses my hand once more and stands to talk to someone in religious garb near the barrier. I'm considering just how I could have phrased my suggestion less suggestively when I feel Bessie leaning in over my shoulder.

"Brace yourself. Here comes your uncle, the Duke of Norfolk."

Her warning barely registers before she disappears behind me, and the seat to my right is taken by a formidable man in his late sixties. He's in an immaculately tailored outfit of all black with decorative silver embellishments. He could be attractive, but there's a wiliness in his eyes and chin that stop him short of it.

"My dear Catherine." His voice is light and carefully measured. He takes a pleasant breath in as he gazes around us. It smells like horse turds and spilled ale, but he sighs like he just caught a whiff of Christmas dinner.

"Our shining day is nearly upon us," he says. "Another niece of mine will be queen. I pray that you won't squander the opportunity as Anne did."

Thanks to Cecily's interactive puppet history lesson last night, I know exactly who he's referring to. Anne Boleyn was Catherine's cousin and Henry's second queen. The king pursued her for seven years before he broke from the Catholic Church and divorced his first wife to marry her. They had a daughter. He fell out of "love." And Anne was executed three years later.

Thomas Howard—the Duke of Norfolk—was a driving force in putting Anne on the throne, then a driving force in marching her to the chopping block. Cecily teased that he would marry the king himself if he could, but since he can't, it seems to be my turn next.

He looks at my dress, particularly my stomach, before speaking again. "I must ask you, niece, are you yet with child?"

I look back at him with thinly veiled derision. He either doesn't notice or isn't bothered. "Not that I'm aware of," I tell him.

He shrugs and glances purposely around the royal seating area, waving to someone farther down the row. "No matter. If you're not, you soon will be. And you must notify me immediately when the event comes to pass."

"I'll be sure to do that."

I'm hoping he'll go join whoever he was waving to, but my gynecologically inclined uncle only makes himself more comfortable, crossing his arms across his chest.

"You've done well, Catherine. Far better than I anticipated when I brought you to court. Indeed, you exceeded all our expectations." He smiles at me in a way that seems heartfelt, but it's hard to trust a pimp in tights.

"If you are ever unsure of anything with regards to the king, know that you can always come to me. His Majesty's happiness is paramount, as yours is now, to a certain degree. The higher you rise, so does your family. Howards stick together. And Howards want what is best for their family."

"Wasn't Anne part of our family?"

The duke looks at me with something close to morbid approval. "Remember," he says, "the sooner you give the king a son, the safer we all will be."

He stands and takes my hand, bowing over it before walking away. I'm a little thrown and plenty pissed off by our interaction. So much so that it takes a few seconds for me to notice that Bessie has taken the seat he just vacated.

"You look pale. Am I to assume that you're not too keen to perform your wifely duties?"

I take in her question, and my gag reflex lodges a strongly worded complaint. "No comment," I answer.

"If you're nervous, I could make a tonic for you to drink. It would relax your muscles and steady your breathing. All my sisters requested it before their own wedding nights."

I give her an astonished sideways look. Did Bessie just offer me the Tudor equivalent to medical marijuana?

I shouldn't be surprised. In any other life, Bessie would be the department head at a thriving ER, but here, she's an under-the-table healer with the smallest sprinkle of drug dealing. The more I consider her offer, the more intrigued I am by it—only not in the way that she proposed.

"Hey, Bessie?" I ask. "Just how good are you at making tonics?"

She follows my gaze, looking over at Henry, who is still talking to Archbishop Something-or-Other. When she turns back to answer, her eyes are fucking fearless.

"I'm very, very good."

Chapter Six

Bessie's room is a jewel box mixture of a brewery and a greenhouse. There's a fire going, with an iron stand and a crossbar set up in the hearth and a hook for boiling. Different species of dried plants are hung upside-down along the windows, letting the sunlight filter in between them. She has something akin to a workbench pushed up along the wall.

"This is not what I was expecting," I say as I keep looking over the mismatched space.

"You're acting as if you haven't seen my room before. Here, breathe in deep." Bessie grabs a cup and a cylinder from her workbench and pushes them together against my chest. She lowers her ear to the end of the cup, and whatever she's made looks very much like the first prototype for a stethoscope.

"Do you know what that is?" I ask, amazed.

Bessie listens through her contraption before tossing it aside. "Just something I'm tinkering with. No matter. You have a rigorous heartbeat. That will help you during your obligatory nights with the king." She fills a cast iron pot with water from a pitcher and sets it to simmer over the fire.

I look over the tools on her workbench and attempt to keep my tone casual. "About that. I was wondering . . . that tonic you suggested to help me relax on my wedding night . . . what if I wanted you to make it a little stronger?"

"How much stronger?" She purposefully doesn't look straight right at me, instead drying her hands off with a nearby cloth.

I take a steeling breath. "Let's assume that I want to sleep through the entire process."

Bessie folds the cloth and places it on a chair near the fire, playing it so cool that I get the feeling this may not be her first rodeo. "I suppose I could facilitate that," she says.

A spark of adrenaline ignites in my veins. "That's good to hear. And the ingredients you would use . . . would that depend on my size?"

"I would obviously tailor the draft to your height and weight. Otherwise, the effects would be ineffective or too effective."

"Too effective. Which would mean . . ."

Bessie leans back against her workbench. "That you wouldn't wake up."

I take a nervous breath at her blunt words. As of now, I'm just trying to not put out. Not murder the king of England.

"I wouldn't want that to happen," I tell her. "But if I wanted you to make the draft two or three times stronger than you would probably make for me . . . is that something you could do?" She doesn't say anything, and I go on, "My body is very resistant to tonics. I need more than the usual dose."

Bessie keeps staring at me until she moves to check on the pot in the fireplace. "I could do it," she says over her shoulder. "What's the desired outcome?"

"Just a nice comfortable sleep for eight to ten hours."

She turns to face me full-on then. A determination fills her gaze that I haven't seen from her before. "You do realize that these remedies aren't exactly allowed. And I take a great risk by making them."

I pause a beat before asking, "Why are you?"

Her resolve falters momentarily. "I have four sisters. The

oldest of us was married to a viscount twice her age. She was very scared of him. She still is. It was the king who made the match personally."

"What's your sister's name?" I ask.

"Margaret," Bessie answers. "She always loved me best."

I take a step closer to her, starting to second-guess my plan. "I don't want you to do anything you're not comfortable with."

"I'm comfortable," she says firmly. "But I also want something from you in return."

I tilt my head just off to the side. "What do you want?"

"I want . . . no, I *need* you to find me a husband."

Did not have that on my bingo card. "A husband?" I ask, making sure I heard her right.

Bessie busies herself with the dried plants hanging in the windows. "Yes. The whole purpose in my coming to court was to find a suitable match. If I don't, my father will marry me off to my cousin Ned. Ned would pinch me as a child and now he always stares at me as he whispers Bible verses. He's barely more than a weedy goat. I'm certain he has hooves."

Ned can immediately fuck off.

Still, I don't know if I can promise results in the role of a medieval matchmaker. While I have more relationship experience than a sheltered Tudor maiden, I can bring little to the table by way of success. During my trial-by-fire dating binge last year, I met several different types of men. Some good. Some bad. Some looking for love. Some looking for a very specific foot shape. The list goes on. And while I don't regret intentionally dating for six months straight, I do regret putting a time constraint on it. Dating is stressful and overwhelming, and when my six months was up, I was so damn relieved.

All in all, I went on dates with eight different men. That's not including the two who never showed for the meetups that they themselves arranged. The remaining statistics were as follows: One thought I looked too much like his ex. One gave friends-only vibes. One drove a van with no license plates and asked me to road-trip with him to a desert wedding in Utah. I politely declined. He called me a cocktease bitch. Two agreed that there wasn't a spark. One said I was the most beautiful woman he's ever seen and named our three children, two boys and a girl, then ghosted me that very night. One was only looking for something casual after his long-term relationship failed, and then there was Brian.

Brian and I dated for a couple of months. He was a fireman who liked that I wore reading glasses, and I liked that both of us were beach bums. The sweatshirts I borrowed from him smelled great, and the sex was good. But even as our conversation flowed, I realized he never asked me any questions. I asked him about it, because that's what I do, and he said he didn't notice. But shouldn't he want to? I asked him. He shrugged and laughed it off, and didn't call me the next day. I didn't call him either. We texted back and forth for a while until it drifted into written silence. I won't be penning a hard-hitting dating manual anytime soon.

"I can try to help you meet someone," I end up telling Bessie, "but I don't have the best romantic history."

She faces me with a scoff. "Are you joking? You're Catherine Howard. You're desired by every man who lays eyes on you. For the longest time, I was certain your breasts somehow offered land grants."

"I'm not sure if that's offensive or not."

"You know what I mean. There isn't a gentleman at court who isn't half in love with you. And I just need one not-evil non-goat to like me well enough to marry me. Surely you can manage it."

Maybe Catherine could have managed it. Me? Not so much.

Bessie lifts her chin. "Those are my terms. Help me to find a decent husband within the month, and I will help you with *this* for as long as I reside at the palace."

Screw it. If she's in, I'm in. I hold out my hand. "I accept."

She gives it an impressive shake. "Good. Brewing first. Boys later. We'll have to take turns during the testing process."

My eyebrows lift in question. "How are we going to test it?"

WHEN I WAKE up, it's to the sound of knocking at the door. I rub my eyes as I force them open, gradually dragging myself up to a sitting position on Bessie's bed. I look out the windows and a crescent moon is just appearing in the sky. Bessie is passed out on the mattress beside me. She rolls over, mumbling something about hating goats' milk, when the knocking starts up again. I shimmy out of bed and totter to the door, slowly opening it to find Simon out in the hall.

My mouth drops. I can barely breathe. Not because of Simon. He looks great and all, but in his arms is without question the most adorable puppy I have ever been blessed to see. Simon chuckles at my reaction, situating the pup-pup angel more comfortably in his hold.

"The king bid me to give you this gift as an early wedding present. One of your maids told me I could find you here."

Henry VIII is good. He doesn't know me in the least, yet he found my goddamned kryptonite. The urge to jump and squeal is so consuming that it almost knocks me down. Somehow I keep a handle on my composure long enough to ask, "Is she really mine?"

Simon's face softens. "He. And yes, I believe that is the sentiment."

He hands the puppy over to me and my heart explodes. "You're a boy?" I coo into his fleecy brown fur. "That's okay. I still love you."

I give him kisses. A lot of kisses, and it's as if I can feel the color returning to my cheeks. I turn to face inside the room.

"Bessie, look! Look at this mushy little bubba!"

My friend scrunches her face as she looks over. "Adorable," she grumbles. "Now close the door. And make a note of the time!" She drops back onto her pillow and is snoring within seconds.

I step out into the hall, and Simon closes the door for me. My hands are filled and will be for the foreseeable future.

"What will you call him?" he asks. I can tell that he wants to pet him but keeps his hands pinned behind his back.

"I think I'll go with . . . Theo."

Simon nods. "It's a good name."

I agree. Every psychologist needs a theory, and my Theo is the cutest. I'm content to carry on with my hallway snugglefest forever when Simon asks, "Shall I see you back to your room?"

That would make sense. But I'm too amped up for tonight to be over, plus I might have just slept for five or more hours.

"I think I'm going to take Theo for a walk," I tell him. "You should join me."

Simon looks down the hall. It's deserted. He pauses for only a moment before answering. "If the future queen insists, who am I to refuse?"

Outside in the gardens, I'm sitting in a soft patch of grass with Theo rolling in my lap. Simon is sitting a few feet across from me, leaning his weight back on his arms.

"Wait, is this the urgent task Henry told you about at the tournament? Bringing me a dog?"

Simon offers a relaxed shrug. "The king honors me with his trust."

"Apparently so." Theo scratches at a shiny pleat in my skirt, and Simon's lips twitch as he watches. My gaze lingers on the cut under his eye, which I'm glad to see has been cleaned up since the joust. I'd ask Bessie to have a look at it, but I'd never hear the end of it if I did. I'm wondering if I could set up an impromptu urgent care appointment between the two of them when Theo begins to squirm in my lap. As I struggle to wrangle him, I realize that he's doing everything in his power to run off in Simon's direction.

"You know, I'm trying not to be offended by just how much Theo prefers you to me, but it's getting difficult."

Simon chuckles as I keep switching my hands under Theo's belly, trying to keep hold of him. "Theo doesn't prefer me," he says.

"Really?" I place the puppy on the ground, and he immediately darts over to Simon, jumping up and down in front of him in a desperate plea to be held. Simon tenderly picks him up and rests him in the curve of his arm.

"That was little more than luck," he tells me.

Not for nothing, but Simon could make a killing selling pictures of himself holding puppies. It's a niche market, but I'm now a part of the fandom.

"Right," I reply. "Was it luck that helped you win the joust today, too?"

"In part. Training is required, of course, but luck is the deciding factor in all things."

"I'd agree with that." I scoot myself closer on the grass, getting myself within arm's reach to scratch Theo's beckoning belly. "I'm starting to think that I'm notoriously unlucky."

Simon looks at me in slight surprise. "Few people would agree with that."

I almost don't say anything, but then I hear myself say, "Few people know the whole story."

He hesitates. "Would you tell *me* the story?"

His question brings an unexpected weight pressing down on me, but I breathe it away as I pet Theo again. I can't be honest, even though Simon makes me want to.

"I guess—sometimes it feels like I'm living someone else's life. Does that make sense?"

Seconds tick by as he looks at me, not just seeing but really *looking*, like he's trying to peel back every layer. I turn my attention to Theo, so I don't instantly regret what I just said.

"It does make sense," he soon answers, "and I often feel the same way."

My eyes flick up to find his. "How so?"

Simon resettles Theo in his arms. "I was originally a second son. I had an older brother. Everyone loved him. Even me. They say second sons are always jealous of their elder brother, but I never was. I liked things as they were. Neville basked in the expectations that were set out for him, and I was left to my own devices. He was meant to come to court, and I was to be a soldier."

"Did you want to be a soldier?" I ask.

Simon gently places Theo on the grass between us. "Not quite."

"Why not?" Theo starts nibbling on the edge of my dress, and I move the material back and forth for him to catch it as I go on. "Soldiering seems like something you would be good at."

He starts to smile, but it quickly falls. "I've seen the fear in men's eyes when they face me. And the aftermath of what I've done to them in a joust." A flicker of something unreadable passes through his eyes—not quite regret, but close—before he pulls a strand of grass out of the ground and rubs it between his fingers. "I don't have a taste for it."

I place Theo back in my lap. "Why did you even start to do it, then? The jousts, I mean?"

"My father believed that doing anything else would be a waste of my strength. And disagreeing with him was . . . an unpleasant experience. It was also what brought me to favor with the king." His voice dips when he mentions his father, and I notice as his jaw tenses.

My eyes meet his, and I inadvertently shift forward a little. "What happened to your brother? If you don't mind my asking?"

"A riding accident," he answers. "Neville recovered at first, but then he fell ill, and he was gone within a week. It never felt right for me to take his place. I wasn't loved as he was. I wasn't bred for a life at court." He pauses before going on. "That's another reason why the king shows me favor. He said we're both living our brothers' lives, and that makes us alike."

Henry lost an older brother, too? I make a mental note as Simon's words make me think of Henry's relationship with the other courtiers who serve him. Does he have little hidden connections to all of them? For the most part, the courtiers seem to be strong young men, full of life and promise. It would make more sense for Henry to push these reminders of his past away, but he chooses to keep them close. They're mirror images of what's gone for him—what he's so desperately trying to get back.

"Do you think you have a lot in common with the king?" I ask him next.

"Not so much as he believes." When I glance up, I catch Simon looking at me. He's unapologetic. He doesn't turn away. "But perhaps we do have some commonalities."

I shift my eyes back to Theo, my pulse jumping. "You mean me?" My chest tightens as I wait for his answer.

"I should like to learn more about you," Simon says.

I take a breath and lean back, mirroring Simon's stance as he keeps his weight on his hands in the grass behind him. "What would you like to learn?"

"Ideally, everything." My hand slips a little, but I don't think he catches it. No guy has ever wanted to learn everything about me before. It's a strange sensation to move through, and more enjoyable than I predicted.

"I like talking to people," I say after a few seconds. "And being there for someone at the right time, when they might not have anyone else to be themselves with. And I especially like to see someone realize that they're stronger than they thought."

I may have just described the best aspects of my job instead of talking about myself, but Simon's smile is warm. It keeps me at ease, until I remember that I'm supposed to be the aspiring psychologist here, not him.

"Tell me about you," I swiftly counter.

Simon sits forward, moving his hand down between us, and Theo immediately lunges over to gnaw at it. "If it were up to me, I'd be outside with horses all day. And dogs."

Theo starts tracking Simon's hand as he moves it from spot to spot, and I can't help my answering grin when he eventually pounces on it. "I can see that," I tell him. "Is that why the king picked you to bring me Theo?"

"Most likely," Simon answers. "The king saw me tame a spooked horse in the midst of a hunt once, and now he relies on me for all things animal related. And for anything requiring brute strength, of course."

"Of course."

Just then, Simon turns his hand up and Theo nuzzles into his palm. He leans down to whisper something near his ear, and I'm intensely curious to know what he said. When he sits back up, Theo is calmer than he's been all night, seeming content beyond reason as he rests his head in Simon's hand.

I'm riveted by the encounter, so much so that Simon then asks, "Would you like me to teach you how to calm him?"

I sit up at his question, hoping I look more intellectually interested than ogling.

"All right," I answer, nudging a little closer.

Simon adjusts his body so that he's sitting beside me. Our dynamic feels more intimate now, but I refuse to make things weird. Or to look at him. If I don't look at him, I won't make things weird.

"With dogs, especially smaller dogs, I bring myself to their level, and I keep my hand open and relaxed."

He leans in a little toward Theo, and I do the same, switching my stance so that my legs are tucked underneath me.

"I also keep my voice low, so as not to startle them, despite how happy I am to see them." He keeps his eyes trained on Theo and speaks again, his tone lulling and gravelly. "Easy there, now. You're safe here."

I'm more affected by his voice than Theo is. I don't know if I want Simon to guide me into a meditation or into an orgasm—except for the fact that I would definitely pick the orgasm.

"Once they've calmed, I make sure my touch is gentle. Approaching overhead can be intimidating." I crane my neck to look at him and find his eyes already on me. "Sometimes under the chin is better."

I don't move. I don't breathe. My skin is vibrating, but I'm perfectly still as Simon slowly runs the tip of his fingers under my chin, tilting my head up and holding my heated gaze with his.

"I don't feel very calm," I tell him, my voice shaking along the way.

Simon's jaw softens as his eyes flick to my mouth. "Nor do I."

He starts to lean in. I let out an uneven exhale, and he's close enough to feel it. My insides are swirling as I lean in, too. His nose brushes mine. I close my eyes. This is about to fucking happen.

And then Theo starts to bark.

Really, really loudly.

We turn toward the noise, our movements abrupt and awkward. Theo is barking into the darkness, and my heart stops as I pray that he's not sensing someone nearby. If anyone just saw us, I'd be dead—literally. I jump to my feet before I can self-sabotage my life *and* Catherine's life any further than I almost just did.

"I'm sorry," I mutter. "That was all me. I apologize."

Simon stands a split second after me, his eyes hazy and his cheeks red. "No. The fault was mine."

"It's no one's fault," I tell him. "Everything's fine. You're good. I'm good. Theo's good. We're all good."

But are we good? My unsteady heartbeat suggests I'm in the early stages of cardiac arrest, and come to think of it, I'm fine with that. I can't marry the king tomorrow if I drop dead here and now.

"I should escort you inside," Simon says.

But I'm already in motion, scooping up Theo and moving in the direction of the palace before walking backward to face him. "I can find my way. Thank you for tonight. For hanging out with me, I mean."

Simon's brow furrows. "'Hanging out'?"

I stop walking. "Never mind. I'm rambling. I had a head injury recently, as you know. You were present for part of it. So if you hear me using strange sayings or words like 'hanging out,' that's why." He only continues to look at me. I hold Theo to my chest like a security blanket. "I'm going to go now. Have a good night."

"Good night, Lady Catherine."

I try to walk away, but my feet don't move, deciding instead to hold me hostage. "Since you keep calling me Lady Catherine, does that mean you want me to call you Lord Gainsford? I will if you want me to."

"No," he says with a little shake of his head. "I like to hear you say my name."

Holy. Shit.

"Then you should probably start calling me just Catherine."

He doesn't say it, but his eyes do. I turn and beeline it back inside as fast as my feet can carry me. This is okay. What I did was okay. It wasn't inappropriate. Henry won't cut my head off for it. It happens all the time. Simon can touch my face and almost kiss me without my wanting it to develop into something more. We can absolutely just be friends.

Needless to say, my freshly horny chinny-chin-chin vehemently disagrees.

Chapter Seven

I am not thinking of this as my actual wedding day. It's only temporary. Temporary for me because I'm going to get home. Temporary for Catherine because I'm going to figure a way out of this for her, too, once she's back and I'm gone. Will she probably have to spend the rest of her life in a nunnery? Yes. But will she get to keep her head? Hopefully, also yes.

In the space of one morning, I've gone from existing here with primarily just Bessie by my side to being submerged in a sea of noblewomen. Cecily explained that the women consist of ladies-in-waiting and maids of honor. Most ladies-in-waiting are married. Maids of honor are not. Maids of honor are the B squad to the ladies-in-waiting A squad—with the B standing for "better get married fast or you're fucked."

I'm paraded through the queens' apartments, which are now mine, as they dress and prepare me for the ceremony. It feels very much like *Toddlers & Tiaras*, and I'm the overstimulated pageant girl with my fifty stage moms buzzing all around me.

There is, however, one queen bee in this group of ladies-in-waiting and younger maids of honor, and that is the ever-somber Lady Rochford. She's a cousin of Catherine's through marriage, and Cecily said the servants refer to her as "Jealous Jane" after she played an integral role in the demise of her sister-in-law, my other cousin, Anne Boleyn.

The primping crowd parts as she approaches me, and I push my tense shoulders into a confident line when she stops across from me and curtsies.

"May I have a word, Lady Catherine?" Her voice is firm and tired at the same time. She keeps her gaze calm, though it could be calculating. I nod in answer and she ushers me away from the group, towards the windows. Her features are pretty and well defined, with a pert little nose and delicate cheekbones. Her almond eyes sweep behind us to survey the rest of the women as they remain a few yards away. Lady Rochford strikes me as someone who would never sit with her back to an exit. Her movements are elegant yet somehow robotic. She looks older than she should in her early thirties.

Finding ourselves in relative verbal privacy across the room as we are, she takes a step back from me. "You're shorter up close than I expected."

"Thank you?" I say, not sure of how else I should respond.

"And you last spoke to our uncle, the Duke of Norfolk, at the tournament."

"Yes." Thinking back to it, I don't remember seeing Lady Rochford there. "How did you know that?"

"I make it my business to know." I digest that information as she moves to sit on the large windowsill. "A word of advice: be very careful with our uncle. Family as we may be, he would cut us both cut down in a moment if it suited his purpose."

"I'm glad I wasn't the only one picking up the creeper vibes." She looks at me with a quizzical raise to her brows. I clear my throat. "And what's his purpose?"

A hint of a smile pulls at the corner of her mouth. "To ascend so high in His Majesty's favor that he touches the heavens." I wonder what her smile means when it suddenly disappears, and her intent eyes focus in on mine.

"Most people at court think you to be a beautiful little fool, but I believe you are much smarter than you let on. And for your sake, I hope that's true. You are going to need every ounce of cunning you possess if you're going to survive as queen." She hops down from the window, checking to make sure no one is listening before speaking to me again.

"But hear this, Catherine: Whatever you require on this new path, I will be with you. I will not falter. My loyalty is to you above all others."

Her voice and gaze are sincere. Super intense, but sincere. "Why?" I hear myself ask.

She thinks a moment before saying, "It's my penance." I'm stunned into silence when she suddenly claps her hands together in a no-nonsense manner. "Now, back to the wedding. The king will be expecting you soon. This is a joyous day, is it not?"

She returns toward the rest of the women, and I'm left reeling in her wake.

Thankfully, Cecily arrives at my side next, holding on a tray two tiny cups that look like antique shot glasses. "You should drink this to get you through the morning," she tells me. "It's mead. A man in the kitchen makes it, and it's strong enough to numb your face."

"I will if you will," I tell her.

She picks up a glass, chugging her drink in unison with me. I see stars for a second, but given what I'm about to do, I'm into it.

"Can you get more of that?" I ask.

"I'm on my way." She turns and leaves, and I'm left on my own by the windows. Something that Lady Rochford said reverberates through my brain.

If you're going to survive as queen.

If you're going to survive.

If. If. If.

Her words remind me of just how serious my situation is, and no amount of high-octane mead will make that fact go away. If I mess up here, I don't get a lawyer. I don't get my day in court. If Henry ever decides that he wants me gone, then I'm gone. Gone from the earth. I'm at the whim of an unstable monarch, and only time travel can get me out.

But I have to do this. For my family. For the timeline.

The entire room is staring at me, though they're pretending they're not, and it feels like their collective gazes are splintering through my skin. My breathing turns shallow. My palms are sweating.

"I need a minute," I say to no one in particular. I turn away from my rapt audience and head to a side door, not caring where it leads as long as I'm alone.

I find myself in a small sitting room, locking the door behind me as I concentrate on my breathing. Inhale for four. Hold for seven. Exhale for eight. I repeat the process over and over until I come back to myself.

I can do this. I can handle a man in a midlife crisis whether he's a king or not. I'm going to make him see what he wants to see, but everything will be for my gain. I don't need to control—I need to steer.

I am in the driver's seat.

It's at this exact moment that a hand covers my mouth and drags me backward. Fear envelops my body as I thrash and flail.

I trip on my skirt, and my attacker holds me up in a tight grip as they haul me against their chest. I'm screaming into their gloved hand as a desperate voice speaks into my ear.

"Catherine. It's me. Don't struggle so and I can let you go."

I struggle harder, kicking and swinging and smashing my head backward until I make contact. I also bite the hell out of the leather glove that's nearly suffocating me.

I hear a curse from the voice behind as I'm set loose. I grab a vase from a table and whirl around to face my assailant.

"Who are you? What do you want?" I keep my voice menacing, and I'm poised to strike. The man covers his nose with his hand, bending at the knees in pain as he looks up at me with shocked, accusing eyes.

"Catherine, it's me! It's Francis! What in God's name are you doing? You bit me!"

"You're lucky all I did was bite you!"

The man stands up, dropping his hand from his face. He's bleeding profusely from the nose. The reverse headbutt worked.

"Why are you acting as though you don't know me?" I try to look past the blood, studying his face to see if I hold any recollection. Then I see it. The pitch-black hair. His stormy eyes. He said just now that his name was Francis.

"Francis Dereham," I whisper.

Silent elation fills his gaze at my hushed words. Francis Dereham was the speck on the road. I met him my first day here. We talked a little, and when he looked at me, at Catherine, it was like everything in the world began and ended with her. He and Thomas Culpepper are the two men who are meant to die with me.

He carefully takes a half step forward. "I just . . . I'm sorry it's taken so long for me to reach you. Believe me, I am doing everything I can for us to be together."

"How did you even get in here?" I look around and realize the only place where he could have hidden was near the window. "How long were you behind that curtain?"

He pauses. "A day or two."

"What did you do about food and using the bathroom?" He glances back at the curtain with a guilty countenance. "On second thought, I don't want to know." I rub my hands over my face. I came in here to decompress and am doing the polar opposite.

When I look back at Francis, he's a step closer to me, and his eyes are streaked with intensity. "Not a moment has gone by where I haven't thought of you. You're just as beautiful as I remember." He raises his hands, like he's about to cup my cheeks, but I move back to dodge them.

"All right, let's just regroup for a second. You're Francis Dereham, right?"

His unyielding gaze burns into mine. "And you are my perfect Catherine."

"And we first met . . ."

"At Lambeth, where I was the secretary to the Dowager Duchess."

He steps forward. I step back. I try to remember what Cecily told me about where Catherine was before she came to the palace.

"Lambeth," I say quietly. "I grew up there. With my stepgrandmother. The Dowager Duchess."

Francis nods. "It's the place where we first fell in love. Where we first kissed. Where we first—"

"Yes, lots of firsts," I say, cutting him off. "And you're here now because . . . ?"

"Because I promised that I would come back for you after they separated us, and after two eternal years, I finally have." His wavy hair falls just above his eye, wild and uneven. It makes me wonder if Catherine used to push it back.

"And you're living here?" I ask. Hopefully not behind the curtain.

"I was given a place at the palace as the undersecretary to the Earl of Sussex." He's standing just in front of me, and when I go to retreat, my back meets the wall. Francis takes a slow breath. He begins to reach for me again but then thinks better of it, resting his arms at his sides. It seems physically difficult for him not to touch me. "I'll never leave you again," he swears.

"Right." This next bit is going to be difficult for him. I keep my voice gentle and steady, leaving room for his disappointment but not for negotiation. "So, Francis, I know this isn't what you want to hear, but I've been doing a lot of reevaluating lately, and I think it would be for the best if we forget everything we ever were to each other."

He begins to laugh but stops halfway. His eyes are unblinking. "You're serious? You want me to forget us?"

"I just feel that we've grown as people during our time apart, and it would be better for all involved parties for us to go our separate ways. Think of it as a clean break."

Francis shakes his head, running a bloodied hand through his unruly hair. "No! I know they're forcing you to marry the king. I know you don't want this union and that if it were in your power, you would leave with me now."

It's safe to say that Francis is well within the denial stage of his grief process. I'm about to explain emotional fixation to him when a firm knock sounds at the door.

"Catherine? Are you in there?" It's Lady Rochford's voice.

My stomach drops. I can't be found in here with an ex-boyfriend. Not only will I lose my head, but I'll lose it ahead of schedule. I walk into Francis, pushing him back in the direction of the curtains.

"You need to go. You need to get back in your hiding spot or leave without anyone seeing you."

He cups a hand behind my neck, and I'm so rattled by the door latch rattling that I don't immediately karate chop his arm off.

"I won't forsake you again, Catherine. I swear it." His voice is all passion and unfulfilled longing, and I really don't have time for it.

"Sounds good. Don't forsake me. Just please hide!"

He touches his forehead to mine, which I make a face at, before he scurries behind the curtain. I move to the door, ready to unlock it, when Francis pops his head back out.

"I'll find a way for us to meet in the coming days." He takes a labored breath before adding, "I have missed you, wife."

Come the fuck again?!

I'm about to tear the curtain off the wall and demand that Francis explain himself when Lady Rochford pounds on the door. I unlock and open it, taking in her suspicious face and praying that she doesn't notice how flushed mine is.

"Are you all right?" she asks, looking at me then past me to glance around the room.

"Me? I'm great." Sure, I might have just found out that I'm already married to Timothée Chalamet's lovesick older brother, who would probably love nothing more than to die by my side. But yeah, other than that, I'm great.

I step out of the room and close the door. My legs carry me forward in a clumsy rhythm as I move past Lady Rochford, hoping against hope that I'm not about to become England's first-ever polygamist queen.

It's official. Catherine is married, and by extension I'm married-ish.

Henry and I are at our wedding feast. Wine is flowing, there's music (thanks to Bartholomew, William, and crew), and the room is full of dancing and merrymaking. As the new Tudor it-girl, eyes follow me everywhere. I'm being looked over and sized up, and after an hour of being queen I have learned that being overlooked is highly underrated.

We're sitting on a little dais at the moment, hovering over the higher-ranking members of court as they partake in the festivities. Henry's arm sleeves are especially puffy for the occasion, and his outfit matches mine in its shade of pure gold.

He places his wine cup down on the table as he turns to face me with a soft, pleased smile. "Are you happy?"

With someone like Henry, I need to use adoration with razor-sharp precision. A man with unchecked power is used to flattery, so I need to feed his ego uniquely if I want him to trust me before anyone else. "Very happy," I answer, placing my hand on the material covering his wrist. "The whole world knows you as a king, but I know you for who you truly are. I get to know your heart. It's the greatest gift you could ever give me."

My words do the trick as pride and contentment sift through

Henry's eyes. He kisses my hand, as he tends to do, and sighs as he looks out at the crowd in front of us.

"A bride should dance on her wedding day. Let me find you a partner."

"You're not dancing?" I ask.

He either doesn't hear me or pretends not to as he turns his gaze to the side. "Thomas! Someone fetch Culpepper to me. I would see him dance with the queen."

Of course that's who he has to go and pick as my partner. My displeasure at his choice is evident on my face, but he sees it as my not wanting to dance with anyone but him, not my specifically not wanting to dance with Thomas.

"Oh, go on, my sweet," Henry says obligingly. "Alas, my leg pains me this evening, and I'd rather save my strength for when we are alone." He gives me a wink, and it triggers an instantaneous bile response in my throat.

My self-preservation instincts kick into high gear as I search the crowd for Bessie. She promised that she'd be finished with the sleeping draft today, and Cecily is milling around under the guise of serving wine as she waits to take part in the drop-off. A group of ladies-in-waiting enter the room. I'm hopeful Bessie is among them when my view is abruptly blocked by none other than Catherine's deadly sidepiece, Thomas Culpepper.

He bows before us with formality and flare. Henry eats it up. "Your Majesty," Thomas drawls, rising to stand tall in all his splendor. "It would be an honor to dance with the queen."

Henry applauds in approval and sends me off with a nudge. I keep my expression impassive as I step off the dais, taking Thomas's softer-than-average hand. We make our way to the middle of the dance floor, and I steal a glance at William and Bartholomew. They make subtle teasing expressions, eliciting a smile from my sour face. Thomas follows my gaze in curiosity, but my boys turn serious before he can catch them. They ready their instruments, and a spritely melody fills the room as dozens of dancers take their place around us.

I momentarily panic as I hear the notes, remembering that the men and women of court have been taught specific music and steps since childhood, thanks to the watchful eyes of their dance tutors. I, in contrast, was never able to fully master the Macarena.

But as Thomas steps forward and everyone moves in a synchronized turn, I'm shocked to find that I do, too. It's the same muscle-memory sensation I experienced during my attempted horseback escape on day one, and, oddly enough, I feel a very similar thrill as I move in tandem with the rest of the dancers.

"Well, you've truly done it, haven't you? Just as you said you would." Thomas's voice is buttered with mischief as he takes my hand and ushers me into another spin. "Catherine Howard, the queen of England."

I'm not trying to dislike him, but it's hard not to. Thomas inherently carries himself with the bravado and entitlement of an Ivy League graduate with no student debt. If I met him in the future, I have no doubt that his chosen mode of footwear would be white tube socks and Adidas Slides.

"I don't know what you're talking about," I tell him.

We step close, pressing the flats of our hands together. "Why are you so cold to me? But a week ago you held me in the breast of your confidence. Now you hardly speak a word in my direction."

God forbid he miss an opportunity to say the word "breast." We move apart then come back together, our hands meeting once more.

"It's for your own good. It's not you, it's me." I speak the words more cynically than I mean to, but Thomas seems to like it.

"What would you have me do to be back in your good graces? I miss the tender touch of your words."

I roll my eyes as we all do a little turn. With arms outstretched, the women move in a circular motion around their partners, and I walk around Thomas with banal curiosity.

"Are you always like this?" I ask.

"Like what, my queen?"

Back in two lines, we walk forward with our toes pointed, moving one step at a time. My fingers rest on the back of Thomas's offered hand. "You speak purely in innuendo. Everything you say and do feels performative."

His returning half smile is almost sincere. "Says the greatest playactor of us all." Now it's the women's turn to stay still as the men walk around them in a little circle. "I don't judge you, of course. On the contrary, I respect you all the more." Thomas is speaking over my shoulder, and I turn my neck to meet his gaze as he steps around to the other side.

"We all do what we must to get by in this world. Don't we, *Catherine?*"

Something inside me sinks at his words. It's the way he says Catherine—like he knows something he shouldn't. It leaves me off-balance, and for the first time in the dance, I miss a step as he spins away with a wry smile. I think about going after him, but just then my hand is caught up in a warm, large grasp as we switch partners. Someone else is standing across from me now, anchoring my feet to the floor with his steady gaze, which I realize I'm starting to crave.

Exhilaration and nerves rake through my stomach as I stare up into a familiar pair of green eyes. He gives me a barely noticeable smile that's just for me, and I'm forced to face a very, very dangerous truth.

I have never wanted anyone as much as I want Simon Gainsford.

Chapter Eight

"Hello." His voice is inlaid with a quiet confidence, and he moves with incredible grace for his size.

"Hello," I answer, trying to conceal my smile.

The men do a turn, and the ladies turn next. I haven't fully gotten my equilibrium back after seeing Simon and spinning when I suddenly stop short. Bessie is standing along the perimeter of the dance floor. My eyes stay on her as she subtly slides a small vial from the sleeve of her burgundy dress, the glass twinkling in the candlelight of the room.

Simon and I switch places as the other dancers do the same. My heart is pounding with jittery energy as I turn to make meaningful eye contact with Cecily. She gives me a nod and moves through the crowd, holding her wine jug securely as she weaves in and out.

I'm a little breathless when Simon and I face each other again, bringing our palms together and stepping forward.

"How is our Theo?" he asks.

Our Theo? His question somehow spikes and soothes my rising nerves. I do what I can to sound level as I answer, "He's living his best life nestled on a pile of pillows."

Simon presses his lips together, amusement slipping through. "As he should. I'm sure he's content in all his finery."

"I like to think so."

We turn and pause with my hand on top of Simon's as a pair of dancers sashay around us. I scan the space until I find Bessie and Cecily. They're on their way to each other, though no one else would notice it. To anyone else, they're just two women sifting through the sea of guests. But as they pass each other, Bessie casually drops her hand and passes the vial to Cecily. Cecily stows the little glass in her apron pocket, and it's the most beautiful drug deal I've ever seen.

My heart soars, drunk with success. From here, Cecily will sneak into my new bedchamber and tuck the draft into a hidden pocket she'll sew inside my robe. I keep eyes on her as she slips from the hall, but my concentration shatters when Simon's hand moves deliberately under mine. My gaze snaps down to look, and I pull in a breath as the rough pad of his thumb brushes the skin of my palm. For a split second, I feel it absolutely everywhere.

In one spot beneath my skirts in particular.

"Are you content?" he asks. "With the events of the day?"

His features stay neutral, and it makes his ghost of a touch feel even more brazen. My breathing stays spiked as we walk in a slow circle.

"I'm more content now." My words come out a little unevenly. His thumb draws along my palm in another slow slide. "Are *you* content?"

"I hardly know what I am anymore." We move apart. The men and women stand in two parallel lines until we move together, and Simon speaks again. "I must ask you something."

I nod my head. He dips his voice low so no one else can hear. "I never existed to you before. We rarely spoke. I doubt you would have called me an acquaintance."

Each couple breaks off to stand in their own small section. Simon and I take two steps in a diagonal to reach our spot. "And your question is . . ." I move the smallest bit closer to him, my arm pushing into his. No one can see it. Only we can feel it.

"What changed that day I came upon you in the gallery? Why do I exist to you now?"

The music is building. It's almost the end. Now that Henry and I are married, I don't know when I'll get the chance to speak to Simon like this again. I take a breath before I answer. "Maybe I lost my memory—and I found you instead."

Just for a moment, Simon's eyes are completely unguarded, flashing with fire, and they're achingly, painfully beautiful. So beautiful that I don't hear when the music stops. So beautiful that when everyone else bows and curtsies to each other, we don't. It isn't until a trumpet blares, almost shaking the room, that we reenter reality. Following the gaze of the crowd, we see that one of Henry's councillors is now standing on the dais. I catch a glimpse of Simon looking between me and Henry, and his eyes flash with something dark.

"My lords. My ladies. It is time for the king and queen to retire to bed!"

Rowdy cheers sound through the room. Simon bows over my hand, gripping it so tightly that it hurts, but I cling to the sensation, if only for a moment.

Slipping my hand away and walking past him is so difficult, I'm not quite sure how I do it. My feet feel weighted down with sandbags as I make my way back to the dais, going up the two small steps and placing my hand on Henry's waiting arm. We turn out to face the applauding crowd. Simon has disappeared, but then I see Cecily standing in a corner.

"Are you ready?" Henry asks, seeming almost nervous in his humming anticipation.

I catch Cecily's eyes once more, and she gives me a nod. I turn to Henry with a dutifully sweet smile. "More ready than you know."

SOME OF THE fancier ladies-in-waiting are the ones who dress me for bed. The wives of earls. The daughters of dukes. Dressing me is an honor now, and the nights of just me and Cecily are a thing of the past. But Cecily is here in spirit, thanks to her handiwork with my robe. As deft with a needle as she is with shadow puppets, no one would ever suspect or notice the little pocket she sewed in. But I feel it. And the little glass bottle waiting inside feels as heavy as a brick against my hand.

The ladies flutter off after a minute or two, sharing sly smiles among each other. Lady Rochford is the last to exit, and she's suddenly holding a small cup like the one Cecily gave me before the ceremony.

"Some servant girl said you asked for mead. Is that true?"

"Oh, yes," I answer, picking up the drink and tossing it back. I need all the liquid courage I can muster. I hand her back the cup, thanking her before she swiftly walks out.

Henry arrives at my bedchamber no more than a minute after she's gone, walking through the door wearing a long nightgown and a fur-lined robe of red and gold.

"My sweet Catherine," he says softly. "What a sight you are." The door closes behind him, and I get the sense that we're two fighters who have just been shut into an arena.

Only Henry has no idea.

"And what a sight you are," I answer in return.

He crosses the room, taking my hands in his and looking

deeply into my eyes. He goes to speak, but I beat him to it. "How about some wine?"

I slip my hands from his and move to a table near the hearth. A restless fire hisses and snaps, keeping the room from falling silent and casting me in silhouette as I stand with my back to Henry. My hands are shaking as I slip the vial from my pocket and uncork the stopper with my thumb. I look over my shoulder. Henry has his eyes on the large four-poster bed as I hold the draft just above his glass. I'm about to pour it in, but then I hesitate.

What if Bessie got the measurements wrong? What if it doesn't work? What if it works more than it should? What if Henry tastes the difference and has me hanged or tortured for attempted royal murder?

If I'm going to do this, it has to happen now. Yes or no. In or out.

Fuck it.

I dump the draft into the cup down to the very last drop. I pour the wine in over it with my other hand next, slipping the empty vial back into my pocket in the process. I swish the cup in a circular motion as I face Henry once again.

When I cross the room to return to him, my insides feel like a broken elevator that's plummeting to the basement. I offer Henry the cup, and I'm close enough that I feel his breath between us. The rise and fall of his chest is inches from my face.

"I hope you like it," I tell him.

"What a sweet little wife you are." He takes the cup with a tender grin and lifts it up in a toast. "To you, my lovely Catherine." Bringing the cup to his lips, he takes a sip as his gaze drops to mine. I wait on bated breath until he sighs. "This is delicious."

Like about-to-kill-you delicious or normal delicious?

He downs the rest of the drink, and I lock my jaw to keep it from dropping. It is entirely possible that I just poisoned the king of England.

Henry hands the empty cup back to me, then rests his palms on my shoulders. "Are you ready to lie down, my heart? I have thought long and often about our wedding night."

My mind goes blank. Bessie said the draft would take a few minutes to kick in. I need to stall him until then, and somehow I forgot to plan for it.

"Sure," I answer weakly.

Henry is all smiles as he makes his way over to the colossal bed. He takes the side that's farther into the room and stands just off from the mattress. He unfastens his robe and drops it to the floor with his eyes trained on mine. It's the striptease that no one asked for.

He lowers himself down with a tired groan, stretching his injured leg out on the mattress. When I eventually reach my side of the bed, I unfasten my robe slow enough to enrage a sloth. I ease the material from my shoulders, and Henry's eyes trail up and down my gossamer nightgown. As they do, I notice the bandage wrappings on his injured leg. The dressing is damp with yellow stains, and this is only on the outskirts.

"When did you hurt your leg?" I ask, sitting gingerly on the edge of the bed. I've only ever seen him limping, and as I breathe in, I catch the smell of rotting flesh and a stronger scent of men's perfume emanating from around the wound.

"It's an old injury. I was unhorsed in a joust many years ago, and the results were quite severe."

I pause. "How severe?"

The king sits up straighter against the pillows, settling himself in the center of the bed. "I was told that I was unconscious for more than two hours. Many believed I would not survive it, but I proved them all wrong."

Unconscious for several hours? He could have a brain injury. There's no way to know the full repercussions of his accident without an MRI, but there's a good chance that the damage was severe.

"And your leg?" I inquire next.

"It never healed correctly and remains putrid. The surgeons keep it open for fear that if it closes, the infection will spread throughout the body."

I'm no orthopedist, but that doesn't sound like a healthy course of treatment. "So, you've been in pain like this for years?"

"It is nothing I cannot bear."

Intense chronic pain can take a massive psychological toll. Couple that with an untreated brain trauma and absolute power—and it's a lethal hotbed for disaster.

"There must be something that can be done," I tell him. "What do you do to fight the infection?"

Henry waves off the questions. "Don't worry your pretty little mind over any of that. I have more physicians than I know what to do with. All you need to worry about is being my loving wife."

I sit back farther on the mattress. "I'm sure your doctors are doing what they can, but if you don't mine my saying . . ."

"Enough, Catherine." He snaps the words out. It's the harshest he's ever spoken to me. His eyes have an unfamiliar streak of resentment, and I watch as the cutting glint flares then dissipates. A moment later, he paints an easy smile on his face as he reaches his arms out to me. "Come here, darling. I wish to hold you." He softens his voice, but he's reminded me of what lurks below the surface. I know what he's capable of, and the truth of it sets a nervous knot in my gut.

As my anxiety rises, I know that it's time to shake things up. "Before we do that," I tell him, "let's talk just a little bit more." His mouth slants downward. "More talking?"

"Mm-hmm." I fling myself all the way onto the mattress with a flying leap, using the element of surprise to my advantage. "Tell me about your earliest childhood memory."

Henry's mouth is agape at my barked-out question, and he labors in a startled breath when I suddenly roll down to the end of the bed, squeezing the foot of his uninjured leg in both my hands.

Feet are some of the most emotionally grounding parts of the body, and if Bessie's sleeping draft doesn't knock Henry out, then God help me, I will foot-massage the king into slumbering submission.

"Why . . . why would you want to hear about that?" he asks a little nervously.

"Because I do. I want to know everything there is to know about you." I push my thumb up and down his instep. He groans in appreciation as his head falls back onto his pillow.

"I suppose one of my earliest memories is when I rode my first horse."

"Tell me about it," I urge.

"About the horse?"

I nod and twist my grip.

"It was brown," Henry muses. "And much larger than I thought it would be. I was always a natural rider. Much more so than my brother, Arthur."

That must be the brother who passed away. "Did you get along with Arthur?" I ask.

"Such a curious girl you are."

I give his foot another squeeze, and his eyes roll back a bit in his sockets.

"I barely knew him," Henry admits. "We lived separately most of our lives. When he died from the sweating sickness, I was suddenly the heir to the throne." He pauses a moment. "I still keep some of his clothes in my wardrobe. It is not right for him to be forgotten."

I'll need to ask him more about Arthur in the future. "You seem to care very deeply about your health. Just how many physicians do you keep on call at the palace?"

Henry lets out a relaxed laugh. "Too many to count," he says through a yawn. "Perhaps I will keep less now that I have you taking care of me. Already, I feel myself at ease in your presence. You are so calming, Catherine." His eyes are beginning to flutter closed, and I pray, pray, pray that Bessie's magic is working. I ease my steady strokes of his foot but don't stop entirely.

"A husband should not sleep on his wedding night," Henry whispers. "Come lay with me, wife. Let me hold you while we rest."

"I'll be there in a minute," I tell him gently.

I move my hand to his ankle, squeezing and releasing the strained muscles. I've barely done it a second time before Henry is dead asleep. I keep my eyes trained on his torso, making sure that he's not actually dead *in* his sleep and find him breathing deeply.

He's alive. He's sleeping. I'm safe.

I carefully stand on the bed beside the king's resting form. "Henry?" He doesn't move or stir. I bounce the bed with my feet as I raise my voice a little higher. "Henry?" Still nothing. I do a big jump up and let myself fall onto the mattress. Henry starts to snore.

I look at the door, well aware that at least twelve noblemen perverts are standing on the other side to ensure that the marriage is consummated. I take a cleansing breath and roll my shoulders.

It's showtime.

"Oh, Henry, yes!" I jump on the bed again, making sure to get the blanket extra rumpled. "Yes, right there! Ah!" I'm moaning like I've never moaned before, in part because I've never had superbly spectacular sex before, but also because I need those creepy door voyeurs to think that Henry is the most fantastic lover in the whole court.

I roll off the bed, and Henry rolls in the opposite direction, snuggling deeper into the pillow. My feet hit the floor and I charge at the doors like they owe me money, smacking my hands against the solid wood. I hear a startled collective gasp from the other side, and it makes me smile.

"Henry, ugh!" I body-slam the door a few more times for good measure before I notice a desk on the far side of the room. Moaning as I make my way over to it, I'm delighted to find a stack of paper, an ink bottle, and a quill pen stationed along the surface. "That's it! Harder! Don't stop!" I crescendo and pound my hands on the desk with a final violent smash.

I let the grand finale linger in the air before I take a breath, then calmly sit in the waiting chair. Setting a piece of paper in front of me, I dip the tip of the pen into the ink. Now that the necessary theatrics are over, I can get down to what's really important.

Henry VIII, I am going to clinical note the shit out of you.

Chapter Nine

When the king yawns the next morning, it's loud enough to rip me out of my uneasy sleep. I bolt upright, looking down at the mountain of pillows I stacked between us. Ripping the wall down, I shove some pillows under my head and hurl the others to the floor before I dive back into a sleeping position.

I close my eyes as the mattress gives under Henry's weight. He's inching closer to me, gently shaking my shoulder. "Catherine? Catherine, my love, are you awake?"

This is for the consideration of the academy.

I flutter my eyes open, smiling dreamily when I meet the king's drowsy gaze. "Good morning," I mumble, stretching against the pillows.

Henry scratches at his arm. "How long was I asleep?"

Sunlight is pouring in from the windows. It wouldn't hurt for me to look drowsy, too. "I'm not sure," I answer, rubbing my eyelids. "I fell asleep right after you. Maybe even before you." I roll onto my side, propping my hand under my head. "I guess we were tired after our marital activities."

"Our activities?" Henry's eyes are still clouded, but he's intrigued now, too.

I keep my voice playful as I answer him. "You don't remember? Henry, you did things to me last night that I never even knew were possible. I just hope that I didn't disappoint you. You have so much more experience than me."

A prideful red blush colors his bearded cheeks. "Well, I *am* a bit older than you, Catherine."

"Barely!" He rolls to face me as I go on, not wanting to miss a word of the verbal gold I'm spewing. "But you were so tender at the same time. When you held me in your arms, after I was literally shaking from wave upon wave of pleasure . . . I just felt so connected to you."

"Wave upon wave?" he asks hopefully, even boyishly.

I sit up taller to emphasize my words. "Wave. Upon. Wave." Henry's eyes are sparkling. He can hardly contain his impish grin.

"I hope I wasn't too loud," I admit a little shyly. "I didn't mean to be, but I couldn't help myself. I'd be so embarrassed if anyone in the hall heard me."

Henry sits up against the pillow and takes my hands. "Let it not trouble you. If anyone heard our cries of love, they'll understand it was because God blessed our union and wished it so."

"It really was a religious experience." Henry lets out a carefree sigh. He folds his arms behind his head and looks up at the ceiling. He's entirely too comfortable. "So how do things work around here?" I ask. "Do I get out of bed first or do you? I'm new to this queen business."

He gives me an oh-silly-Catherine smile and sits up again, seemingly full of energy. "I will get up first, my love. Your ladies will attend to you shortly, and I'll see you at dinner this evening."

He slowly but resolutely makes his way off the mattress. I hop out of bed after him, helping him to put on his robe.

"I miss you already!" I tell him with a gentle shove toward the door.

He gives me a smirk over his shoulder as he knocks and waits.

The door swings open to reveal at least ten lords in the hallway. It's utter silence until they erupt in boisterous cheers. Henry dives into the crowd like a returning sex hero, allowing Bessie and Cecily to sneak in behind him. They close the doors on the frat-like vibe that's tangibly pulsating through the hall.

"I suppose it worked, then?" Bessie asks.

"Oh, it worked," I tell her, falling back into bed. "It worked, and I worked, and now I'm ready for a very long nap."

Cecily rounds the mattress and pulls me up by my arms. "There's no rest for the wicked, Your Majesty, especially when there's a roomful of women waiting to attend to you."

"What do you mean?"

My arms are still slack in Cecily's hold when Lady Rochford whips the door open, stomping into the room like an inconvenienced drill sergeant.

"Good morning, Your Majesty. I see that you're only just out of bed, so once you are bathed, fed, and dressed, we can carry on with your daily goings-on as queen. If it pleases you, we can attend mass straightaway. I've already attended twice this morning, but who's counting. Or, if you prefer, there's a choir visiting from Wales that is rather good. They're assembled in the Great Watching Chamber."

I'm so tired after being on Henry-please-stay-comatose watch all night that the thought of listening to high-pitched singers sounds as tempting as a rougher-than-normal pap smear.

I rub my hands over my weary face. "I have a different idea. What if we don't do any of that, and we decide to have a girls' day instead?"

Lady Rochford watches me with a mixture of bewilderment and disgust. "What's a girls' day?"

There are now over a dozen of us women lounging around in my inner receiving room. Blankets and pillows are strewn on the floor; we're fully dressed but with warm washcloths on our faces or cucumbers on our eyes. I'd like to say that the ladies are embracing the experience, but they look more like a collection of statues that have tumbled to the floor. William and Bartholomew are providing what's meant to be a relaxing soundtrack via a lute and flute, but they seem equally uncomfortable. Bessie is the only one who appears somewhat at ease, but that's because she's leaning backwards as she enjoys a snack.

"Bessie, stop eating all the cucumbers."

She ignores my request and munches on another one. "It seems a shame to waste them."

"It really does, Your Majesty," says Lady Wessex. Lady Wessex is in her mid-thirties and is never not scowling. She's also the only lady-in-waiting who doesn't suck up to me, and I like her tremendously for it. "And why must we all have food and cloth covering our faces when *she* doesn't?"

The group turns to look at Lady Rochford, who is perched on a chair in the corner with her arms crossed. "I'm special," she says, straight-faced.

I sit myself up from my reclining position to address the room while repositioning Theo, who's sitting comfortably on my lap. "Okay. I admit that maybe the self-care concept is a stretch in the current sociopolitical climate, but I really just want us all to get to know each other."

"In what way?" Bessie asks.

I give Theo's coat a pet as my fingers begin to fidget. "I think it would be beneficial for everyone if we could connect more. From what I've observed, it seems that most of us are a bit suspicious of each other, and it would be great for our mental health if we could support each other and let our guards down when we're together."

"When you say 'mental health'..." Lady Wessex asks, trailing off at the end.

"I mean how we're feeling in our minds. Our psychological, emotional, and social well-being. No one should neglect their mental health."

The room breaks out into laughter, and it takes a good twenty seconds until they settle.

"How about this?" I try. "Let's do a group exercise."

"Anne of Cleves didn't make us do group exercises," Lady Wessex complains. She's referring to Henry's fourth queen (the one before me), whom he was married to for six months before he had the marriage annulled. It was a political match, but Henry immediately deemed the twenty-four-year-old Anne too "unattractive" for him. Clearly his self-awareness waved bye-bye and hit the Hampton Court road a long time ago. Anne was given a settlement and then referred to as the king's sister.

Some people are just born lucky.

"So, we're going to play a game called Stand Up, Sit Down. Everybody, stand up." I hop up from my place on the floor, setting Theo down beside me. Slowly but surely, the rest of the ladies do the same. "In this game, one of us talks about a challenging experience we've faced, and then whoever has had the same experience sits down, too. I'll go first. I sometimes experience depressive episodes."

I sit down, and everyone does the same.

"See, this is great. Lady Wessex, when is one of the times that you've felt depressed?"

"This game is inspiring a depressive episode as we speak."

A number of the women try to hide their laughs. "Okay, well, I'm glad you're speaking your truth. It's your turn now. Everyone up."

Lady Wessex takes an exhausted breath. "Fine. I sometimes worry very deeply about my son, so much so that I make myself sick over it." She sits down, and half the ladies do the same.

"Thank you for sharing that, Lady Wessex. Do we have any volunteers to go next?"

One of my younger maids, Margaret Sutton, speaks up. "I will. I have trouble sleeping at night for fear of being killed by an angry mob." She sits down, though no one else does.

"Thank you for sharing that, Margaret," I tell her. "May I ask why you have that fear?"

"On account that I watched as my entire family was killed by an angry mob."

William and Bartholomew stop playing. The room falls wholly silent.

"I feel like I should have been prepared for that possibility. I'm very sorry for your loss, Margaret, and, if you're comfortable with it, I would be happy to unpack that with you privately in the very near future." She stands back up with a nod, and I slowly look out at the rest of the group. "Would anyone else like to go?"

Elizabeth Norworth steps forward. She's one of my oldest maids of honor and is also one of the quietest. "I will, Your Majesty. When I displeased my father last year, I was forced to fast for a week to show my repentance and obedience."

Every woman in the room sits down, apart from me.

What the actual fuck?

Every woman in this room has been starved as a form of punishment at some point in their lives.

"I'm sorry you all had to go through that," I tell them.

"It is not just that," Elizabeth goes on to say. "What happened was, the fasting made my insides hurt so wretchedly that even now, whenever I see food, I hide a bit of it in my garters. Especially cheese. Most of the court thinks I emit a retching smell, but I don't. It is just the hidden cheese."

I'm silent for a moment. "Do you think you could maybe pick something else to store in your garters? Maybe fruit or a slice of bread?"

She stares unsmilingly back at me. "I much prefer cheese."

"As do we all."

The women are all looking at me, and I give my head a shake. "You know what? Upon further investigation, I think it's best that we switch over to individual sessions."

If there's one thing I've learned from this exercise, it's that this traumatized Tudor court is in desperate need of a psychologist. And guess what? They just got one.

"What do you mean by 'sessions'?" Elizabeth Norworth asks.

"What I mean is . . . embroidery sessions. I would like to embroider with each of you, one at a time."

"May I ask why, Your Majesty?"

I shrug and tuck my hands behind my back. "No reason in particular."

<u>Client name:</u> Agnes Fitzhugh
<u>Occupation:</u> Maid of honor

Presenting concerns: Agnes reported difficulty maintaining trusting social relationships after King Henry executed five of her family members on five separate occasions. When Agnes relayed her anxious thoughts to her father, he assured her that he is a close personal confidant of the king and that Henry would never abandon his friends.
Interventions used: Guided visualization was employed. Will follow up with Agnes's father about his avoidant coping behaviors and the dangers of continued denial.

Client name: Sarah Empson
Occupation: Lady-in-waiting
Presenting concerns: Sarah expressed anger and resentment toward fellow lady-in-waiting Anne Calthorpe. Sarah stated that Anne relayed details of their private conversation to a member of the king's privy council, in the hopes of getting Sarah banished from court. Violent inclinations were noted, with Sarah stating she would like to part Anne's hair with a broadsword.
Interventions used: Cognitive Behavioral Techniques were introduced. Emotional labeling was practiced: "I felt disappointed and betrayed"; "I don't *really* want to cut Anne's head open with a broadsword."

Client name: William Finch
Occupation: Musician
Presenting concerns: William communicated feelings of near-crippling anxiety after reoccurring dreams where he plays out

of tune at the king's wedding ceremony. William conveyed that while being taught how to play the organ as a young child, he was struck with a thin tree branch by his music instructor each time he made a mistake, which was quite often.

Interventions used: Employed 4-7-8 breathing technique to manage anxiety. Introduced the concept of journaling to help decrease rumination.

*Sidenote: Speaking to William outside of a professional capacity once our session was complete, I gave a grisly description of my plans to hammerfist-punch his music instructor in the back of the head at the earliest possible opportunity.

My sessions last for hours, and I've embroidered a solid quarter of a bedsheet by midday. I'm stretching my fingers out when I look up to see an elegant woman standing in front of the vacant chair across from me.

"May I embroider with you next, Your Majesty?" She seems to be in her early thirties, with pale blue eyes and a composed countenance.

"Of course," I tell her, gesturing her to sit.

She makes herself comfortable and begins to stitch the handkerchief she's working on. "I'm Lady Barrow," she says. "I'm one of your ladies-in-waiting and a close acquaintance of your cousin Lady Rochford."

That's why she seems familiar. When Lady Rochford is talking to someone, it's usually her. "I'm sorry. I'm still in the process of learning names."

"Think nothing of it," she says. "I'm sure you have plenty of more important things to worry about as you adjust to life as queen." She pulls a graceful stitch, her mouth curving as she looks up at me. "I'm also a relation of one of your maids of honor, Bessie. It's wonderful to see my young cousin so at ease at court."

I glance over now to see Bessie sound asleep on the floor with Theo on her chest. "I'd be lost without her," I tell Lady Barrow, and we share a quiet chuckle.

"Bessie and I share a common interest in herbs," she says. "We often confer with each other over healing properties and such."

Something in her tone makes me freeze for a beat, but then I continue to embroider. "That's nice," I reply.

"I wonder if you would be able to assist me in a tea I'm hoping to create."

I slowly pick my embroidery back up, but I don't begin a new stitch. "How could I assist?" I ask.

"At present, I'm unable to acquire wild carrot seed. But as queen, I'm sure that you would be able to."

I hold my needle in my hand, though I still haven't used it since she sat with me. "And what do you need the carrot seed for?"

"Would you prefer an appropriate answer or the truth?"

"The truth," I tell her.

She nods and leans in the smallest degree closer. "I was married very young, you see. And my husband was quite eager to beget an heir. Praise be to God, we were granted my son. A healthy, strong baby boy. But while he thrived, I did not. The birthing was incredibly difficult for me, and the doctors believed that having any more children would be impossible."

"I'm so sorry." No sooner do I get the words out than she immediately brushes me off.

"What are you sorry for? It's all just a part of life." I see her sweeping her trauma aside and under the rug like unsavory dust, because that seems to be the only thing done in this century.

"Miraculously, we went on to have four more children, and each birthing has been more painful than the last. My husband hopes for more children still, but..." She pauses. "But I feel quite certain that if I'm to go through another, I will not survive it."

I take in a quiet breath at her words, still not positive where this is going.

"Wild carrot seed would protect me, as it would protect other ladies in your court who bear a plight similar to mine. Will you help us?"

I see the fear behind her serene eyes. She wants something preventative. Something to protect her from becoming pregnant.

"Of course I will," I tell her. "You have my word."

Lady Barrow takes a shaky breath and straightens the handkerchief in her lap.

"I am most thankful," she replies. She goes to stand, but I catch her wrist, stopping her before she can leave.

"Can I ask you something?" She pauses and sits back down. "Why are you trusting me with this? How do you know I won't tell other people what you asked me to do?"

She looks at me before quietly responding. "Lady Rochford believes you trustworthy, and my cousin Bessie is a bit unusual but a good judge of character." I watch as her defenses momentarily crumble, a small smile once again pulling at her cheeks. "But more than that, if something is going to befall me, I want it to be done by my choice, rather than my inaction."

I don't ask her anything else. She takes her embroidery and calmly walks away. I'll have to ask Lady Rochford about the carrot seed and how I can go about getting it. If it does the job that Lady Barrow thinks it does, maybe I'll try some of her tea, too. Just in case.

I'm replaying our surprisingly frank conversation in my mind when there's a knock at the door. One of the guards on the outside opens it, and Simon walks inside.

I hate how I innately respond to seeing him. My heart rate jumps. My chest grows tight. I've been attracted to people before, but this feeling, this strange high that he sparks . . . I don't know what to do with it.

He looks around at the room filled with women, straightening his back as his eyes focus on me.

"Forgive my intrusion," he murmurs, "but I have a message from His Majesty. He wishes to see the queen immediately."

Lady Rochford springs into action and gets up from her chair before I can even move. "I will come with you," she says.

She's already set her embroidery down when I put up an arm to stop her. "It's fine. I'll be right back."

She looks at me in a curious way before sitting back down. "Yes, Your Majesty."

I give her a reassuring smile before walking to the door. Simon turns when I approach, and we leave the room side by side.

Our commute to the king's room is a quiet one. At least, it is for us. We pass plenty of people, and everyone bows or curtsies as I walk past. It's unsettling. It isn't until we're well out of the queen's rooms that Simon eventually speaks.

"Are you all right?" he asks.

My gaze snaps in his direction. His eyes are studying me, like he's making sure that I'm whole. My pace eases. His expression is protective and impossibly gentle. It makes my throat tighten. I have to swallow before I can say, "I'm fine. Thank you for asking."

Simon tempers his pace to match mine. He doesn't speak again for a few seconds until he says, "The king was in high spirits today. Married life must suit him."

"Maybe it suits him too well," I mutter. "And that's why he keeps getting married."

Simon gives his head a small, disbelieving shake. "You speak of him with no fear. Do you have that much faith in him?"

His voice isn't at all scared, yet he seems to think mine should be. I face ahead as I answer. "I don't think Henry wants to hurt me. Not right now, in any case."

Simon stops walking then. He keeps looking at me, and I wish he wouldn't. His looking at me leads to my looking at him, and when I do that for too long, my mind wanders where it shouldn't.

I'm grateful when he starts walking again, and I move beside him when he lowers his voice.

"This is a dangerous road we're traveling down, Your Majesty." His tone is thick. It feels hard to talk when I clear my throat and throw him a playful look.

"You mean this hallway?"

"No, not this hallway" he counters easily. "I mean the way I feel about you."

My pulse jumps at his words. I slow my pace down again. I need to make this stroll last. "How do you feel about me?" I ask. I'm hyperaware of every sound, every footstep, every breath between us as I wait for his answer. When he speaks, he keeps his eyes forward.

"How honest would you like me to be?"

"Very honest," I tell him.

Simon nods, inching the smallest bit closer to my side and dropping his voice again so no one can overhear. "Well then, very honestly, I feel as if there's everyone else in the world, and then there's us. And we belong more to each other than we do to anyone else."

There's a rush of heat to my cheeks and ears. We belong to each other. He belongs to me, and we haven't even kissed. These Tudor guys don't waste any time.

"And you think that's dangerous?" I ask quietly.

Simon looks down at me, his gaze assured and unshaken. "I know that it is. But I'm accustomed to grave peril. Are you?"

I'm taken aback for a second. "You're accustomed? Like, you've done this with queens before?"

Simon's eyes widen in confusion. "What? No, I mean with jousting. I could die each time I joust."

"Oh," I answer quickly. "Sorry, I should have figured that." With my jealous nerves quelled, I lean my head toward him subtly as we cross through a corridor. "What if I told you I wasn't worth the risk?"

Simon moves closer to me, letting our arms touch. "Then I'd tell you that you were a liar." A smile starts to spread across my face, and I have to bite my lip to keep it at bay as Simon goes on. "I don't know how it happened or what changed, but I don't want to go back to the way things were before. But if you want me to, I will. I think I'd do just about anything you asked me to—even if it's staying away from you."

We're entering the king's rooms now, just outside the Presence Chamber.

I cast a few quick glances around the room. We're not alone, but no one is close enough to hear. My shoulders tense, but not from discomfort. I just know that our stolen moment it almost over, and whatever I say next needs to count.

I should think this through more. I should think long-term and endgame, but I don't want to. Not now. "No," I quickly tell him. "I don't want you to stay away. I want the opposite."

I murmur the words so quietly that for a second, I wonder if Simon's heard me at all. But then I look at him. His eyes grow warmer. The muscles in his neck tighten. His controlled stillness has me lingering somewhere between exhilaration and panic. I want to do or say something, but I also want to keep watching him as long as he's willing to stand there. I could look at him for hours.

It's just us now, despite everyone around us—like he said. It feels like I've taken a bite of something I shouldn't have, and I already want more.

Just then, the doors swing open in front of us, and Archbishop Cranmer exits. Dressed in clerical vestments, he has a narrow nose and a dominant chin. His blue eyes seem too small for his face. He's one of the king's most loyal sycophants and I can't tell if he loves or hates me.

"Your Majesty," he says with a bow. "The king awaits your presence."

I give him a small smile and a curtsy, walking into the Presence Chamber and looking back at Simon over my shoulder. His hands are pinned behind his back and his legs are tense, like he's forcing himself to stay where he is as the doors close between us. They seal shut with a *click*, and when I focus forward again, I realize what purpose the Presence Chamber serves. It's Henry's throne room.

Lavish tapestries adorn almost every wall. The gilded ceilings instantly draw the eyes up before they're demanded back down by the formidable throne sitting front and center. It looks more eerie than it does powerful, and I don't like being in here one bit.

"Henry?" I call out through the empty room.

"Back here, Catherine."

My shoes echo against the stone floor as I make my way through, coming to a narrow hallway lined with guards as I enter the king's Privy Chamber. This is the inner sanctum. The room where I was brought to Henry, when we played cards and he told me we were to be married.

It seems different than it did that night—somehow grayer, despite the fading sun. The guards close the door behind me, and I find Henry sitting in his high-back chair, his mouth tilted with quiet satisfaction.

"Hello, my love. What a tedious day it has been without you." He reaches his arm out, beckoning me over to the chair facing him. I do as he wishes, and he squeezes my hand as I sit down to join him.

"I was told you wanted to see me."

"I always want to see you," he says teasingly, "but I sent for you now because I just concluded the plans for my upcoming travels with the archbishop."

I go still as unease ricochets inside me. "What travels are you talking about?" Solo travels? Group travels? I can't leave the palace when I'm meant to see Matthias in three days. Do royal astrologers go on road trips?

"Unfortunately," Henry says, "you will have to remain here. I have urgent business to attend to in Buckinghamshire that should take around a month."

A month?!

"Oh, no." My voice is shaking in unexpressed excitement. I keep my gaze downcast. Henry leans forward to brush a comforting hand across my knuckles.

"You must know that I would never leave you so soon after we were married if it wasn't necessary. This hurts me as much as it hurts you."

I grip the chair with my free hand. If I don't hold on, I might float away on a cloud of bliss. I look up at Henry like I very well might die from missing him. "I'll do my best to manage the pain."

"My brave girl." He gives my hand another comforting squeeze before reaching for a decorative wooden box on the table between us. He hands it to me with a knowing smile, and when I open the lid, I'm met with the most elaborate diamond necklace I have ever seen. It's precious stone after precious stone and has to weigh at least four pounds. That's the weight of a prize-winning summer squash.

"I promise you," Henry murmurs, "when I return, we will go on and progress just as we intended. The people of England want nothing more than to honor their perfect new queen. And I want nothing more than to spend every waking moment with you."

I place the jewel box in my lap, taking a pained breath for Henry's sake.

"I just don't know how I'm going to say goodbye . . ."

His face fills with tenderness as I look down, brushing away a fake tear.

Chapter Ten

"Bye! Goodbye!"

I'm on my tiptoes with Theo in my arms, waving Henry off as his royal retinue departs for Buckinghamshire. The morning sun is beating down on me, and my forest green headpiece greedily absorbs the heat, making my scalp sweat. I should be doing a better job of looking heartbroken, but there's an undeniable lightness in my chest as I watch Henry's carriage move farther and farther away from the palace.

Lady Rochford is standing beside me as it seems like a hundred mounted horses ride out behind Henry's carriage, with another hundred in the front.

"Where are we off to, then?" she asks me. "More embroidery, I presume?"

The sounds of Henry's Thanksgiving Day parade begin to quell as most of his entourage has left the yard, and a sense of freedom washes over me as I turn to Lady Rochford. "Yes, I would like to embroider, but I just have something I need to do first. Alone."

A dignified eyebrow lifts in question as I pass Theo over into her not-cuddly arms. "What could you possibly need to do on your own?"

"Matthias! Please, open up!" I've been pounding on his door for almost a minute when the alleged astrologer finally swings it open. His hair is more askew than usual, and his eyes are noticeably bloodshot. "Are you drunk?" I ask.

IN MY TUDOR ERA

"I'm always a little drunk." He leans his shoulder against the door, fumbling a step when it opens wider.

I sniff the air between us. "You smell like a music festival."

"Well, you're two days early. I was going to bathe before I saw you."

I scrunch my eyes. "Why don't I believe you?"

"Because I'm lying," he admits. "Come in, come in. Let's have a talk."

He moves aside and I enter the room. I don't know if the space is slightly cleaner than the last time or if I'm just getting used to it, but I have a feeling it's the latter. His raven in the corner bites at the cage like it's just itching to peck my face off.

"I'm pretty sure your bird hates me," I tell him, moving to the center of the room to sit on the less dirty high-backed chair.

"Sorry. I've trained her to root out time-traveling abominations."

"I should have assumed." Matthias sits down in the chair across from me. He's smiling and saying nothing as he rests his hands in his lap. I don't know if I'm about to get good news or bad news.

"So," I prompt him. "Did you find anything?"

For a second his eyes are totally blank until he says, "Ah, you mean about how to send you home. Yes and no."

I wait for him to elaborate. He doesn't.

"What does that mean?"

He sits forward in his chair, rubbing his hands together. "It means yes, I did find something, and no, because I'm not quite certain how we can use it to bring Catherine back or to send you forward."

I open my mouth to speak but then stop myself. "I'm going to need more details than that."

Matthias gets up to grab a bottle of wine from a nearby table. He sniffs it, makes a sour face, then pours himself a glass. "What I found was a passage in a text that focused on the matter of souls. Souls coming, souls going, and the possibility of controlling the destiny of a soul." I inch forward as he goes on. "You see, the more I think of it, the more I'm convinced that what happened to you didn't happen by chance. I believe that Catherine's spirit must have somehow *chosen* to send you here."

I sit back in my chair. The surface is sticky, but I can't bring myself to care. "No," I tell him.

Matthias takes a sip of his wine, almost gags, then swallows it down. "No?"

"No, that makes no sense. Why would Catherine choose to send me back? I don't fit here. I hate it here."

"Well," Matthias says, returning to his seat, "alternatively, Catherine might have sent you back to punish you. Maybe she saw you in the palace in the future and didn't like you."

I give him a glare, and he goes on. "Or maybe it was just the path of least resistance. Your spirit *is* more bendy than most."

"You can sense that?"

"Of course not," he scoffs. "The mist told me."

"Fantastic." I'm the one to get up now, putting my hands on my hips as I begin to pace. "You're telling me that there is no way for us to bring Catherine back? I thought you said you found something."

Matthias's gaze turns slightly optimistic. "Yes, I did read a passage that suggests that summoning a spirit can be done . . ."

"That's great!"

"The issue being, we would need a piece of Catherine's soul in order for it to work."

I'm cursed. My mom didn't invite an old witch to my christening after I was born, and, because of that, I was cursed in my crib as a baby. That or Matthias is right, and Catherine Howard is actually trying to kill me.

"Her soul?" I repeat for clarification. "We need a piece of Catherine's soul?"

"Correct. Or something connected to her soul."

I cover my face in my hands to stop myself from screaming. When I lower them back down, my eyes are raging. "What the hell, Matthias?"

His affronted gaze shoots right back at me. "Why am I the one taking all the blame? I'm doing the best I can here."

I inhale a ragged breath and close my eyes. I know this isn't his fault. I just want to go home. I at least need to have hope that I can get home. When I open my eyes back up, Matthias is watching me with a curious flicker in his gaze.

"Wait," he says quietly. "I just realized . . . you never told me your name. What is it?"

My throat instantly turns tight. I hadn't realized just how badly I needed someone to ask me that question until I heard the words.

"It's Lily," I answer. Matthias smiles. He even chuckles a bit. "Why is that funny?"

He shrugs. "It just suits you, is all. You remind me of a lily of the valley."

"It's my mom's favorite flower."

Matthias chuckles again. "It's quite poisonous, isn't it?"

"Just a little. And only when ingested." I move over to look at one of his tables, picking up and perusing a scroll that appears to be written in Latin.

"What was your mother like?" he asks.

I accidently squeeze the paper at his question, crinkling it along the edges before I place it back onto the table. I've done a good job of not thinking about my mother here, afraid I'd instantly break down. Picturing her now, it doesn't hurt like I thought it would. Instead, I feel safe and calmer.

"She's tall," I tell Matthias. "Taller than most women. And she loves the ocean. She can identify seashells within ten seconds of looking at them." I glance down at my empty hands, half expecting to find one there. "She has freckles on her nose, and all around it, too. Her hands are uncommonly soft, and no matter what she's doing, she smells like lilacs and library books."

I think about crying then, but sadness isn't the only thing that can bring tears. Love can, too.

"You're lucky you have such vivid memories," Matthias says. "I hardly remember my mother at all."

I'm about to ask him what he does remember about her, but he downs his drink and throws the cup into the fire. Whatever emotions he's feeling, I want to give him the time and space to sort through them. I turn away and walk to the windows, noticing a long row of tents set up in the distance.

When I hear Matthias approaching, I ask, "What's going on over there? By the base of that hill?"

He stands at the window a few feet away, opening it up and gazing out. "Those are the revels. Still going on, it seems."

I move closer to the glass in front of me for a better look. "What are the revels?"

"Music, jugglers, games of chance. I lost a fair bit of coin there yesterday." Matthias closes his window and faces me. "You wouldn't happen to have any I could borrow, would you? My debts have been stacking up as of late."

I look back at him with a wry stare. "I will steal every jewel in this palace and drop it on your doorstep if you help me get back home."

"I need more time," he says, moving deeper into the room. "I haven't given up hope. In the meantime, look inside yourself and see if any bits of Catherine are still in there. Maybe she's just as trapped as you are." I look down at my stomach before cynically glancing back up. "Or if you have any theories," he continues, "feel free to keep testing them. Not that I don't work well under pressure, but I'm not exactly the most dependable person, so to speak."

"Not even with the mist?" I tease.

Matthias smirks. "The mist likes to deceive me sometimes."

I offer him a quick smile and head over to the door. My hand is reaching for the handle when I twist back around. "The king is gone for a month. I'll check on you again in a few days."

He makes a scrunched-up face. "You see, I'm feeling the pressure that we just talked about."

"Oh, are you? *Are* you feeling the pressure, Matthias? Show of hands, which one of us is meant to get their head chopped off in a public forum after being forced to marry a jealous erratic king?" I raise my hand. Matthias half raises his, then lowers it back down. "Look at that, just me."

"Anne of Cleves was much nicer than you are," he says, shifting to pour out more wine but finding it empty. "Maybe I can find a ritual to bring her back instead."

"Whatever it takes," I tell him.

I've just stepped into the hallway when Matthias walks up

to the door himself. "Farewell, Your Majesty! I look forward to your next visit!"

Then he slams the door in my face.

When I get back to my sitting room, about ten ladies are engaged in reading or embroidery. I sit down next to Lady Rochford, who is nestled off to the side, absorbed with a book. I don't say anything right away, and she's completely at ease in the silence.

My leg is bouncing up and down. After my talk with Matthias, I'm feeling restless. I miss my family, and I need to let off steam.

"Can we get a drink?" I ask her.

Lady Rochford doesn't look up. "I'll call an attendant in a moment."

"Not here," I explain. "We should go out."

She snaps the book closed. "What do you mean by *out*?"

"I want to see the revels."

She exhales an amused laugh. "That's impossible. The crowds are too rough, and I will not risk your safety in such a way."

I turn to her with a pleading stare. "Jane, I need to get out of here. Just for an hour or two. Just for tonight. *Please.*"

She sighs at my request and pinches the bridge of her nose. "If we do sneak out tonight, Catherine, you have to promise that it will be just you and me. Under no circumstances are you to invite anyone else."

"About that . . ." I say, dragging the words out. "I think we should invite a few more people."

When she twists to face me, her brow is so furrowed that I think I might be aging her. "I truly miss Anne of Cleves."

I nod in empathy. "I think we all miss Anne of Cleves."

Chapter Eleven

We end up as a group of six. Me, Bessie, Cecily, William, Bartholomew, and Lady Rochford (who absolutely missed her true calling in life to work in espionage). She knows the palace like the back of her hand and has taken us through no fewer than ten shady hallways and down three flights of stairs until we step out into the brisk night air. She, Bessie, and I are all dressed in plainer clothes than usual, with long hoods and capes keeping us mostly in shadow. When we slip out through a creaky garden gate, I breathe deeper than I have in a week.

We're free. Just for tonight, we're free.

"I can't believe we've snuck out of the palace," Cecily quietly screeches in elation. "Do you think we're the first to do it?"

"We did it last night," Bartholomew says.

"I went involuntarily," William adds.

It's a good long walk from the castle to the revels. Lady Rochford and Bartholomew argue for most of the way, but the trek is more than worth it. The open space is lit by torchlight, music is playing, and there are entertainers everywhere—some even juggling fire. The row of tents is nearly half a mile long, with countless vendors selling trinkets, food, drink, and some other carnal services that may or may not be legal here.

"Could we try some honeyed lamb shank?" Bessie eagerly asks as we pass a group that's eating. "I've always wanted to try lamb right off the spit. Will you join me, William?"

William nods. "I do enjoy a lamb shank." Bessie takes his

arm, fully prepared to lead him off, when Lady Rochford pulls them both back.

"No! We are not separating. We are staying together and then we are going back to the palace as soon as we've had a drink." She's breathing harder than usual but freezes when she sees a small circle of revelers playing dice. She looks away, then turns back, twisting her neck slightly. "On second thought, let's all meet back here in an hour. No one is to go off on their own. No one get hurt. Be here in one hour."

She swiftly walks off in the direction of the gambling, and we stand in mystified silence for several seconds as a result.

"All right, see the rest of you in an hour." Bessie and William walk off next, and Bartholomew offers his arms to me and Cecily.

"Shall we, ladies?"

We set out as a trio, heading deeper into the line of tents. A laughing couple rustles past us, and the woman hands me a cup. I smell it, and I'm eighty percent sure that it's some kind of spiced wine. I take a small sip and brace myself, but the drink goes down smooth. I take a large gulp, and Cecily and Bartholomew share a look.

"Honestly, that was really good," I tell them. "We should find more."

I pull them along with me, determined to find the Tudor equivalent to a dive bar. If this is my one night of freedom, I'm going to revel the shit out of it.

Forty minutes later, Cecily and Bartholomew have had two drinks each, and I'm three cups in. We find ourselves at a large gathering area. The music is thumping, and there's a massive bonfire. Dozens of people are dancing—and not toe-pointing choregraphed dancing, but moving-their-bodies-and-having-fun dancing.

Bartholomew chugs his drink and tosses his cup to the ground. "All right. This is what we're here for."

He grabs ahold of me and Cecily and pulls us into the mix. The crowd comes together in a wave of excitement. The three of us can't stop laughing as we sway and jump, moving to the sounds of lutes and drums like they were Diplo.

I lift my hands and close my eyes. For a second, I could be home, out dancing at some sketchy club that Zoe dragged me to after I refused to come out of my study cave for months. I smile as I think of her. The crowd surges and I'm jostled around. When I open my eyes, I can't find Cecily or Bartholomew. I keep looking, even calling their names, but I can't spot them anywhere in the throng of people.

I move out of the crowd, standing along the edge in the hopes of getting a better view. Half of my eyeline is on the bonfire when I suddenly see Simon through the flames, walking on the other side. My breath catches. He doesn't see me yet, and I move toward him like I'm being pulled by a magnet. But then I stop myself. I get that nervous swirling sensation in my belly, the one that always seems to manifest right before I decide to do something risky.

I think of disappearing into the crowd. I could just ease away and be gone. I start to do it. My foot is inching backward when Simon looks up. Our eyes meet in the jumping sparks of the bonfire, and in that split second, we both know that I'm not going anywhere.

Simon is startled at first, but it doesn't last. It takes him all of two seconds to stride forward. He makes his way around the fire, stopping when we're only a few feet apart.

"Catherine? What are you doing here?"

I try to appear nonchalant and not tipsy, gazing out at the surrounding festivities. "I decided to venture out a bit."

"Clearly," he says with a strained chuckle. "Everyone is still celebrating your marriage."

"Are they? And here I thought it was my birthday." I take a sip of my drink, and Simon lifts his cup to do the same. "Is that you drinking to my future happiness?"

"Always." He places his now-empty cup on a log behind him, and I pass him mine to do the same. He glances around before speaking again. "How did you even get here?"

I give a little shrug. "I'm mysterious like that. Are you going to tell me I should go back to the palace?"

He continues to watch me, his gaze light but intent. "Not if you don't want to."

"I don't want to," I tell him. "Lady Rochford gave us an hour."

"Lady Rochford is here with you?" he asks, amazed. "The surprises never cease." Then, "In that case, should we have a look around while there's still time?"

Simon and I have time. It's a really nice feeling. I give him a nod and follow his lead as we begin to head back in the direction of the entrance. We have a fair walk ahead of us, but we slow down near a table of jewelry. It isn't diamonds or rubies on display here—more beads and wooden charms, or special woven ribbons for your hair. One bracelet catches my eye, the sea green color of the beads against the linen cord reminding me of my favorite beach. I touch it with the tip of my finger before moving along, and Simon falls into step beside me.

"Let me guess: This outing tonight was your idea?"

"And what makes you say that?" I ask teasingly.

A crooked edge pulls at his mouth. "Just a feeling I have."

We twist through a cackling group of revelers, and Simon's hand brushes my wrist, making sure I stay beside him. My stomach flutters at the sensation. "I like that you're comfortable talking about your feelings. Emotional intelligence is a good strength to have."

He looks down at me to catch my gaze, and I have to crane my neck up to meet his. "You bring it out in me," is all he says.

A flickering wave swooshes through my abdomen. "I'm sure you say that to all the girls."

"No," he answers confidently. "Just you."

A smile tugs at my cheeks, but before I get the chance to reply, a fight breaks out between two revelers beside us. The shoulders of one of the men knocks into me hard, and Simon immediately shoves him with so much force that the man goes tumbling to the ground. Before I know that it's happened, he's blocking the entirety of my body with his – a shield between me and the world. More fighting erupts, but Simon takes my hand and pulls me away, moving us into a nearby tent a few yards off.

The entrance flap drops down behind us as we move to stand in the center of the empty tent. We're all alone now. Everyone and everything is shut out around us as we gaze at each other in adrenaline-spiked silence. The commotion outside slowly dies and fades, being replaced by the chords of music once again.

There's room in the tent but we don't use it. We're so close to each other. Only one of us would need to step forward for our chests to touch. Simon lifts his arm slightly, and the tips of his fingers brush mine. "Do you want to leave?" he asks. There's a rasp to his voice. It draws me in and under as I shake my head.

"No," I manage. "I don't want to leave." Our hands weave together. The air around us feels so thin that I wonder if it's there at all.

"Do you know how many times I have imagined us alone like this?" Simon brings his hand up, running the tips of his fingers under my chin, barely grazing the surface of my skin. "Thoughts of you fill my mind."

I should stop this. I know that I should. If the wrong person saw us hidden away in here together, we could be killed. But Simon wasn't executed with Catherine in the past, so he should be safe this time. Maybe that's just what happened when Catherine was here. Maybe she and Thomas Culpepper flaunted their affair, and that was why they got caught. Simon and I can be careful. What happened to them doesn't have to happen to us.

Looking at Simon now, I step forward until our bodies meet. I've never felt a pull like this. I doubt I will again. My arms feel heavy as I raise my hands to his warm chest. His heart is thundering under my palm, and I want to make it go even faster.

Simon gazes down at my face like he's trying to memorize me—the curve of my cheek, the suppleness of my mouth. "Are you scared?" he asks.

I tilt my head as I look up at him. The closer we get, the more intoxicated I feel. And we're so close now that my body is humming. "No," I tell him.

Simon's smile is almost restrained, yet his eyes hold nothing but hunger. "You're fearless, aren't you?"

I take a beat before I answer. "I never used to be."

He slides his hand behind my neck, drawing me all the way forward. I take a quick, shuddering breath and close my eyes. I don't care how much this will hurt once it's over. I'm going to let it happen.

Our lips touch, my mind sighing *finally*. Simon's mouth moves over mine in an unhurried rhythm that lulls me into a deeper haze. I slip my hands farther up his chest, and the firm surface trembles under my touch. When I rake my fingers into the hair at the nape of his neck, I'm rewarded with a muffled groan in his throat.

His languid nips increase in pressure, and I match every slide of his insistent mouth. His lips slant over mine as his tongue strokes inside. A dizzy, coiling sensation knots in my stomach. I slip my tongue forward to meet his, and he drags me impossibly closer. It's like I'm free-falling. If I had a parachute, I'd throw it off.

He keeps one hand pressed to the back of my neck while the other slides to my hip. His grip tightens on the waist of my gown as he pulls me up flush against him. Lightheadedness clouds my mind and all I can think is that giving in never tasted so sweet. I can feel every inch of Simon against me, including his hard length. He nudges closer as his fevered mouth travels the line of my throat. I forget that anything exists outside of this. All my worries and fears evaporate into a searing fog. We're invisible to everyone but each other.

I arch my back and mold my body into his. He has to duck low to reach me, his lips never parting from my skin and savoring every inch he can reach. He drags a hand up over the fabric of my bodice as a low tugging feeling starts to unfurl inside me. I inhale sharply when he squeezes my breast. More. Everywhere. That's what I want and where I want it. Words seem far away, so I bring his other hand to the stays at the back of my dress. Maybe he can rip them open. His middle finger slips under one of the strings when a voice calls out over the music.

"Catherine?"

It's a girl's voice, right outside the tent. Simon and I freeze, neither saying a word until we hear it again. "Catherine? Where are you?"

It takes me two seconds to realize that it's Cecily.

"I can't stay," I blurt out. I begin to backstep in a panic, but Simon slips a hand to the small of my back. He holds me steady, his eyes a mix of hunger and control.

"We'll leave together but separately," he says, his voice deeper than I've ever heard it. "You go out through the front, and I'll leave from the back. I'll stay unseen as I make sure that you reach your companions and that you all get back to the palace safely."

He lets me go, and I follow his instructions even though it physically hurts to leave this tent. Still, I lift the flap and walk. I'm a little wobbly as I exit, and the music-filled air hits my flushed face. Everything is a blur. The people. The lights. And Cecily's body as she hurls herself into me, swearing that she doesn't know how we got separated. Lady Rochford is glaring at me over her shoulder, and I repentantly step in front of her.

"Is our little adventure done with, then?" she asks.

I nod and straighten my hair. She shakes her head and spins me around to begin walking back toward the palace, pulling my hood down in front of me.

"Keep your wits about you," she says. "In this court, those who are governed by their hearts are the first to lose. You are playing for your life now, Catherine, and the game never stops."

Her words send a nervous wave through me, helping to cool my overheating skin. I know that she's right. I need to focus.

I do my best to appear composed, and not like someone who was minutes away from have moaning, screaming, summon-the-ancestors tent sex with a courtier named Simon Gainsford while in the completely wrong century.

Chapter Twelve

William, Bartholomew, and Cecily are off to bed, and Lady Rochford and I are dropping Bessie off at her room.

She claims to be flying high from all the delicious food she ate, but it's more likely due to the generous amount of ale that she downed.

"That was so much fun," she muses, her arms wrapped steadily around our shoulders. "I have honestly never had more fun in my entire life."

Lady Rochford grunts as she lifts Bessie up higher. "I'm glad we all enjoyed ourselves."

Bessie giggles as she pulls us closer. "Is this what it's like to be a man? You can go out when you want, you can do what you want, and you don't get in trouble for any of it?"

"Basically," I answer.

Bessie sighs. "Incredible. Well, at least I have something to look forward to. I should think that I'll have more liberty once I'm a married woman."

Lady Rochford barks out a laugh. "That's some wishful thinking if I ever heard it."

"No, it's true," Bessie insists. "I'm going to marry someone level-headed and kind and not a tyrant. Catherine is going to help me."

If it wasn't borderline illegal for Lady Rochford to roll her eyes at me, I'm positive she would. "Right, because Catherine's husband selection skills are so extraordinary."

"I resent that," I tell her.

"I'm sure you do."

When we're a hallway away from Bessie's door, Lady Rochford sets our companion on her own two feet to walk ahead of us. "There now," she says. "We've gotten you back safe and sound, so let's all get to bed, and this frightful day can at last be over."

No sooner does she finish saying the word "frightful" than we round the corner and nearly collide with a waiting Mistress Marshall. I scream, because she's scary as fuck, and Bessie screams retroactively. Even Lady Rochford flinches.

"Mistress Marshall," she says, moving to stand a bit in front of us. "What are you doing awake at this late hour?"

The somber woman turns her head painstakingly slowly. This must be her audition tape for *The Exorcist 12*. "A curious question, Lady Rochford, considering it appears that you are all just returning to the palace with Her Majesty."

Lady Rochford juts her shoulders back slightly. "Yes, we were talking a late-night stroll about the gardens with *Her Majesty* and would very much like to retire."

I can't be sure, but Lady Rochford and Mistress Marshall may be about to square up. The tension is that intense.

"I understand," the older woman says. "But in the event of future late-night walks, I would like to be informed if one of my girls accompanies you. Bessie is, after all, my responsibility as mistress of the maids."

"And you are *my* responsibility as queen." I had no intention of entering this chat, yet here I am.

Mistress Marshall smiles at me, and it is entirely feline. "For the time being," she says.

I tilt my head as I take in her veiled threat. "I'm sorry Mistress Marshall, I think you must be overworked this evening. That has to be the reason you think it's acceptable to speak to me the way you are." Bessie gasps in an *oh shit* kind of way, and I take a step forward. "As queen, I hereby relieve you of your duties as mistress of the maids. For two months. Lady Rochford, is there someone who could assume the role while Mistress Marshall takes her much-needed rest?"

"Of course, Your Majesty," Lady Rochford answers. "I'd be happy to settle the matter for you personally."

"Wonderful. Enjoy your time off, Mistress Marshall."

I walk around and past the woman, who looks like she's swallowed a fuzzy lemon, and my heart is pounding at such an unnatural rate that I might actually keel over. I'm still wheezing when Bessie catches up to me and grabs my arm.

"I can't believe you just did that," she whispers.

I tuck her farther into my side. "Was I too harsh? Should I apologize? I'm going to go back and apologize."

"Don't you dare," Lady Rochford orders. "I've been going dagger to dagger with that scaled fish for years. Watching her get soundly scolded was nothing short of glorious."

I wish I could enjoy the moment as much as she is, but I'm still in a state of shock.

"See how my hand shakes," Bessie mutters.

"Yeah, mine, too."

LADY ROCHFORD LEAVES me to seek out her own room after she's helped loosen my gown. She untied the strings at the back so I can undress when I'm ready, but for now, I'm wide awake. In part from my run-in with Mistress Marshall, but mostly from my time in the tent with Simon.

I'm still thinking of him as I stand in front of a mirror near the hearth, though I'm looking down at the moment. I touch my hand to my neck, remembering how it felt to have his mouth there. He was so unrestrained. So hungry for me. My hand dips lower to my midsection, remembering the warm churning I felt when Simon touched my breast. I slip my hand upward to brush over that very spot, and when I turn my gaze up, Francis Dereham is standing behind me in the mirror. I gasp and almost scream, and if he was close enough, I would have smacked him through the fucking wall.

"Francis, what the hell are you doing?" I seethe, whipping around to face him. He just stares in response, completely transfixed. When he does speak a few moments later, his voice is steeped in cold determination.

"Where—is—Catherine?"

A chill shoots up my spine, so cold that it stings. "What are you talking about?"

"Tell me, *Catherine*, when did you first say that you loved me when we were at Lambeth? What did I gift you on our second midsummer? What was your exact answer when I asked you to marry me?"

He waits, and I say nothing. My throat is bone-dry. My heart is racing. I can't let him know that I'm rattled. "I don't have to answer your questions," I tell him.

He doesn't make a move toward me, and somehow his stillness is even more nerve-racking. "You won't answer them because to do so would prove your treachery."

How can he know? He can't know. He's just making a desperate guess. I need to stick to the script. "I hit my head and lost my memories. Bessie said that it's common."

"Stop lying!" he shouts. Theo starts barking from his place on my bed, and I run over to soothe him. Francis and I nervously stare at the door, waiting to see if anyone comes. Miraculously, they don't. Francis lowers his voice as he steps in my direction. "I know everything there is to know about Catherine Howard. How she moves. How she speaks. How she sees and interacts with the world. I know all of this and more. I have been watching you for days, and I can tell with absolute certainty—you are not *her*."

He's backed me into a corner, but not a physical one. I could keep lying. I could gaslight him into thinking that he's wrong. He's compulsive and infatuated, and trusting him would most likely be a fatal mistake.

Theo finally lies down again, and I keep my voice even as I turn back to Francis. "I get that you're upset, but you need to leave now."

"I will not go!" he whisper-yells, moving frighteningly close to my face. "I will have the truth! Where is she?"

Something inside me snaps. Maybe it's his aggression breathing down on me. Or maybe it's the spiced wine that I drank at the revels. Or maybe it's the fact that I'm so damn tired of lying that if I do it one more time, I'll scream and rip my hair out.

I move in closer to Francis's looming form. I glare back at him, matching his ire with plenty of my own. "I. Don't. Know." I emphasize each truthful word with approximately zero fucks.

Francis leans back with a disbelieving tremor. "You admit it, then? You took her?"

I come close to laughing. "I didn't take her. All I know is that I fell or fainted, and when I woke up, I was Catherine Howard. I'm from the future, and trust me, if I could bring her back and be home again, I'd do it in a second."

I watch as Francis starts to breathe hard. His eyes are wide. His neck muscles are tense. If I had to guess, I'd say he's in the early stages of a panic attack. I wait for a telltale verbal cue.

"You've gone mad," he mutters.

And there it is. I should try to soothe him, but I just don't have it in me. I sit down on the cold stone floor, pulling my knees into my chest. "Maybe we both have," I tell him.

He stays where he is for several seconds until he slowly joins me on the floor, sitting down across from me. He looks at me for a long time. "What happens to Catherine?" he eventually asks, his voice soft. "If you're from the future, then what happens to her?"

I take a moment before I answer. "She's killed. Henry has her executed. He executes you, too."

His stunned eyes flick open wider at my admission. They stay with me until he turns to stare at the fire in the hearth. "So, in your future . . . Catherine is dead. Were she and the king married for many years?"

I just told him he was going to be murdered, but he's still thinking only of Catherine. I hesitate again, wondering if I should cushion this for him. Ultimately, I decide to continue with the truth. "No, they're not married for long at all. She dies young."

Francis pushes both hands into his hair. He grips it so tight, I'm worried that he'll hurt himself. I'm about to stop him when he suddenly stands, pacing the space between us like a horse penned in too tight. "I won't let this happen. She and I are meant to be together. You need to bring her back. Bring Catherine back, and she and I will run away."

His tone is frantic. I keep mine steady. "You think Henry and his men wouldn't find you?"

"I don't care!" he counters. "What can we do to bring her back?"

I stand up as well, moving deeper into the room to sit in a chair against the back wall. "I wish I knew," I tell him. "I've tried going back to the place where I was transported, but that doesn't seem to work. I have someone who's trying to help me, but what he did find is impossible."

I gesture for Francis to sit in the chair opposite me. He begrudgingly does, and his posture is weighed heavy with defeat. His hands are balled into fists.

"Can you tell me about her?" I decide to ask. I may be trapped inside her body, but I barely know her at all.

Francis shifts up at my question, slowly bringing a hand to rest on the arm of his chair. It takes him a while before he answers.

"The day we first met, I had only just arrived at the Dowager Duchess's estate to begin employment as her secretary. I was alone in the library, answering a letter regarding a new tax on the Dowager's land when the door opened and Catherine peered inside. I glanced up, and she was there watching me like I was an unknown creature—some lawless beast she had never yet encountered.

"The room was full of dark tomes and the windows were shut. The curtains were mostly drawn. The airlessness of it was stifling. Then Catherine came in, strode right up to my desk, and asked me to walk with her. 'We should talk and take in the sun,' she said. And suddenly, I could breathe again." His eyes have only now begun to warm since he's talking about Catherine.

"It must have been nice," I offer, "to feel a connection like that."

Francis nods and looks down at his lap. "My first few months there, she was the only one who bothered to speak to me. The others thought I was strange. She was the one person to really see me. And in exchange, I saw no one but her."

His voice is reverent. Almost pure. Speaking about Catherine is holy for him.

"What did she like to do in her free time?" I ask, trying to lessen the formality.

It takes a moment, but Francis lets a small smile slip— more to himself than to me. "Not many people knew this, but Catherine was an excellent storyteller. She would come up with tales about princesses and bandits, or princesses who *were* bandits, and the stories were romantic, but they had such humor in them, too. I had never heard anything like it. I begged her to write any of them down, but she only ever laughed at me."

Catherine was a writer—or she could have been. I lean my elbows onto my knees as I wait to hear more.

"Until one day," Francis continues, "she did it. Her story was . . . It was beautiful. Her words were so skilled, and fair and true, just like her—it was as if she poured her soul into the paper itself."

I'm glad that Catherine showed her writing to someone. Art is meant to be shared, and the fact that she decided to share hers fills me with a proud kind of warmth.

Then I sit up absolutely straight. "Wait, what did you just say?"

Francis spares me a distracted glance. "That her story was beautiful?"

"No," I snap back. "You said something about her soul . . ."

"Oh," he answers, "I said it was as if she poured her soul into the paper."

I lunge forward at Francis and grab ahold of his shoulders. "Holy shit! That's it! That has to be it!"

Francis tries to pry my fingers off him, to no avail. "What do you mean, 'that's it'?"

"The story! Her soul!" I stand and drag Francis up to stand with me. "Where is it? Do you still have it?"

"Her story or her soul?"

I give him a surprisingly violent shake. "The story, you idiot!"

He does break free from me then, stepping away and holding his hands up to defend himself. "I don't have it. I sent it back to her at Lambeth."

I can taste the disappointment in my mouth. "No," I groan. "Why would you do that?"

"Because she asked me to. She asked me to send it back to her in the letter she wrote saying that she never wanted to see me again."

"Francis, I need that letter. If you can get it . . ." My words abruptly trail off. "Wait, did you just say that Catherine broke up with you?"

He doesn't answer, which is telling.

I rub at my eyes as I try to gather my shifting thoughts. "Also, I should have asked this earlier, but why did you call me 'wife' the last time I saw you? Did you and Catherine secretly get married?"

Francis looks to the ground before leveling his heavy stare in my direction. "We both knew that her family would never approve of the match. But they couldn't prevent us from being married in our hearts."

I breathe out a torrential sigh of relief.

"And our bodies," he adds.

I can't keep my nose from scrunching as I give him a slow blink. "Okay, well, that's private information. The important thing is that you and Catherine weren't lawfully married. That's an important distinction we should both agree on."

Francis straightens his shirt, even though there are hardly any wrinkles.

I venture a step closer, keeping my voice calm. "So, why did you come to the palace if Catherine called things off with you?"

"Because I loved her," he answers automatically. "I still love her."

I nod as the subtle hurt etches across his cheeks. "And do you accept the fact that she might not love you back anymore?"

Francis opens his mouth to answer, then stops. He turns to look toward the hearth, speaking more to it than to me. "Neither of us can know how she feels until we save her."

If we were in session together, this would be where I'd dive into some Emotionally Focused Therapy with Francis. We'd identify unhelpful thought patterns and work on balanced thinking. But unfortunately, we're not in session, and right now I need Catherine's writing if there's any chance of my getting home.

"You're not wrong," I tell him. "But if we want to find out how Catherine really feels, then getting that story is our biggest hope of bringing her back."

Francis pivots to face me, planting his feet. "I sent the story back to her at Lambeth, but I'm sure the Dowager Duchess intercepted all my letters. And I'm certain they're still in her keeping."

I've watched enough crime shows to know how deadly a paper trail can be. Those letters might have been used as evidence to prove Catherine's "guilt" in her lifetime, which means they could also be used to prove the guilt in mine.

"Why would the Dowager keep your letters to Catherine?" I ask.

"Because it furthered her purpose of having Catherine believe that I forgot about her. And the Dowager likes to keep things. As her secretary, I saw that she would often withhold and steal correspondence from her wards as a form of punishment."

I'm assuming this wasn't a federal offense in Tudor times.

"I need you to get those letters, Francis. I need to read them to see if they can help us." As in, they're going directly into the fire. Except that story.

"I'll leave tonight. If they're there, I'll easily find them, and the story," he swears. He heads to the door, but then quickly stops to turn back around. "One more thing . . . if Gainsford ever touches you again, I'll kill him."

I let out a sigh. "When you get back, we really need to talk about healthy attachment styles and emotional regulation. Let's block out a consistent time."

He nods with confusion and slips from the room. I'm left in silence and can only now begin to process the fact that I just told Catherine Howard's obsessed ex a secret that could earn me a one-way ticket to a sixteenth-century insane asylum. I have no idea if it was the right choice, but what I do know is that my head is spinning and there isn't a shot in hell that I'm falling asleep anytime soon.

Jitters and adrenaline clash in my lungs. I have to move. I have to do something. Francis just left on a whole-ass side quest to bring Catherine back, and I need to take action, too. I think for all of ten seconds before coming to a decision.

I'm going to haunt the Haunted Gallery.

Chapter Thirteen

I'm not here to run. I'm not going to hurl myself against the doors either. Tonight, I'm taking a different approach. That's why I'm lying on the ground, and the only thing I hear is the sound of my own voice as I quietly start to sing.

> "Pastime with good company, I love and shall
> until I die. Grudge who lust but none deny,
> so God be pleased thus live will I . . ."

I pause as I try to remember the rest. Giving up with a sigh, I pick up the paper beside me and glance over it. I had Bartholomew recite the lyrics of "Pastime with Good Company" the other day while I jotted them down, and I'm still in the process of learning. Sidenote: jotting things down with a quill and ink converts to twenty-eight minutes for four sentences.

For idleness is chief mistress of vices all. Then who can say, but mirth and play, is best of all?

I tilt my head forward a little, doing a quick portal check in the otherwise empty hall. Nothing has materialized. I ease my head back down, preparing to take this not-catchy song from the top. I look at the paper again, and as I do, I catch the sound of footsteps. They're alarmingly close.

I tense, not sure if I should jump up and run or play dead. I twist my neck to follow the sound when Simon comes into view. He looks at me and I look at him before I lie back down to gaze up to the ceiling. His upside-down face appears in my eyeline a few seconds later as he stands over me near my head.

"Dare I ask what you're doing on the floor?" His voice is serious, but his eyes are teasing. It's tricky to decipher from this angle, but I can tell.

"I just wanted a change of scenery."

"It would seem so," he says. "I wasn't aware that you were fond of singing."

He reaches a hand down, and I take it as he gently pulls me up. "I wouldn't call it fondness. More a project I'm working on. I couldn't sleep."

My hand stays enclosed inside his large grasp. It reminds me of how I just imagined his hand touching me as I stood in front of the mirror in my room, until Francis interrupted. My cheeks burn red, and it almost feels like Simon can guess my thoughts as his eyes turn a little stormy.

"Yes," he agrees, moving the smallest bit closer. "Rest seems out of reach tonight."

Rest may be out of reach, but I no longer am. Part of me wants Simon to grab me and drag me off somewhere. The other part of me . . . also wants him to grab me and drag me off somewhere.

"Do you want to walk a bit?" I quickly ask him, trying to overpower my hormone-crazed mind. He releases my hand, and I rub it along the skirt of my gown.

"I should like that," he agrees.

We move through the Haunted Gallery, and I only give a quick look to the chapel doors as we pass them. "I meant to ask you, why didn't you travel along with the king? I assumed most of his privy council members would go with him on the journey."

"I thought I would accompany him as well," he answers. "But then the king informed me that he would rather I stay behind... in case any gentleman thought to get too close to you."

My eyebrows shoot up and Simon tries to hide his own amusement. "You're meant to be my bodyguard?" I ask, hardly believing it myself.

Simon nods. "Thomas Culpepper was asked to stay behind as well. The king requested that he write to him weekly informing him of how you fare at court."

"Wow," I mumble as we continue down another corridor. "So, Thomas is Henry's eyes and ears, and what does that make you? His fist?"

A low laugh echoes in Simon's throat. "I suppose that could be a way of looking at it. Though I'm hardly doing a good job, am I?"

I glance over to him at his question, and his humor slowly falls away. I try to guess what he's feeling, but I can't quite do it. His expressions are so hard to interpret. I've never had trouble reading people before. It's my party trick. But not Simon. I wonder if that's part of what draws me to him—the fact that I have no choice but to switch out of psychologist mode and just be present in the moment. I'm not actively trying to interpret his words, and I don't have to be so careful with mine. Our dynamic is easy when it shouldn't be.

"Is your life at court usually so interesting?" I ask him.

Simon's pace mirrors mine even though he's not quite looking at me. "Not in this way."

We go down a twisty stairwell, and as we follow the curved

walls, the tension thickens between us. Our bodies move nearer. Our steps slow. The stairwell is dark, and it makes me think of the tent. The tent where we both felt on fire. I start to feel that way again now. I steal a peek over at Simon, and judging from his tense muscles and flushed cheeks, he feels it, too.

Still, when we reach the landing, I try to cling to sanity one more time before it's too late. "Let's wait a second," I tell him, catching hold of his wrist. "Simon, are you sure about this? I mean, are you really, really sure? Because this... whatever we're doing, it could end really badly. So if you've changed your mind, I understand."

Simon steps in closer, his green eyes absolutely endless. If I was wearing Tudor panties, they would drop of their own volition.

He stays quiet as he steps back and away from me, moving to a door along the wall. He carefully swings it open to reveal a small room. When he turns to look back at me, his gaze is decisive. "Get in," he says.

And I've forgotten how to breathe.

He doesn't say anything else, just keeps holding the door open. On some level, I knew what was going to happen on this walk, even if I pretended I didn't. And Simon is making it clear that he knew, too.

A quiet breath slips through my lips as I move past him and into the room. Moonlight sifts in a narrow window. With all the bags of wheat piled on the floor, this must be some kind of a space for storage. We walked a decent distance from the royal apartments and are now closer to the servants' hall. It makes me like the room all the more.

Simon shuts the door, closing us in. When I turn to face him, he's already in front of me, dipping down to claim my mouth in a drugging kiss. The air around us feels charged with electricity. My arms instantly wrap around his neck as his hands fall to the small of my back, anchoring me against him. Before I'm too far gone, I pull back slightly, my eyes searching his as I take a disjointed breath.

"I need to ask you something: When it's just the two of us, can you call me Lily?"

Simon pauses at my words. It's a big, weird ask, but it feels necessary. When he and I are alone, I need to be me. I don't know what he's thinking as his hand shifts up to cup my cheek. I turn into the comfort of his palm.

"Can you actually say it now?"

He strokes his thumb up and down the line of my jaw. "Lily," he murmurs softly.

A serene, sad smile crosses my face as he says it, and I'm still smiling as he bends down to taste my lips again. His mouth moves over mine in a sinful, soft possession. An anthem of *more, more, more* plays on repeat in my brain.

Within the confines of this tiny room, with the door bolted shut, everything feels heightened. Dangerously desperate. Someone could catch us. So many things could go wrong, but none of that matters. All that exists is the slow glide of his lips as he urges mine open, and the tightening in my stomach when his tongue teases mine.

A consuming need flares through me, blazing outwards. My impatient hands tangle into the hair at the nape of his neck and a low moan reverberates in Simon's throat as I draw his tongue deeper into my mouth. Then we're both moving, crossing the space until my back meets the stone wall. My hips buck forward, rocking restlessly against his. The cold surface behind me is the opposite of Simon's engulfing heat, and even through my layered gown, I start to feel Simon's hard length straining against me. My thigh instinctively lifts to bring him closer. He bears into me with a half roll of his hips, and my head falls back against the wall. Simon covers my mouth with his as he kisses me harder. I'm nearing delirium when his lips make a tantalizing trail down my neck, licking along the column of my flushed throat.

"Lily," he growls, his hands reaching down to pull at my skirts with a barely controlled urgency. "Why can I not stop? Tell me now if you want me to stop." His nimble fingers slip under the last layer and catch the soft flesh of my bent thigh, pulling it up higher and locking it around him as he keeps me pinned against the wall.

I can barely form a cohesive thought, let alone speak, but somehow I manage it. "I don't want you to stop," I answer, my voice breathy and shaking. "Please, don't stop."

Simon lets out a low chuckle into the soft juncture between my neck and ear. "Thank God." His nose skirts across my cheek as he leans back to kiss me again, his lips nipping at mine in relief. "What would you have me do?" he asks, his voice faltering as much as mine. His hips push into me again, moving in a driving rhythm that sets a twitching sensation in the softness between my thighs. "What would you have me do, Lily?"

"Just keep touching me," I all but beg. "I want to feel you everywhere."

I can't believe I just said that. I'd be embarrassed, but as I watch his eyes fill with an almost menacing level of longing, I let the fleeting feeling go.

"I can do that," he drawls. His hand leaves my leg to run along my front, over my hip, and up my stomach to stop just under the curve of my breast.

I heave in a labored breath as he stops there, his head dipping low until I feel the wet brush of his tongue against the surface of my cleavage. A flood of heat washes through me as my nipples harden against the material of my chemise. With the strings being loosened as they are, Simon is able to take full advantage as he delves his hand inside my dress's front, drawing the neckline down and one breast up.

The night air meets my burning skin as he cups me in his palm. His hand rotates, his thumb and forefinger lightly pinching and pulling as they work the small bud. A whimper builds inside me, and when he lowers his head to suck the swollen flesh into the warmth of his mouth, I can't help myself from letting it out.

I roll my hips, looking for any kind of relief as his tongue continues to mercilessly lick at my chest. With his free hand, he exposes my other breast and begins his delicious torture of flicking and teasing all over again. Moisture pools between my legs as my gaze turns down. Simon devouring my tits may be the most erotic thing I've ever seen.

I clasp his head and pull him up for another mind-numbing kiss when his hand moves down low. He bunches up the right side of my skirts even more and pins them between us with the driving press of his hips. His hand is free to brush the skin of my outer thigh, then my inner thigh, until his wandering fingers find the wet heat of my folds. I gasp and push my head into his shoulder when one finger slips inside. My walls squeeze around him. His free hand grips the hair at the nape of my neck, tilting my head back up. He meets me in an untamed kiss, his tongue pushing into my mouth as his finger does the same to my center. He eases out and moves back in, and as he does, the pad of his thumb rubs around my swollen clit. I moan into his mouth, because he won't stop kissing me, and my voice pitches when he curls a second finger in at the perfect angle. I'm close. It's right fucking there, and when I push down as he twists his wrist, a white hot current washes over me in a shaking, scorching rush of sensation.

This. This. This.

This is what it's supposed to feel like. How the fuck did I ever go without it?

My mouth is parted in the aftermath, my shoulders still squeezed up, and Simon's eyes are molten as his fingers keep moving in small, slow circles.

He eventually stills, and it takes me some time before I pull in a breath to speak. I'm not entirely sure if words are even possible when we suddenly hear a noise through the door.

Holy shit! There are people on the stairs.

We're unmoving and breathing heavy as we attempt to stay quiet. Simon's fingers are still inside me. The voices are right outside, laughing and talking for a moment before they eventually begin to weaken as they continue past.

Simon's gaze stays with mine, both of us knowing just how close we were to being discovered. His fingers slip from my center as he kisses me again, this time much more softly.

"Thank you," I hear myself say when he pulls his head back.

A slow smile tugs at his mouth. "I assure you, no thanks are necessary."

A few seconds later, our breathing has leveled to a manageable degree. My leg unhooks from around his waist and my foot touches the floor, feeling unstable as I gradually get my bearings.

Simon drops his head forward, nuzzling his nose against the swell of my breasts as I tuck them back inside my gown. He stands up straight, readjusting himself inside his pants with a half-pained exhale.

"I will walk you back," he tells me.

I wish he could, but I shake my head.

"We have to be more careful," I tell him. "No walking me to my rooms."

He isn't happy but begrudgingly nods. I take a step forward, and he pulls me back to kiss me again. When I eventually do make my way toward the door, a bittersweet smile crosses my face as I imagine how our goodbye tonight could have played out if we were in my time.

Simon would have walked me to my door. We'd kiss one more time, maybe a few more times, and make plans to see each other in a couple of days. He'd text me that night and I'd smile in bed when I saw it, hopeful and curious of what the future held. I know that's not something we can have here, but just for now, for tonight, I'm going to make believe that we can.

Chapter Fourteen

"Why did you ask for an embroidery session if all you want to do is sleep?"

Bessie pulls the embroidery hoop off her face to look at me, wincing her eyes against the light of the room. She's sideways in her chair, half reclining with her legs dangling over one end. Theo is biting at her shoes. "Alice Wharton was practicing the lute directly in my ear. If I stayed sitting over there, I would have emptied my stomach onto the floor. It may still happen now."

I complete my feather stitch and give her a knowing look. "That's what chugging ale gets you. William said he almost had to wrestle you to the ground when you tried to steal a full barrel out of the pub tent. He was drenched when he brought you back."

"Oh, shut it," she grumbles, putting her embroidery hoop back on her face.

I put my own embroidery hoop in my lap. "Couldn't you go straight to jail for saying that?"

"Apologies. Kindly shut it, Your Most Regal, Royal Highness."

Satisfied, I pick up my hoop, ready to start the next stitch, when the sitting room doors open, and a messenger enters. "The Duke of Norfolk," he announces.

My least favorite uncle enters behind him. Lady Rochford stands from her seat in the corner and gradually moves in my direction.

"Good afternoon, Your Majesty. Ladies." He attempts a relatable smile, but the embedded insincerity of his face fights it hard. "I am here bearing news. The Italian ambassador is to visit our court. Indeed, he will be here in the coming weeks. I will be meeting with him on political matters, but in his absence, the king wishes you to arrange an entertainment for our guest."

The fifteen women in the room, some ladies-in-waiting and some maids of honor, look to each other in excitement as the duke goes on, his attention now entirely directed at me.

"The king bid me tell you that no one could better display the beauties of our court than his beloved, perfect Catherine. And in less than a month, he will be ever by your side."

Oh joy.

Bessie excuses herself as the duke approaches, and the room is doused in an eager flurry of whispers as he steps forward to greet me in relative privacy. "Niece, are you well?"

"I'm well," I answer, albeit unenthusiastically.

He steps the smallest bit closer. "How well?" He lowers his voice and makes an invisible baby bump with his hand over his belly. "Are you *very* well?"

His cringe level knows no bounds. "Not that well," I tell him.

He heaves a sigh and glances absently around the room. "That's disappointing to hear. When the king returns, you will have to increase your efforts."

My stank face is blatant by the time Lady Rochford arrives at my side.

"Hello, uncle," she says sternly.

"Jane," he replies with a scowl-smile duo. We then silently simmer in our toxic family dynamic until the duke eventually steps back. "And now I must leave you. Good day."

"Please, don't go," Lady Rochford says lifelessly.

He glares at her before he turns and leaves. Lady Rochford and I exchange a look until Bessie barrels into us.

"Catherine! This is wonderful news."

"That my uncle left?" I ask, confused.

She shakes her head, moderately out of breath. "No, about the ambassador. We must have a masque."

I give an unsure glance to Lady Rochford. "A masque?"

Bessie nods with a wild kind of fervor. "Everyone loves a masque. There is nothing more exciting to be done at court."

"It's not a bad idea," Lady Rochford mutters. "It's more acceptable for me to ignore people when I'm wearing a mask."

Bessie clasps my wrist and shakes it. "A masque is an ideal place for you to find me a husband."

I lift a brow. "How so?"

"There will be drinking, dance rehearsals, and half my face will be obstructed... What better conditions could we ask for?"

She makes a solid case.

"A masque it is, then," I agree.

"Yes!" Bessie claps her hands together and turns to face the women in the room. "Everyone, the queen has decided that there's to be a masque! I will inform the Master of the Revels. Expect rehearsals to begin in a few days!"

An enthusiastic murmur rustles around us as Lady Rochford crosses her arms. "So," she says, "you are to turn the masque into a husband-hunting ground for Bessie?"

I give her a noncommittal shrug. "What better purpose could it serve? I'm sure only a few men will volunteer anyway."

WHEN WE ENTER the receiving room that's being used for dance rehearsal days later, Bessie and I are met with at least twenty waiting courtiers and noblemen. They turn as we step inside, varying in age as each of them bows at my arrival.

"I like our odds," I whisper to Lady Rochford, who is standing behind us. "Bessie was right about this being the perfect venue to find a husband."

"And what did Bessie do for you that you agreed to such a task?" I think about answering, but before I can, she quickly walks past me, refusing, as any good defense attorney would, to listen. "On second thought, don't tell me. I don't want to know."

Bessie takes my hand, nearly vibrating in excitement. "All right, Your Majesty. Where to first?"

I remind myself of just how much she risked in making the sleeping draft for the king. For what she saved me from, she deserves the best reverse-harem speed-dating experience this palace can offer. I roll my shoulders and stretch my neck.

"Let's do this, Bessie."

When we approach bachelor number one, I'm fairly optimistic. Between being Zoe's loyal wingwoman and then having my own date-a-palooza last year, I'm more or less indestructible at intros. There is no ice I can't break. No awkward silence I can't overcome.

"Hello there," I say, approaching the first twenty-something Bessie steers me toward. He has dusty blond hair and a nonhomicidal face. "So, this is exciting, right? Have you ever danced in a masque before?"

He looks back at me with a wide smile and offers an extravagant bow. "With people, Your Majesty? No, this is my first. And I am so keen I can barely stand still!"

I tilt my head a drop. "What do you mean it's your first with *people?*"

He chortles. "Silly me. I just meant that this is my first masque with a partner. At home, I frequently arrange my dolls in dances of delight. We are quite an energetic crowd."

"That sounds so fun," I reply, keeping my voice friendly. I turn and give Bessie a protective shove in the opposite direction.

Bachelor number two could be promising. He may be the youngest man here, in his early twenties, though his eyes appear older. He sort of reminds me of a basset hound. But who doesn't love a basset hound?

"Lovely weather we're having lately," I comment.

He glances over at me, seeming tired as he stiffly bows. "Indeed." Okay. Maybe he needs some time to warm up.

"Out of curiosity, are you married?"

He shakes his head. "I am yet to marry, though my father is keen that I find a bride within the month."

"How interesting," I say, my voice rising a note or two.

"My mother, however, insists that I take my time in selecting a wife. She will miss me quite dearly when I wed."

"That's nice." I give Bessie a nudge with my shoulder. "It's always a positive attribute when a man is close with his mother."

Bachelor number two sighs. "Yes, I fear the bed will be quite cold without her."

"Pardon?" I ask, hoping I misheard him.

"We still share a chamber, you see, but that will obviously have to end once I marry. As will the breastfeeding."

I'm losing steam when we reach bachelor number three, a skinny man in his early thirties with a very eager countenance.

"And what are you mainly looking for in a wife?" I ask.

"Your Majesty," he says, bowing down low. "I would love to find one who has all her teeth."

"Anything else?" I ask.

He seems perplexed. "Not particularly, no."

Bessie smiles a big toothy grin to show off the goods, and I quickly take her hand. "Don't do that."

Five minutes later, I'm wondering if convent life is the safest choice for my friend when we approach bachelor number four.

"What do you like to do in your spare time?" I ask, speaking to him without so much as a hello.

His eyes startle to find us standing beside him, but he clears his throat and straightens out the front of his gray doublet. He bows politely before standing up tall. "It's a pleasure to meet you, Your Majesty. I like to read. And I go out riding when the weather is fine."

"Really?" I ask with cautious interest. "That sounds very pleasant. And are you close with your family?"

He shrugs. "As much as the next person is, I suppose. My father, Baron Dorford, is quite scholarly and prefers to stay away from court. My mother spends her days caring for my sisters."

Bessie locks my hand in a hopeful death grip. Bachelor number four—do not break our hearts.

"And everyone has . . . their own rooms?"

"Of course," he says, noticeably confused. "Why wouldn't we?"

"No reason at all! Forget what I said. What's your name?"

"Richard Lumley," he replies with another bow.

"That is a great name. Richard, may I present my dearest friend, Bessie Stanley."

I pull Bessie forward. Richard bows once more, and she curtsies. They shyly gaze at each other, and as they do, I'm pretty sure Taylor Swift flies past us on a unicorn, strumming the intro of "Love Story."

Several minutes later, a man in a very stylish doublet and cape claps his hands in the center of the room. "Attention, please, we are ready to begin pairing up the dancers!"

After deciding on a masque as our chosen mode of entertainment, Bessie explained that the most important aspect of the masque is when there's a big, choreographed dance performed by some of the highest-ranking nobility. I grow a little queasy at the performance part of it, but with my Catherine-muscle-memories firmly intact, I know that I'll survive. The dance portion—I know that I'll survive the dance portion.

The man I assume is the choreographer claps his hands again. "Please fan out so I can see you. Then I can begin my selections."

We follow his instructions, all of us spreading out in a circle. We're a full house now, having since been joined by any ladies-in-waiting and maids of honor who want to participate.

The choreographer has matched half of us when I look over to Lady Rochford as she stands along the side. I nudge my chin toward Bessie and Richard, who are still in quiet conversation together. Lady Rochford nods and casually approaches the choreographer. She whispers in his ear, and a moment later, he announces Bessie and Richard as dance partners.

I'm trying to hide a satisfied smirk when he makes his next announcement.

"And now we'll have Her Majesty dancing with . . ." He looks around until an *of course* smile crosses his face. "Mr. Thomas Culpepper."

My eyes dart to my far left, and there's Thomas, keeping his face composed except for a small tic on his cheek. He's trying not to smile.

I groan and walk over to the far side of the room, where William, Bartholomew, and the rest of the musicians are setting up.

"Why are you scowling like you sat on a thistle?" Bartholomew asks.

"Because I can't stand my partner."

He looks over my shoulder. "Thomas Culpepper? Are you blind? You should be pleased."

"No, I'm not blind. But I am a good judge of character, and for no specific foreboding reason, I get the feeling that he's the worst."

William looks around me to sneak a peek at Thomas as well. "I could fix him," he murmurs.

Bartholomew nods in agreement. "I could help."

"No," I counter. "Both of you deserve better. Trust me."

William shakes his head. "I strive to settle."

"I'm happiest when I'm unhappy." Bartholomew is still staring at Thomas when the choreographer claps for the third time.

"Everyone! Find your partners, if you please."

I drag my feet as I move to the center of the room. We're in two lines, women and men. And Thomas is soon standing across from me.

"What a pleasant surprise," he says.

I give him a forced smile. "A remarkable coincidence." I take a beat before asking, "How did you manage it?"

Thomas looks affronted until he smirks. "The dance master owes me a favor."

Weird flex, but sure.

The music begins, and even though my mind doesn't recognize it, my body does, and I seamlessly step forward to touch hands with Thomas, just as I'm meant to.

"I see you were quite busy this morning," he muses, "attempting to marry off your friend. With some success, it seems."

I look across the floor to see Bessie and Richard dancing, and they can't help but smile every time they touch. "I was just helping her find some prospects."

"Yet you didn't consider me for a suitor?"

Thomas and I circle each other as I struggle to contain my laugh. "Yeah, that would be a very strong no."

"And why is that?" he asks.

My gaze falls to the couple dancing beside us and finds Elizabeth Norworth, my favorite cheese-pilfering maid of honor, paired up with an older gentleman. I catch a whiff of Stilton from her suspiciously drooping sleeve just as I notice that the man's hand is dangerously low on her waist. I'm deciding if I should tackle him or shove him off when Thomas suddenly steps forward and speaks close to her partner's ear: "Mind your hands or I will cut them off."

The man flushes as Elizabeth smiles and purposefully stomps on his foot. Thomas takes my hand as he returns to my side.

"My apologies. Do go on."

I slip my hand under his so that I'm the one leading, still a little startled by his defending Elizabeth. "I was only going to say that Bessie is one of my closest friends, and you don't seem like the marrying kind."

Thomas positions his hand back under mine as his aristocratic face tilts in feigned regret. "I'm precisely the marrying kind. No man here loves love more than me."

I shake my head slightly as we both do a turn and bring our hands back together.

Thomas keeps his eyes locked on mine when we face each

other again, peering at me more closely than usual. "I'm beginning to wonder if your fall has something to do with your newfound disdain for me. Was I the villain in a bad dream you had when you were asleep? Tell me what I did to offend you."

I feel a nervous twinge in my belly. I can't tell him what fate has in store for him if the real Catherine were here and not me. That their mutual death was waiting just around the corner.

"My priorities aren't what they used to be, that's all."

"Stop, stop, stop!" The music halts as the choreographer addresses a couple near the front. Most of the partners begin to talk among themselves, and Thomas checks that we're a safe distance away from listening ears before he approaches me.

"You are the only person at court I can truly talk to. When we first met—when we would talk as we used to do—we swore to always trust each other. I miss our friendship, Catherine. Tell me what I did wrong so I can fix it. Please." His eyes are still trained on mine, and his voice sounds honest.

"Is friendship really all you're after?" I ask.

"Is that so hard to believe?"

I feel the tug of a nagging feeling that maybe I've been too hard on Thomas. Knowing what I know about his shared fatal future with Catherine, I was determined to protect her and me by cutting him out of the equation. But what if I was being too mercenary? Since I've been here, I've been trying to rearrange the chessboard of Catherine's life to set us up to win, and in the process, I labeled Thomas as a hollow pawn, not an actual person.

"Fine," I tell him before I can change my mind. "Maybe I have been a little unfair to you."

"I'm sorry, what was that? My hearing goes in and out." He

leans in closer to me for a better listen, and I give him a blank stare back.

"You're making me instantly regret my decision, and we've only been friends for five seconds."

"We're friends again, then?" he asks with a sly smile. "I knew it was just a matter of time until you succumbed to my charms. I don't blame you, of course. Everyone's first instinct is to hate me, but I always grow on them. I'm like a very distinct, handsome chin mole."

"That is a super specific choice of metaphor. Still, if we're going to be friends, I have ground rules. No more flirting, and no more innuendos."

Thomas's face scrunches like he was force fed something bitter. "So I'm never supposed to speak again?"

"You can speak," I tell him. "Just be friendly about it. Platonic and friendly."

"To everyone or just you?"

"Just me is fine. Outside of you and me, you're free to seduce away to your slutty heart's content."

"I can accept that," he says. He then turns and looks toward the musicians, giving William and Bartholomew a wink. Bartholomew drops his lute as Thomas turns back, very pleased with himself.

"I like to keep my options open."

DANCE REHEARSAL GOES on for an hour, and it was more enjoyable than I thought it would be. Thomas is tolerable, even entertaining, and Bessie and Richard have yet to stop talking. The vibe in the room is relaxed and chipper as people start to disperse. As they do, Simon enters, seeming unnoticed, but not to me. To me, the air shifts, electric with his presence. I watch as he approaches, and my legs go a little loose.

"Good afternoon, Your Majesty," he says with a respectful bow.

The gesture is so formal, in no way reflecting the fact that we were dry humping in a closet a few days ago. The back of my neck grows speckled with heat as I think about it.

"Good afternoon, Lord Gainsford. I'm going to assume that you didn't volunteer as a masque dancer?"

"Unfortunately not," he answers. "I fear I'd do any lady a disservice by being her partner when there are much better ones to be found."

"I thought you danced very well," I tell him.

He looks back at me in a way that makes my stomach tighten. "Perhaps I was especially inspired that evening." I think he's about to go on when he suddenly bows again, only saying, "Good afternoon, Your Majesty."

He takes my hand, and I almost pull him back to make him stay when he pushes a small piece of paper into my palm. My breath catches as he walks away. When no one is watching me, I move over toward the windows with my back to the rest of the room.

I unfold the tiny parchment, seeing six words written in neat, hurried handwriting:

Tomorrow. Meet me in the garden.

Chapter Fifteen

I walk along the gravel path, listening as my shoes crunch against the tiny stones. Tall, neatly trimmed hedges shield me on either side as the sun drips through the green cracks. I'm not too far from where Simon and I sat with Theo that night, and I'm hoping this is where I'm supposed to meet him. I walk through the hedges until I reach the garden wall, and when I do, I hear the sound of footsteps behind me.

I exhale in relief when Simon comes into view, his small smile both soothing and fanning my fluttering nerves.

"You could have been a bit more specific than saying 'meet me in the garden.'"

"I'm sorry," he answers. "Are you well, Lily?"

I don't think I'll ever not feel a thrill when Simon says my name. I take a quick breath in as I look around at the hedges. "I am," I tell him. "So, are we going for another walk?"

"In a way." He moves in my direction, and I stay still when he suddenly strides past me. He steps right next to the stone wall and bends his knees, leaning down to cup his hand in front of me like a stirrup.

"Your foot goes here," he says.

I take a second, looking at his offered hands and then to the wall, which has to be about seven feet high. "You're going to fling me over the wall?"

"I'm not going to fling you," he assures me. "Just help you over."

"To see or do what on the other side?"

Simon stands up straight again. "You'll have to trust me if you want to find out."

I look back to the path we just came down, and at the palace beyond. I told Lady Rochford that I needed privacy. Some time alone in nature to clear my head. Technically, I'm still in nature even if I jump the fence. But I could also be in unimaginable trouble if we get caught. I look at Simon—his hand is reaching out, waiting for mine, and there's a soft hum beneath my skin when I take it.

I can't go back just yet.

"I guess we're going over, then."

Simon smiles and leans down once more. I raise the hem of my gown, putting my foot in his palm and my hand on his shoulder as he easily hoists me up. I swing my leg over the wall, which is no easy feat in these heavy skirts. With my back to the garden, my feet dangle down in front of me as I look out at the deep green fields and the dark trees of the king's woods in front of us.

Pulling himself up on his own, Simon settles beside me. He gazes forward before turning his eyes in my direction. "Hello again."

"Hello," I answer with a smile.

He jumps down a moment later and reaches up to help me after. His arms wrap around my waist as he lowers me to the ground, and he weaves his fingers through mine as soon as I'm steady. We walk through the field in a comfortable silence that doesn't feel like silence at all.

We've gone maybe a quarter of a mile into the woods when Simon gradually comes to a stop. "We're here," he says, his gaze resting ahead of us. I follow his eyeline and see a massive tree. Its pale leaves are dangling down, touching the ground and carpeting the wide area it encompasses.

"It's a weeping willow," Simon goes on. "I like to come here when I want to be alone."

I can feel him looking at me, but I can't tear my eyes away from the tree, which seems straight out of a storybook.

"It's beautiful," I tell him.

Simon gently squeezes my hand in his. "You haven't seen the best part."

He urges me forward until we're standing just before it, looking through the curtain of soft, swooping leaves. He brushes a section aside and we step inside. It feels like we're back in our tent, but it's somehow better. When we stop in the center of the surprisingly open space, I do a full circle as I look around.

"This is possibly the dreamiest place to ever exist."

Simon walks in a wider circle around me in confident comfort. "I would have to agree with you."

I stop taking in my surroundings to turn and focus on him. "Am I the first girl you've brought here?"

"You are," he affirms, giving no indication that he might be lying.

"Really? You're saying I'm the only person to experience your weeping willow seduction?"

"What makes you think I took you here to seduce you? A bit presumptive, isn't it?"

"You're right," I agree apologetically. "Did you bring me here to talk about science?"

He steps toward me with a smile, his hands clasped behind his back. "Maybe I did."

I give him an assured smile of my own. "In that case, I can name every muscle in the brain in alphabetical order. Or by location. You pick."

Simon stops walking, only a couple of feet away from me. "Fine. Perhaps in the deepest, furthest corners of my mind, I did consider seducing you."

"And the truth comes out," I say lightly. I'm the one to close the distance between us. We're chest to chest when I stop before him, and Simon pauses before slowly bringing his hands up. I think he's about to touch my cheeks, but instead, he carefully lifts off the veiled headpiece that I'm wearing, revealing the small white cap underneath.

"Will you let your hair down for me?" he asks.

I think for only a moment before I pull off the cap. I take out each of the pins from the wound-up bun at the base of my neck, and my hair spills down my shoulders.

Simon reaches forward and runs a curl through his fingers. "You really are the first person I have brought here."

"I believe you," I tell him, sincerity softening my voice. "The palace is nice, but this is better."

He drops the strands he was holding and brushes his fingers into the hair just above my ear. Goosebumps shiver down my spine at the soft contact, and my eyes fall closed. His lips touch mine in a quiet kiss. Delicate and fragile.

"Will you rest with me for a while?" he asks. "I've missed you."

I nod in answer, and Simon lowers himself to the grass below us, holding my hand as I do the same. We lay down, side by side, gazing up at the blanket of leaves that look more like stars as sunlight flickers in around them.

After a while, we turn to face each other, and Simon stretches his arm out so I can lean my head on it. He's a very comfortable pillow.

"Tell me something that makes you happy," I prompt him.

His eyes drift to mine, a hint of a smile passing over his mouth. "I am happy when I'm out riding. On nights when I can't sleep, I rise early, even before dawn. I go out on my horse, bringing him to full speed just as it becomes day, and I pretend that I'm racing the sun."

His voice is so light. It makes me feel light, too. "Do you ever win?" I ask playfully.

"Not as often as I would like." A distinct warmth fills his eyes. He shifts closer to me, spanning his free hand over my waist. "Tell me about a time when *you* were happy."

Moments and snapshots of my old life flip through my mind's eye like a cherished photo album. The one that pushes its way to the front is my mom and me. And my grandma. The memory is quiet and tender. As faint as soft music playing in another room.

"When I was young," I tell him, "my mother and I, and my grandmother, would lie outside before we went to sleep to look at the stars. Kind of like this. We would find different shapes and patterns, and when one of us would find one, the rest of us would try to find it, too."

"Do you miss your family?" he asks.

I don't answer, but I nod. A tear slips down from the inside corner of my eye, trailing down and over my nose until it drops into the grass between us. Simon lifts a hand up to my face, wiping the wet path away.

"I'm sure that they loved you very much." I nod again, not trusting myself to talk. He edges closer, pulling me into him in the process. "I didn't mean to upset you."

"You didn't," I assure him. "It's nice to talk about my family. It helps remind me that they were real."

"Would you like a handkerchief?" he asks, holding his wrist between us.

I look at the cuff of his sleeve and see one tucked away inside. I pull it out, and it's my handkerchief—the favor I tossed to him after he won the joust. The thought that he keeps it with him makes something in me melt in a toe-curling way. I smile as I move the soft material through my fingers and then cover his face with it. "Did you make me cry just so you could show off your hidden hanky?"

I hear him chuckle under the fabric. "What kind of a monster do you take me for?"

I pull the handkerchief away and fold it into a semi-tidy square. "A very romantic one," I tell him.

He smirks before sneaking the material out of my hand and tucking it back into his sleeve. "Unfortunately, you can't keep it. It was a very special gift."

He urges me closer with a tug, and I nestle into his chest. "You're also a selfish monster." I run my hand up his arm and let my fingers trace the base of his neck. "I wonder what life could have been like if things were different. If you were a farmer and I was a dairymaid."

Simon smiles, his hand shifting to roam up and down my side. "I can't imagine you as a dairymaid."

"No one would have bothered us. We could have said and done as we wanted."

He slides into the small space that's left between us, his nose brushing mine as the closeness of his body surrounds me. "There's no one to bother us now," he says.

A consuming look clouds his hazy eyes. It pulls me in so deep that it's almost hard to breathe. I lean forward to meet him in a devastatingly gentle kiss, one that's meant to build up slowly and then ignite into a blaze. My lips play with his like we have all the time in the world—like where we are now is a permanent state of being and not a fading moment. He rolls me onto my back and settles over me. The ground is soft. He's so warm. Leaving is incomprehensible.

Our kiss starts to intensify, and when I delve my tongue into his welcoming mouth, I'm rewarded with a low echoing moan. The muscles in my body tense at the sound of it, and I want to hear it again.

I spread my legs, and his knee nudges into the apex of my thighs. A delicious tension takes root in my abdomen, and I hitch my hips up against him. We linger in the kiss, drawn out and consuming. Time slips away until Simon's lips fall to the underside of my jaw and down the length of my neck.

"I'll never get enough of you," he whispers against my oversensitive skin. "I'll never get enough of this."

I feel his hand on the hem of my skirt, scooping under each layer and dragging them up to my knees. His hand keeps moving, grazing over the side of my thigh and leaving goosebumps everywhere he touches. I gulp in a breath when his fingers brush along my entrance. He traces a soft lazy circle, and my back arches off the ground.

"Do you want me here?" he whispers, his fingers stroking up and down my trembling flesh. He lowers his mouth to kiss my breasts as they strain against the neckline of my gown, his hand between my legs gliding higher. His thumb strums the heated skin just below my clit, and I claw my fingers into the ground. He slides down my torso and farther still. My eyes stay glued to the sight of his chestnut hair disappearing beneath the wall of my hitched-up skirts.

If the first lick of his velvet tongue makes me twitch, then the second one causes a full-body spasm. His head turns, and I feel the press of his nose nuzzling the highest point of my inner thigh. He focuses back on my center and spreads me wider as he lifts my legs over his shoulders, pulling me down to settle more comfortably against his eager mouth.

He dips low again as his tongue laps at my warm slit. I feel his fingers between me and the grass as his hands slip under me, cupping my ass in both hands and tilting me upward for unfettered access.

I look down to watch him and can't hold back the whimper it elicits. He pulls back to gaze up at me, appearing almost drunk.

"You have no idea how much I regretted not doing this the other night. It's all I have thought about since."

His words leave me feverish in the best of ways. Simon is caring, deeper than he lets on, and is arguably the most attractive person I have ever met . . . and he's been thinking about eating me out all the livelong day.

I know that my being sent back in time is severely unlucky, but at least I get to have this.

He lowers his head, delving back into to my warmth. I can't keep still. I thread my fingers into his tussled hair, and I imagine what we would look like if I was watching us from above. Me half naked and him nestled between my legs, which are splayed open on the forest floor. The image sends a coiling heat coursing through me, and his mouth drives me closer to oblivion with every unceasing drag of his decadent tongue.

I hold my eyes shut, my head thrashing from side to side. I can feel myself climbing that inner peak. My stomach dips, and a shallow breath rips from my lungs as I go higher and higher.

Simon grips my thighs in a greedy hold as he laps at me with a driving need. The careening pressure sends my hips jaunting up, but he pins me back down with a forceful push from the palm of his hand. I struggle against his hold for a split second until his mouth latches around my throbbing clit. The taut pleasure inside me contracts and bursts, and I scream Simon's name into the leaves above us as I come harder than I have in my entire life.

I'm still shaking in the aftershocks as he crawls up my body a while after, somehow seeming as satisfied as I am. He leaves my skirts as they are and my skin exposed to the open air as he pushes up on his arms to kiss me. I taste myself on his tongue, and the headiness of it makes me feel feral, even in my drowsy state. Simon soothes me with gentle pulls from his lips as he shifts to lay beside me.

"We should stay here," he eventually says. I turn away from the arbored canopy over our heads and find him watching me.

Snuggling into his chest, I feel his leveled breathing as I listen to the strong beat of his heart under my ear.

"I wish we could," I tell him. "But we both know that we can't."

He takes a defeated inhale, listlessly stroking his fingers through my grass-tangled hair. "Parting from you strikes a pain in my chest. Each time, it grows sharper."

That makes two of us.

I push myself up a little to look at him, already losing the will to leave. "We'll come here again," I promise him.

His eyes have an indulging tint. "Will we?"

"Yes," I say, only half believing it myself. "Every week."

He waits a beat before he runs his index finger along my cheek. "Every week, then. I'll be here."

The journey back to the palace is a quiet one. When we reach the garden wall with our clothes and hair back in place, he hoists me over as he did before. Walking through the maze of hedges, I'm the first to speak.

"I should head back the rest of the way on my own. If we're seen together, people will talk."

Simon nods in stoic agreement but then takes my wrist to stop me from walking. There's a fearful sort of hunger in his gaze as he pulls me into another demanding kiss. I give myself over to it, a moan lingering in my throat, when someone starts calling my name.

"Catherine! Are you here?"

I instantly recognize Bessie's voice and tear myself out of Simon's arms. Her footsteps draw nearer, and out of sheer panic, I shove Simon with all my might into the shrub behind him. He goes down with a muffled crash, and I see nothing but his feet in the air until they disappear between the leaves. I'm about to check if he's all right when Bessie rounds the corner.

"Catherine, what in the world are you doing? Lady Rochford is on the hunt for you, and if she found you first, I'm sure she would have you flayed."

She links her arm through mine and pulls me in the direction of the palace. I look back over my shoulder and see the top of Simon's head popping out over the bush. There's some dirt on his cheek, but other than that, he appears fine.

I give him an apologetic wave when Bessie isn't looking and then turn my head forward as we continue on. It's not the most graceful thank-you I could have given him, considering the world-altering orgasm that he just gave me, but desperate times call for desperate measures.

Chapter Sixteen

Pregaming is a rite of passage. That's what Zoe told me when she religiously blasted music in her dorm room every Friday night, requiring me to drink no fewer than two shots of Tito's before I was allowed out the door. I didn't expect to like it, but somehow I always did. I don't know if it was the ritual aspect or the camaraderie it built with the other girls on her floor, but something about pregaming just feels good.

That's what I'm trying to convey to my ladies-in-waiting at this very moment.

It's the night of the masque, an hour before it's set to begin, and I have all the women who are participating gathered in my sitting room. We've rehearsed for at least an hour almost every day for the past two weeks, and we deserve a victory lap. We're dressed in matching gowns that are a far cry from comfortable, but they're strikingly beautiful. Each is white with sparkling specks of silver and gold—very Drew Barrymore circa *Ever After*, and I'm feeling it.

Bartholomew and the boys are playing what sounds like elevator music in the corner, and I walk over to them with a half-formed plan.

"We need a change of pace," I tell them. "If I hum a song, do you think you could play it back?"

Bartholomew scoffs. "I should think so, Your Majesty."

"Perfect." I proceed to hum the melody to my favorite Chappell Roan song.

Bartholomew watches me and listens with his arms crossed across his chest. When I'm done, he pauses for several seconds until he nods. "Let us confer." He turns and convenes with William and the rest of the musicians, and I return to the ladies.

"More wine?" I ask, pouring another cup for Lady Wessex.

"I don't understand why we're all here when the masque doesn't start for an hour yet. Wouldn't we be better off rehearsing?"

"What's to rehearse?" I ask. "We already know all the steps."

"Maybe we should have a snack before we go," Elizabeth Norworth suggests.

Lady Wessex rubs her temples. "Fill your garters all you wish, Elizabeth. I'm returning to my room."

"Wait!" I call after her. "Come on, pregaming is all about bonding and building excitement and reducing social anxiety. Everyone, stand up. Just stand up for one minute."

The ladies do as I ask, and as I lift my cup in a toast, Bartholomew and Co. drop the beat to "HOT TO GO!" It's a banger that is impossible to deny, even via flute and lute. Lady Barrow's hips inadvertently start to sway, and I lift my cup higher in optimism.

"Here's to us. We're not going to worry about our husbands, or our suitors, or anyone else. Tonight is for the ladies."

"And the maids," Elizabeth chimes in.

"The ladies and the maids," Bessie says with a smirk.

We tap our glasses together, and then it's time to shake what God and country gave us.

The musicians bring the heat as we start to dance with abandon. We drink and we move, and Bessie is up on a chair at one point. The musicians dance with us as they play, and Lady

Wessex makes lewd gestures with a flute. This is the best team-building experience I could have hoped for.

The past few days, I've noticed that many of my ladies-in-waiting were more relaxed than usual. It could be due in part to the wild carrot root I delivered to Lady Barrow. She gratefully accepted it and set right to work blending it into tea, also promising to supply me with a fair amount. Maybe with that constant worry off their shoulders, my ladies can finally let loose. And letting loose they are as they whirl and twirl around the room.

I'm considering introducing a Tudor twerk when I suddenly see a tear-stained Cecily standing at the door. Everyone is having too much fun to notice when I rush over to her.

"Your Majesty." Her voice is shaking, and her eyes are glassy. "I'm so sorry to disturb you, but I need your help."

I grab her hands, moving off into the hallway with her for privacy. "Cecily, what's the matter? Are you hurt?"

"No, not me, Your Majesty. It's my sister, Maggie. She works in the laundry, and she's been ill for days. Her fever won't break, and I don't know what to do." Her tone is desperate, and I immediately nod.

"Of course. Where is she? We'll go now."

I begin to walk off, but Lady Rochford catches my arm. "You can't, Catherine. What if it's the sweat?"

Cecily moves over to face her. "It isn't the sweat, Lady Rochford. Maggie has no rash or coughing. She had a babe less than a month ago and says there's a burning pain in her chest, especially when the child feeds."

"I'll get Bessie," I tell her. "Just wait here."

When Cecily leads me and Bessie (and an unhappy Lady Rochford) to the north side of the palace, we're not too far from the kitchens. We go up one staircase and then up another. There's a chill around us, and the air is damp. Cecily pushes open a squeaky door, walking inside a narrow room filled with stale air. The thick wooden eves are so low that crouching every three feet is an accepted way of life.

As we go in deeper, we follow a long row of beds, "beds" being a generous word. These are small wooden frames with barely more than thin pallets of straw. Blankets are stained and threadbare if a bed has a blanket at all. We keep walking, and I piece together that this must be a women's dormitory. Two girls are asleep in a shared bed with their aprons covering their eyes. Another woman is holding a screaming toddler as she walks him back and forth. An older woman sits on a wooden stool near the smudged window, and her stare is sharp as she looks at me. Not wholly unwelcoming but also not curious. Maybe she's too tired for either.

We make it to the far end of the room, and I feel obnoxiously elitist in my gold-trimmed dress. We're looking down at a young woman curled up in a fetal position on the bed, moaning in pain as she keeps her arms pinned across her chest.

"Maggie," Cecily says, kneeling by her side. "I've brought some people here to help you." A baby lays beside her in small, simple crib, awake and squirming with a thin cloth resting over her. I freeze as I look down at the scene in front of me, not knowing what to say or do. Thankfully, Bessie isn't thus afflicted.

She pushes past me and pulls up her sleeves, moving close to Cecily's sister.

"First thing's first, Maggie," she says confidently. "Let me see those breasts of yours."

Sometime later, Bessie has determined that Maggie has a

blockage in one of her milk canals. Working in the laundry, she goes long spans of time without breastfeeding, which led to the infection. Bessie will prepare an herbal compress to treat her symptoms until it clears.

Cecily wipes her face as she gently rocks her niece. "Lady Elizabeth, I mean Bessie, I can't thank you enough."

"No thanks are necessary," Bessie assures her. "It's barbaric that women are forced to endure this nonsense when it's so easily preventable."

Cecily lays the babe back in her crib as I look around the dim room again. "Is this where you live, Cecily?"

"This is home," she answers with a smile. "It's not much, but we're better off than many. My younger brother sleeps on the floors of the kitchen, or really anywhere he can find a place for himself."

"I'm going to fix this," I tell her. "I don't know how, but I am."

She wraps her arms around me with a hard squeeze, and Bessie joins in after her. It's nice to know that group hugs exist in every era.

WHEN THE THREE of us rush back to the great hall, the dancers are in the corridor just outside, waiting for the masque to begin. Everyone is already lined up, since Bessie and I are almost an hour late. The choreographer is glaring at me with his arm shaking, like he's actively restraining himself from throwing his shoe at me.

Our dance partners are donning light full-body armor with silver masks over their eyes. I spot Thomas as he makes his way toward me. His outfit is giving very strong 1996 Leonardo DiCaprio Romeo vibes.

"Is there a reason you supplied us with an army of drunken fishwives?" he asks when he arrives at my side.

I look around to see what he's talking about and find that more than half of my ladies are laughing hysterically. Their posture is slouched. Some are still dancing. Elizabeth Norworth is doing high kicks.

"How dare you call us drunkards," Lady Wessex says lazily, moving very close to Thomas's face. "You may be handsome, but your ears offend me."

She saunters away, walking in a zigzag pattern as I face Thomas again. "I'm sorry I'm late. I had something important to do."

"More important than impressing the Italian ambassador? Your uncle Norfolk was just out here searching for you and looked ready to spit fire."

"My uncle will have to get over it," I tell him. "Regardless, I'm here now and I'm sure everything will work out."

"Oh, will it?" he asks humorlessly.

I shrug. "Probably not, but it's good to stay positive. So, should we get this show on the road?"

Thomas looks to the still-closed great hall doors, signaling the choreographer with a wave and taking my hand. "Come on, then. You and I will open the dance." He steers us toward the front of the line and squeezes the two of us in front.

"Why do we have to go in front?" I ask, feeling sudden nerves whooshing through me.

"Because out of all the women, you seem the least in your cups, and we're also the most pleasing pair for the crowd to look at."

He wiggles his eyebrows at me, and I give his hand a little pat.

"Never lose your wonderful sense of modesty, Thomas. It might be your most endearing quality."

His mouth tilts in a smirk, and the music begins to play in the great hall. It's the opening notes of the dance, and Thomas quickly looks forward and takes a deep breath. As he does, I see a sense of nervousness pass his typically haughty face.

"Are you getting stage fright?" I ask, surprised.

"I don't get stage fright" he answers. Then he adds, "My family is in attendance tonight."

I find myself oddly excited at the prospect. "Really? Who?"

"My father and my older brother, Thomas."

My head tilts slightly at his words. "You and your brother are both named Thomas?"

This Thomas nods. "If one of us died young, my father wanted to ensure there would still be one Thomas Culpepper."

That's morbid but makes sense, I suppose. "Do you get along with your brother?"

Thomas looks down at me, his eyes unexpectedly serious. "My brother is a monster."

I want to ask him what he means, but before I get the chance, the doors in front of us swing open. Thomas turns to face the waiting crowd and smiles charmingly as he leads me in. The rest of the dancers follow behind us, with Lady Wessex only subtly tripping along the way.

The performance goes . . . all right.

We might not have been the most graceful group, but we had gusto. Before the next party, I'll have to convey to my ladies that one of the key principles of pregaming is that you eventually stop.

After I'm introduced to the Italian ambassador, my uncle

Norfolk quickly asks me for a private audience. He's leading me off to the side before I've agreed, his grip harsh on my wrist.

We stop along the wall, and he rounds on me to block the view of the room with his body. "This is the entertainment you've prepared?" he seethes. "Half your women were floundering about like newborn calves and the others seemed ready to fall over. And you . . ." He leans in close and sniffs the air between us. "Why do you smell of sour milk?"

I meet the anger in his eyes with some of my own, and I step around him so that I'm no longer hidden from view. "I have no idea," I tell him. "But speaking of sour milk, you should know that I'm going to be making some changes around here. When I was in a servants' room tonight, I saw firsthand how unacceptable their living conditions are, as well as the lack of childcare."

The duke's cheeks flame in frustration. He looks around, seemingly remembering that we're in view of the court, and flattens his expression. "What were you doing in a servants' room?"

I casually wave to the Italian ambassador, who merrily waves back. "I was helping a friend," I answer with a smile.

"A *friend?*" My uncle shifts his body again, blocking both our faces from view and dropping his voice. "Let me remind you of something, Catherine. Your only job is to obey the king and give him children. Nothing else. No doing. No speaking. No friends. Nothing. Just be pretty and stay quiet."

I can feel the rage taking hold inside me. I harness it. I breathe it in. And I look at my uncle with calmly confident eyes.

"Yeah," I tell him, "that's not going to work for me."

We stay locked in a passive aggressive stare fest until the duke turns and faces the inside of the room.

"I've noticed you've grown quite close to Bessie Stanley. An odd creature, though it seems she has met her match. Does she not look happy, Catherine?"

I follow his calculating gaze over to Bessie and Richard. They're laughing and whispering back and forth to each other. If my uncle wasn't here, I'd smile.

"Young ladies are drawn to a handsome face," he goes on to say, "but that is why men must handle their affairs. I wonder if Lady Elizabeth might not secure a more advantageous match? A friend of mine, though he's advanced in years, is just now looking for a bride. His first two wives died before they could give him heirs—perhaps his hand was too heavy with them—not that it matters. But he grows impatient to secure his line. I'd wager that little Bessie would be an excellent candidate for him. I will suggest it to the king. With his blessing on the match, I'm sure the union would happen in all possible haste."

I can hear his threat. My shoulders tense. "Do you think so?" I ask.

The duke looks down and over at me. "Just stay in line, Catherine. Heed my advice and all will be well."

I nod at his words and move to his side to look back out at the festivities.

"The thing is," I tell him, "I don't think the king will bless the match. Especially since he's already approved the match between Bessie and Richard. I wrote to him last week through a private messenger and received word yesterday that he immediately granted my request. Henry is so *very* eager to please me." I lean in a bit toward the duke, making sure that he can hear me. "Just stay in line, uncle. Heed my advice and all will be well."

I give his arm a squeeze and walk back into the crowd. I'm so high on satisfaction that when I see Mistress Marshall standing along the inner wall, I feel brave enough to approach her. I take a glass of wine from a servant's tray as they pass me, and when I stop to stand in front of the glowering woman, I hold it up between us.

"It's a peace offering," I tell her.

She waits a while but eventually takes the cup. "Thank you, Your Majesty."

I adjust my stance to stand beside her, partly because she's too intimidating to make solid eye contact with and partly because watching the dancers makes the silence between us feel less tangible.

"Are you having a good time?" I ask.

She takes a sip from her cup, and I don't think I've ever seen her eat or drink anything before. "I don't particularly enjoy social events." She stretches her shoulder blades, seeming out of sync with her body as she tries to relax. "I'm usually more occupied, seeing to my girls, but I've had a fair bit of free time to contend with of late."

She's not looking at me, but if she was, I'm sure I would see the hurt in her eyes. I take a breath and angle myself to face her.

"About that," I say. "I want to apologize for how I treated you the last time I saw you. Tensions were high that night, and I think I took my reaction too far. I didn't mean to hurt you."

Mistress Marshall shakes her head. "No, it was deserved. I shouldn't have spoken to you in such a manner. I'm not very . . . skilled, when dealing with people." She flashes me the most minuscule smile, but it feels like a tremendous victory.

"I can forgive and forget if you can," I tell her.

She turns her gaze to the ground, then briefly looks at me before turning back to the dancing. "I'd like that," she says quietly. "Perhaps I could do with a bit of a change."

My head juts back in surprise. She's still watching the partygoers, but this time I pick up on the small hint of longing. "In that case, you should get out there and dance."

A laugh snaps out of her, and she covers her mouth with her hand until it's gone. "I can't change that much," she says sternly.

I nod in acceptance. "Fair enough."

Quitting while I'm ahead, I move from her side and continue to mix through the crowd. I'm in a more isolated part of the great hall when I feel a featherlight touch on my hand—a touch that I'd know anywhere.

I stop walking and look up. Simon gazes down at me, then pivots so that we're standing side by side. "You're not dancing, Lord Gainsford?"

He's close beside me, but not so close that people would think anything of it if they saw us. "Alas, I'm not sure I'd survive the dance floor this evening."

Following his chin that he nudges forward, I see that my girls are still tearing it up. They're dancing and jumping and spinning and having the times of their lives despite everyone looking at them with more than moderate concern.

"That might be my fault," I admit.

"They're enjoying themselves," Simon replies. "That's all that matters."

He might be the only person here to think so. I let my hand fall to my side, and when our fingers touch, he doesn't move. He only leans closer.

"Would you allow me to give you something?" he asks.

I'm too taken off guard to answer as Simon lifts my hand up and discreetly slips a bracelet onto my wrist. I keep my hand low while I bring it closer to my stomach. It takes a moment, but I recognize the bracelet. It's the sea green one from the revels. The one I looked at while we were walking together.

"How did you get this?" I ask a little breathlessly.

"I went back for it after I was sure you made it to the palace safely."

I let the pads of my fingers brush over the soft beads. They glimmer in the candlelight, and my breathing catches as I watch.

"I know you have much finer pieces," Simon says, "but I hoped this one would make you smile."

"No," I tell him quickly. A flash of anxiety crosses his face until I go on. "No, I don't have a piece that's better than this one."

We look at each other, and it might just be the two of us here. No one else. But the sensation passes as soon as it washes in, with Thomas Culpepper suddenly bowing before me.

"Pardon the intrusion," he says smoothly. "May I have the next dance, Your Majesty?"

I want to say no, and because of that, I know that I need to say yes.

"Of course," I answer with a smile. Thomas nods to Simon and takes my hand, gently pulling me back out to the floor.

We move in time with the rest of the dancers, my body taking me where it's meant to go. When Thomas and I face each other, moving backward and forward with a little hop, he speaks so only I can hear: "You need to guard your emotions, Catherine. Especially in public." My heart stutters at his words, but I keep moving to the music. "If I didn't come over when I did, it wouldn't have taken long for someone else to see you. Especially your uncle."

I look out to the crowd, watching as my uncle Norfolk stays in deep conversation with a group of three other noblemen.

Thomas is waiting for my response when I gaze back at him. "I am guarding my emotions," I tell him. "I'm trying to."

He leads me into a turn. "Well, try harder. And smile as you do it."

"Is that your technique?" I ask him. "You prefer to lie with a smile?"

"It's what I do," he answers easily. "But I never said I like it."

We do another couple of hops, moving along with the dancers. "You continue to surprise me, Thomas. I'm really starting to question whether you're diabolical or decent."

He walks around me in a circle, as the other male dancers do with their partners. "I often wonder the same thing about myself."

Then it's my turn to walk around him. Thomas keeps his face so at ease, it's as if he doesn't have a care in the world. "So, which is it?" I ask. "Diabolical or decent?"

He takes my hand, giving my knuckles a gentlemanly kiss as the final notes of the song echo through the crowded room. "I'll let you know when I decide."

Chapter Seventeen

Hours later, I'm tossing and turning in bed. I'm holding my wrist over my head, moving my bracelet in the moonlight as I think of Simon. We didn't get to talk much tonight, but our few hidden moments are fresh enough in my mind that I feel them on the top layer of my skin. The teasing touches. The whispered words in my ear. I want to lean into them, but I can't. I'm so fidgety that I roll onto my back with a groan. I try to take soothing breathes to clear my head. They don't work. I know there's only one thing that will cure my pent-up energy, but I haven't done that here. Not yet at least.

I tilt my head over and Theo isn't anywhere in sight. He must be sleeping in his favorite chair in my sitting room. Reaching down and under my blanket, I run my fingers up the top of my thigh over my nightgown. The material dances across my agitated skin, and just when I begin to bunch the hem up to find what I'm after, there's a quiet knocking on the door.

I instantly sit up, but I don't move otherwise. My ears strain to decipher if the sound was the wind or an actual knock. I hear it again a moment later, and I cross the room knowing that I probably shouldn't. It could be anyone at the door. The king might have come home early. Mistress Marshall could have decided she hates me again and is here to murder me. My curiosity still wins out, and I open the door by the smallest degree.

Simon is standing outside, and I swing the door wide in shock. I have no idea how he got past the guards and into my apartments, but as I frantically look behind him to see if anyone's around, the outer room is completely vacant.

"Lady Rochford snuck me in," he says. "I told her I had to see you." I shake my head and pull him into my room, shutting the door behind him. I don't know if I'm more stunned by the fact that he's here or that Lady Rochford was the one who got him here, but I'm in a near daze as I take in the sight of him. He's wearing just his britches and a white linen shirt. His cheeks are rosy, and his breathing is faster than normal. He's just as restless as me.

"I know I shouldn't be here," he says. "I know it in my mind, but when I try to stay away, I feel pulled back to your side and I have to find you." He takes my hand and pushes it against him, over the thrumming of his heartbeat. "Whatever this is, I've not felt it before. Do you feel it?"

"I feel it," I tell him.

An endless beat goes by as we stare at each other. My chest is tightening, and I slip my arms around his neck, drawing him down to me and pressing my lips to his because if I don't, I might implode.

Our kiss is a balance of need and fear. We know the consequences, but they're not here now. We're trying to keep our feet on the cliff, but we've already jumped. His tongue steals inside my mouth to collide with mine, and when he gathers me against him, I can feel the heat of his skin in a way I haven't before. The material of my nightgown is hardly a barrier, and the thin shirt that he's wearing allows me to uncover every sculpted muscle.

I pull at the hem of his shirt, ready to lift it up and off him when he stills my hands and leans back.

"Lily, wait." He's breathing hard. His pupils are dilated. It takes real restraint to not launch myself at him again, especially after he's called me Lily.

"Are you sure about this? About me?" he asks.

His question makes me want him even more.

"I'm very sure," I answer.

His mouth edges up in a smile, and it sets a warm floating feeling through every inch of me. I lean in, anticipation sparking as his hand catches the back of my neck and pulls me forward. His lips move over mine with uninhibited recklessness and the world goes quiet. It's just us now. Fever dream or real life, it doesn't matter. All that matters is that our bodies are finally pressed tight, straining and clawing as we race against time, even as we try to make it go on and on.

His mouth plunders mine, and I groan at the sensations it sets loose inside me. I tangle my hands into his hair, tugging at the roots, and he lets out a small hiss. His hands shoot down to clutch the fabric of my nightgown, bunching it at my waist in a rough, urgent grip. The cold air blows across the bare skin of my ass, and he fills his hands up with each round cheek. I feel so exposed, and I want more. A swirling breathlessness sweeps through my abdomen when he squeezes hard and lifts me from the floor, and a moan rises from deep in my throat. Simon swallows it down with a grunt and grips me harder as my legs wrap around his waist.

I shimmy down and move closer, already able to rub the hard length of him where I want it the most. He twitches inside his britches and lifts an arm to grasp a handful of my hair, tipping my head back. "I have dreamed of this. You have no idea how much."

I think I do, but I don't say it. Instead, I slip down again, dragging myself over him in a slow, torturous churn of my hips. He blinks his eyes closed and takes a labored breath. When his eyes open, they're deep-set with fire and barely managed restraint. His hand tightens in my hair. "Don't rush this, Lily. We are going to take our time."

I wasn't aware that I wanted to die via a heart attack instigated by dirty talk, but apparently I do. I don't say anything. Only take his hand from its hold on my hair and press it down between us to slip along my too-ready entrance.

There's a wolfish edge to his smile as he walks the room to gently place me down on the bed, flat on my back. He steps as close to the mattress as possible, gazing down at me as my shift stays gathered halfway up my body. Trailing the tips of his hand past my knee, up the outside of my thigh, and delicately between my legs, he leans down on one arm as he slowly slips a finger inside me. He circles and stretches the walls of my folds, and I push my head back hard into the mattress.

"Tell me you were made for me," he whispers, curling his finger and bringing his face close to mine.

"God, yes," I answer, lifting my hips and forcing him deeper. "I was made for you." His thumb slides up in a small circle, thrumming around my clit, and my stomach clenches. I'm trying very hard to keep still, but it's starting to feel impossible. Simon is still hovering over me, watching me with measured dominance as he works me with his deft fingers.

This isn't how I usually am in sex. I like to be on top. In control. In this moment, I feel almost completely at Simon's mercy. I need to get the upper hand, and as much as it pains me to do it, I ease his fingers out from my soft flesh. Pushing up against him, I climb onto my knees, bringing us close to eye level.

I keep my gaze trained on his as I reach down, pulling my nightgown up and dropping it to the floor at Simon's feet.

His eyes trail my body, so focused and intense that I can almost feel him under my skin.

"Tell me you were made for me," I say in a hushed voice, feeding his own words back to him.

He takes a beat. "I was. I'm yours."

I take his hands and pull them to me. Two of his fingers are still wet as I draw his palms to my now-bared chest. Simon's stormy eyes flick to mine as he massages my breasts. His thumbs brush at my nipples and an icy-hot shiver races through me, settling right at my core. The more he teases me, the more he seems bewitched, almost in a dream.

"You're overdressed," I tell him.

He shifts a hand lower to the underside of my breast, propping it up higher as he dips down. He sucks the peak into his mouth, and I swallow hard to stifle a groan, tilting my head down to watch him. He turns his attention to my other nipple, giving it the same ravenous attention before looking at me again.

"I'm afraid you'll disappear if I take my hands from you."

His words shock me into momentary silence as my skin starts to tingle.

"I can help you." My voice is barely above a whisper, but Simon hears me.

He only draws his hands away when I take the bottom of his shirt and lift up, pulling it fully over his head. I place it down onto the mattress beside me, paying no attention to where it falls because I'm too busy taking in the sight of him. I always knew that Simon was toned, but the truth of his perfectly developed muscles is another thing completely. I run my fingers across his skin as I watch him in a near daze.

"You're very beautiful," I murmur. "But I'm sure you already know that."

"The only thing I'm sure of is how much I want you."

My hands ghost down his stomach to pull at the strings of his britches. "Show me how much."

I hear his breath catch, and as I look up into his eyes, the fire is back. The one that promises to consume me, and I'm ready to go up in flames. I've only just got his pants open when he hooks his hands behind my knees, pulling my legs out from under me so that my back hits the bed. He pulls his bottoms off with deliberate slowness before he leans forward, covering my body with his as he nudges me up the mattress until my fingers can reach the headboard.

Simon pushes onto his arms, caging me in as he gazes down at me. "You are just as I pictured you," he says. "The world could burn, and I wouldn't leave this bed."

He kisses me like the world really is burning, and I'm not leaving this bed either. My head spins, and my legs wrap around his hips to pin his weight against me. So much for my staying in control.

He lines open-mouth kisses down my throat, along my collarbone, and back to my heaving breasts. He lavishes each rosy peak, tugging one then the other into his worshiping mouth. My hips whip forward at the jolting heat it shoots though my veins, and I need him inside of me before I pass out. I feel his iron hardness on the base of my thigh and I'm almost shaking with how much I need him.

"Simon, please," I say, pulling him up and kissing him for all I'm worth.

I'm rewarded as I feel him brushing along my entrance. The tip of his cock is wet and warm, and I can't stop myself from reaching down to grasp him in my hand. His head drops down onto my shoulder as I seal my hold around him, pumping up and down. He's breathing hard into the hollow of my neck, and it sends a tingle up my spine.

"If you mean to kill me," he says, drawing back, "know that I'll walk to my death gladly."

I let out a quiet, panting laugh. "We haven't even started yet." I slant my wrist to lead him to my heated core, and he blinks his eyes like he's trying to focus. "Are you sure you're up for the task?"

His roguish smile reappears. Simon doesn't back down from a challenge.

"Quite sure," he replies. I'm about to taunt him some more, but the words slip into a groan when he surges forward, filling me up to the hilt. It takes me a second to adjust. He's bigger than I anticipated, and I feel so tantalizingly full of him that my back arches, wanting to get him somehow deeper.

His cheeks are red, his mouth at half-mast as he takes his time pulling back before he drives forward again. He eases in and out of me with an unpredictable rhythm, changing the angle every time I think I can anticipate what it is that's coming next.

"I'm never going to stop," he mutters, falling forward slightly to lick at the thin arc of my ear. "This is all I want."

"Don't," I whine. He pauses for a second, turning to look at me, but I'm quick to clarify. "Never stop."

He lets out a relieved breath and kisses me, starting slow but building into something desperate with every scorching swing of his hips. I curve myself up, meeting each of his thrusts until my stomach starts to shudder. He takes one of my legs and hooks it up, pushing it forward with his hand while his mouth reaches down, his tongue swirling over my chest. I look down to watch him—to watch us. My nipples are wet with his kisses as he pushes my leg up higher, sliding in deeper and affording me a clear view of him as he drives into me at a punishing pace.

My hands dig into his hair as he pulls his head back to look at me.

"Have you dreamed of this as I have?" he asks, his voice raw. "Did you touch yourself and see my face? Did you imagine me filling you up?"

His fucking mouth. I'll never get enough of it.

"Yes," I tell him, thinking back to when I thought about him as I stood in front of the mirror. But my hands never would have done justice to what he's actually capable of. "Simon," I pant, turning fitfully into the column of his throat. He tilts his hips at a particular angle that rubs against my tingling clit. I jolt up, but he pushes me back down.

"Did I find somewhere special?" he asks. "What would happen if I touched that place again and again?"

His forehead lowers to rest on my shoulder, and I grip the back of his neck. He lets go of my leg and arches his back as he sinks in and out of me. I wrap my stretched-out limbs around him as I rock my hips in a deliberate circular motion that makes him shake. I close my eyes, but he nudges my cheek with his nose.

"Lily," he says. My eyes shoot up to look at him. "Stay here with me."

He starts to move faster, and the air around us feels more like steam, becoming almost unbreathable as the pressure stretches and builds. Simon pulls his head up and lets out a groan that's almost a roar. He rushes forward, slamming into me over and over as he pulses inside me. I suck in a sharp, trembling gasp and clench down around him, shaking in earnest as the world disappears into a sea of white behind my eyes, carrying me off on an unending release.

Minutes later, I slowly feel myself coming back to earth. I'm sated and spent as Simon rests his head on my chest, which is only just starting to rise and fall at a calming rate. I stroke his hair as he settles his cheek against me.

"I don't want to sleep," he says, his lethargic tone already contradicting his words. "We can't sleep."

"We won't," I tell him. "Or if we do, just for a minute."

When I wake up from a dream some time later, Simon is sitting on the edge of the bed beside me, pulling up his pants as he stands. I watch in silence as he ties them closed and slips his shirt on. When he turns to look at me, he seems happily surprised that I'm awake.

"Hello there," he says.

I sit up on the mattress, holding my blanket over my breasts even though he's now intimately aware of every inch of me.

He looks to the still-dark window before turning his gaze back to me. "I should go before it's daylight."

I nod in agreement. "You should."

I expect him to go, but he doesn't. He just keeps looking at me and sits back down on the edge of mattress. "I wish I didn't have to."

His voice is so genuine, his eyes soft—it makes me turn my own gaze away. "I know," I tell him.

He reaches his hand out, tilting my chin up towards him as

he kisses me. We're both slow to pull back. "Are you always this beautiful when you wake?"

"Yes," I answer honestly. Because Catherine always is. This is the first time I've thought of her today, and it leaves me feeling off-kilter. "What if I wasn't?" I then ask him. "What if I woke up and I was a little older, and my skin wasn't perfect, and you couldn't even recognize me?"

"It wouldn't make a difference," he tells me. "My heart would find yours."

He gives me another kiss and gets up from the bed. I get up, too, still wrapped in my blanket as he sneaks out the door. I'm about to close it when I suddenly open it back up halfway.

"Simon," I whisper, leaning my head out. He looks over his shoulder, most likely expecting me to whisper a sweet farewell when I actually say, "Just so you know, I'm pretty sure he's out of the palace at the moment, but I do have a slightly murderous ex-boyfriend who may or may not be hiding behind a curtain somewhere in the vicinity. I'm sure you'll be fine, but you should walk to your room fast to be on the safe side."

He turns all the way around, his eyes widening in confusion. "What?"

"Just be aware of your surroundings. If you see something, say something. Good night!"

I close the door and turn to lean back on the wooden surface. My muscles are sore, and my mind is racing, but I've never felt better since I've been here.

Of course the best sex of my life just had to be waiting for me in 1540. It would be way too easy otherwise.

Chapter Eighteen

Through heavy questioning and consistent annoyance on almost every level of Hampton Court hierarchy, I have learned that this palace is in desperate need of an HR department. They need a caffeine-addicted, no-nonsense corporate warrior named Cindy. Cindy, who will flag the shit out of every nonexistent department and make them bleed with the biting rhetoric of her interoffice memos.

As it stands now, I'm in a standoff with the Master of the Household, Lord Fowley, a tired man in his mid-fifties in a very expensive doublet and cape. I continue to air my grievances to him as he rubs his well-trimmed beard.

"I don't understand what it is that you're asking of me, Your Majesty."

I sit back in my chair. "All I'm asking is for humane, safe living conditions for our servants. These people dedicate their days and lives to helping this palace function. They see to our every need, and yet we're not even remotely seeing to theirs."

"Servants of Hampton Court are given food and board, as well as a salary. Those are extremely generous terms."

"In theory, yes, but not in practice. To my knowledge, the only options servants are given are unjust, unhealthy, and unacceptable."

Lord Fowley continues to glance at my sitting room door, no doubt in eagerness to leave. I nod to Lady Rochford, who then makes a show of locking it. The man sighs at his blocked escape and turns his gaze back to mine. "What is it exactly that you want, Your Majesty?"

I cross my arms and wait a beat. "I want to make improvements," I tell him.

One of his oiled eyebrows shoots up. "What kind of improvements?"

"WHAT ARE THESE rooms used for?" I ask Lord Fowley. We're in one of the buildings surrounding the Great Gatehouse courtyard. Senior nobles are seldom here unless they're passing in or out. The courtyard is public and is more of a transitional space into the palace than a place for the higher-ups to linger.

"Base court is primarily reserved for an overflow of guests."

The Master of the Household looks at the primarily empty room we're standing in. It's modest, with just a few beds and hardly anything else, but there's sunlight and the air is breathable. Curtains could be hung for more privacy.

"So, what you're saying is, most of the people who stay here could pay for a room somewhere local? Which would benefit innkeepers and other small business owners, while giving hundreds of servants a decent place to sleep?"

"Possibly," he answers sheepishly.

I look over at Bessie, and she makes a note in the hard book she's carrying around with us.

WE'RE STANDING IN a back room outside the kitchens. Several servants are wiping themselves down with wet cloths and small buckets, no more than a couple of feet apart. I'm standing beside a particular man who just washed his armpits with a cloth and then used that same cloth to wash his face.

"Tell me, how are servants meant to stay healthy when they don't have regular, adequate opportunities to bathe, nor the time or facilities to do so?"

"I'm not entirely sure, Your Majesty." A woman walks past Lord Fowley, ferociously scratching her hair along the way.

"And there's another prime example. Do you enjoy headlice, Lord Fowley?"

He looks at the woman and quickly moves several feet away.

"Our workers need better sanitation and washing facilities. Improved health prevents the spread of disease and exhaustion and increases morale." I then walk past him, giving a purposeful look to his scalp.

"I think I see some nits ready to hatch."

He itches his head so violently that he might draw blood.

WE'RE NOW IN the midst of the bustling noise and heat of the kitchens. Cecily is holding a bowl out to Lord Fowley, showing him the food servants were offered for lunch today. It looks like a mixture of wet dog food and dirty broth.

"Everyone working in the palace needs nutritious, regular meals," I tell him. "There must be proteins, vegetables, and clean water or ale. No half-chewed scraps. No gruel."

Lord Fowley glances down at Cecily's bowl again, his face twisting in disgust. "Would you care to take a bite?" I ask him.

He shakes his head, and Cecily holds up a spoonful. "Take a bite," she demands.

AS WE WALK through the hall back toward the royal apartments, Lord Fowley is now taking his own notes as Bessie and Cecily follow along behind us.

"What are your thoughts on childcare?" I ask him.

His defeated eyes look up from the paper he's working on. "I don't know what that means."

I stop walking a moment, giving him the chance to catch his breath. "It's not sustainable for our workers to continually become sick due to poor post-birth care or by forcing them away from their children. Women need allotted times to breastfeed and family-friendly accommodations to live in so their husbands can assist them."

Bottled-up anger flashes in Lord Fowley's eyes as he lowers his notebook. "It is simply not how things are done, Your Majesty. The palace has been running successfully exactly as it has for years. You can't just change our every way of life based upon a whim."

I give him an obliging smile and move a step closer. "Watch me."

Lord Fowley balks at my words, staying absolutely still as I walk off. I only make it a few feet before Thomas Culpepper suddenly falls into step beside me.

"Well," he says, glancing down at me, "you seem quite pleased with yourself this afternoon."

I struggle to hold in my little smirk. "I am pleased," I answer.

"Indeed. Saving Hampton Court Palace one swill bucket at a time is undoubtably very rewarding."

He offers me his arm, and I take it despite his snobbish comment. He veers us to the left, leading me into the Long Gallery. Stately portraits and tapestries line one wall and tall, narrow windows line the other.

"Tell me about when you first came to court," I decide to ask him. We move past other noblemen and -women walking the gallery, all of whom bow or curtsy as I pass. Thomas stands up a little taller, clearly enjoying the deference being shown.

"When I first came to court," he says, "I loved everything about it."

"Now why doesn't that surprise me?"

He casts me a sly grin. "Of course, it helped that the king took a keen interest in me soon after I arrived. I had helped obtain a hawk for him, and before long, I was a Gentleman of the privy council. Suddenly all at court knew who I was and wanted to befriend me. They practically begged me to exert my influence over the king."

I look up at him, knowing the validation must have been delicious to him. Probably addictive. "Do you think of Henry as your friend?" I ask curiously.

Thomas doesn't answer right away, but the self-satisfied lift of his brow does. "I wouldn't dare to presume so."

"But you said people would ask you to exert your influence over him. Did that make you feel powerful?"

"It would make anyone feel that way," he says. "But I also know how precarious it all is. He who sits in the clouds one day may be wallowing in the dirt in the next. Or under it."

"That's very prophetic." We stop near a particular portrait of a woman in an extravagant gown with her hair free-flowing. She's standing straight, and her hand rests on the back of a tall golden chair. Her expression is unreadable. Written in the bottom corner in curling script is *Sub rosa, veritas*.

Thomas studies the portrait as well before speaking again. "The king said I remind him of himself when he was a young man. That when he looks at me, he sees himself."

I look over at him myself, trying to imagine Henry and him standing side by side. From what I've heard of Henry in his youthful prime, perhaps they did have some similarities. Well-liked, athletic, charming—but whereas Henry must have always had some level of dormant cruelty hidden beneath his pleasing facade, I'm not fully convinced that Thomas does. But I've been wrong before. Hopefully I'm not now.

We're moving on to the next portrait when Lady Rochford approaches us from the far end of the gallery. She's unsmiling, and her eyes are all business.

"Your Majesty, I need a word with you at once."

"Duty calls," I tell Thomas. "Thank you for the stroll." I give him a little curtsy and he bows. I start to walk toward Lady Rochford when I opt to turn back around. "You know, you could head down to Base Court and help with hanging the new dormitory curtains or something."

"Oh, yes. I'm on my way." He walks off, and I call after him as he goes.

"You're going in the wrong direction!"

"Am I?" he asks over his shoulder without stopping. I press my lips together and exhale through my nose as Lady Rochford settles beside me.

"We have a little problem," she says. "And by we, I mean you."

I wheel around to face her, still cocky from my staff improvements. "There are no problems, only solutions."

"Your grandmother, the Dowager Duchess of Norfolk, is here. And she brought Francis Dereham with her."

I drop my head back. God fucking dammit.

"I'm assuming she caught Dereham trying to retrieve your letters."

"You're probably right," I groan. Then, "Wait, how do you even know about the letters? And how do you know about Francis?"

Lady Rochford gives me a deadpan look. "I know everything, Catherine."

She's calling me Catherine, so in truth, she doesn't know *everything* everything. Though with her, you can never be too sure.

"I feel like we should embroider together sometime."

Her eyes narrow into slits. "I would sooner rot."

LADY ROCHFORD LEADS me down a flight of stairs and through a hall I've never seen before. At the very end, we arrive at a sitting room. Walking inside, I'm met with a sheepish-looking Francis, and a woman who I can only assume is the Dowager Duchess.

Francis is sitting in a chair with Catherine's grandmother—my grandmother—standing to the right of him, leaning down on the support of a cane. My first impression is that she's stately, elegant, and noticeably dressed in all black. She's smiling at me, but there's also something subtly menacing about her. I wouldn't be surprised if her cane doubled as a shank.

"Well, my girl. You have certainly come a long way since Lambeth, haven't you?" Her voice is rich with age, and in a way, it reminds me of my own grandmother's voice. It hurts to hear, but I want to hear more.

"That's one way of looking at it," I reply.

She crosses the room, stomping her cane with each step until she sits in a chair by the fire. Her skin is wrinkled, but her eyes are young and teasing. "My granddaughter, the queen of England. How does the crown feel?"

I think a moment before answering. "Heavy."

She chuckles at my response, settling her skirts around the chair. "Yes, well, my stepson, the Duke of Norfolk, is certainly tickled to be related to royalty once again. But I'm sure you already know that. Tell me, has he been in here whispering threatening riddles into your ear this afternoon? If not, don't fret. The day is still young."

When I look behind me, Lady Rochford is standing by the door. I move deeper inside the room, taken off guard by the Dowager's frankness. "I'm surprised to hear you talk about him like that," I tell her.

She taps her embellished cane on the floor, resting both her hands across the handle. "I am well aware of the sort of man my stepson is. He's tortured enough squirrels on our estate through the years to know that it was only a matter of time until he moved on to ensnare bigger beasts. And now you are the one who's caught up in his web of ambition, it seems."

Her candor is as refreshing as it is concerning.

"Accustomed to mischief as I am, I was still surprised to find this surly field mouse sniffing around my library under the cover of the night." She nudges her cane toward Francis, and he flinches a little. "If you're trying to destroy evidence, you should at the very least try to send someone with a little more finesse."

The Dowager reaches into her pocket then, pulling out a tied-up stack of letters. I look over at Francis, and he grips the arms of his chair as his mouth parts. Those are *the* letters.

When I glance back over at the Dowager, she's watching me with an expectant gaze. "Well then? What do you have to say?"

My heart is beating too fast in my chest. My fingers twitch with the urge to snatch those letters right out of her hands. But I need to stay calm. I need to play smart. Those letters very well might be my execution warrant, and Catherine's story inside one of them could be my ticket home. But I can't let the Dowager know just how badly I need them.

I take a steadying breath and walk the few feet to sit in a chair across from her, folding my hands in my lap. "I don't know what you're talking about," I tell her innocently.

The older woman only chortles. "Don't you try your pretty little trickery on me, girl. For all the love this one swears he bears to you, he sang like a skylark when I questioned him."

Our collective gazes shoot over to Francis, who squirms back in his seat.

"I'm sorry, Catherine," he says, his voice sounding feeble. "She practically beat it out of me."

"Oh, indeed," the Dowager laughs, stomping her cane on the floor again. "I said but one stern word to him, and he told me all in an instant."

My blood turns cold at her statement. "All?" I ask, turning my betrayed eyes back over to Francis. His face goes white, but he gives his head a barely noticeable shake.

"Yes, he told me how you sent him to Lambeth to rid me of the letters. 'She needs to keep her reputation pure,' he said. And you wouldn't be wrong, of course."

Her last sentence gives me hope. "Does that mean you'll let me have them?" I ask.

She nestles the letters more securely in her lap. "What pained me the most keenly in all this is that you thought me capable of using them against you in the first place."

The letters are still in her vise grip.

I keep my voice soothing as I speak to her. "I didn't think that you would use them against me. I just wanted to be careful. I wanted to protect our family."

"Yes, our precious family," she muses. "I suppose your uncle's whispers have reached you well enough after all."

I nod in solidarity as a thick silence covers the room. I stand up a second later, smiling at the Dowager in what I hope is familial friendship.

"So, can I have the letters back?" I hold out my hand, and the Dowager slowly stands to bring herself to eye level. My hand is shaking ever so slightly in anticipation. I can't be sure if the woman notices, but she tucks the letters back into her pocket.

"I'll have a think on it," she says. "I've traveled long and I'm tired."

My hope collapses in on itself, my limbs feeling heavy as the Dowager makes her way to the door. When she's halfway there, Lady Rochford steps forward to block her path, prompting the older woman to turn around to look at me.

"Is this your henchwoman?" she asks. "If she thinks to scare me, I'd have to warn her that I've dispatched much more unsightly creatures than her, and I have plenty of fight in me yet."

I shake my head, swallowing down my disappointment. "It's all right," I tell Lady Rochford, who then steps aside, clearing a path for the Dowager.

"Good night, Catherine. I'll see you again soon enough."

She exits the room in all her state, leaving Lady Rochford to close the door behind her.

"Did that sour-faced hag just call me an unsightly creature?" she asks, aghast.

I sit back down in my chair. "She might have."

I look over at Francis, and his posture is the most relaxed it's been in this entire conversation. "She really isn't a very nice woman at all," he says.

If I was in possession of the Dowager's cane, I'd hit him with it.

"Thank for that observation, Francis, and for absolutely nothing else. I thought you said you could easily get the letters?"

He finally stands up, pushing his shoulders back and running a hand through his tangled hair. "Well, it's not ideal circumstances, but at least the letters are here at court. It should be all the easier for us to get them back now."

"Or for them to get discovered," I counter.

Lady Rochford takes a decisive step closer. "I'll get the letters," she states. "But not tonight. From the looks of her, that crone will stuff them in her hindquarters now that she knows we're after them."

I wince at the thought. "That is a disturbing visual," I tell her. "But you're also right. It has to be soon. Bessie and Richard pushed up the wedding, so that'll be happening in three days. I'll make sure the Dowager is invited and you can sneak into her room during the wedding feast."

Lady Rochford nods, and Francis moves toward us. "What about me? What should I do?"

I scrunch my face as I try to think of something, but Lady Rochford is quicker than me.

"Perhaps you can sit and cry over the fact that you were bested by a tired old woman who's likely half blind, yet still managed to find you sneaking into her home in the dark."

Her insult lands with stunning accuracy, and I take a step nearer to Francis to soften the blow. "Don't take it personally. She's only mean because she cares."

I turn to Lady Rochford in the hopes that she'll agree, or stay silent, but instead she answers, "I assure you, I'm dead inside."

Well, that settles that. I give Francis's shoulder an encouraging squeeze and steer him in the direction of the door. "I'll let you know if we hear anything," I tell his retreating form.

Once he's gone, I turn back to an ill-tempered Lady Rochford and clap my hands together. "So today was eventful, huh?"

It takes a fair amount of time before she speaks again. "I won't say it out loud, but you do know what I'm thinking, don't you?"

"That you still miss Anne of Cleves?" I venture quietly.

Lady Rochford nods and closes her eyes. "I really, really do."

Chapter Nineteen

Bessie makes a beautiful bride. In a pale blue embroidered gown and French hood, she's the perfect fusion of live-action Cinderella and cartoon Cinderella. When I arrive at her wedding feast, I take both her hands and kiss her cheeks.

"Congratulations, Bessie." I lean back to look at her, and when I do, I notice her nervous smile. "What's the matter?" I ask. "You look stunning, and Richard is obsessed with you."

"No, it is nothing like that," she mumbles. "It's just . . . I am worried about being a wife."

"Marriage jitters are completely understandable. But I promise, you are going to be a wonderful wife." I take a beat. "Unless you're not telling me something about Richard. If he ever hurts you, just say the word and I'll have him arrested. I have the power to do that, you know."

"No!" She grabs at my wrists and pulls us over toward the side of the room. "It has nothing to do with him. I'm just nervous about tonight. The wedding night."

"Ohhhh," I answer slowly. "Which part are you nervous about?"

Bessie turns us so that our backs are facing the inside of the room, lowering her voice. "All of it. My mother said the act will hurt terribly, but I must endure it. She said to keep my eyes shut and not to scream or God won't see fit to give me a baby."

Loss of virginity, terror, and religious guilt—an infallible trifecta.

"I see. And by any chance, do you know how it physically

happens when God gives you a baby? Maybe from a medical standpoint?" Pretty please say yes.

"Not entirely," Bessie answers, "but a maid at my family's estate once told me that the motions are similar to a strange bunny hopping in and out of its hole. She also said that the first time it happens, it will feel as if I'm being stabbed in my unmentionables."

Oh, my sweet sister in Christ.

"Right. So, I think it's very important that we go at your pace with this conversation. You tell me exactly how much you want to know about what goes on in a sexual relationship and that's what I'll tell you."

Bessie's eyes bulge. I forgot that queens of England aren't usually sex-positive psychologists.

"How much am I supposed to know?" she asks, a little panicked. "How much did you know before you . . . married the king?"

It's safe to say that we're both aware that my wedding night with Henry wasn't my first sexual encounter. But I also can't tell her that I lost my V-card at a prom after-party my senior year of high school.

"I think I knew slightly more than you do now."

"Please, tell me," Bessie pleads. "If I know what's going to happen tonight, at least I can prepare myself."

Explaining the birds and the bees to Bessie at her wedding venue certainly wasn't on my bingo card today, but what in my life ever is? Ten minutes later, we're in a secluded side room, sitting in two parallel chairs, and my innocent friend is looking at me like she's just seen a ghost. A horrifying ghost with a very big boner.

"But . . ." she stutters, "but I'm sure that's not physically possible. It's mortifying! I can't let him do that to me!"

I lean forward in my chair, keeping my voice smooth and calm. "But that's the thing—it doesn't have to be *him* doing that to *you*. You should be an active participant. Sex can be an extremely enjoyable act that you and Richard do together to express yourselves. At some point, you might even want to do it every day."

"Every day?" she asks disbelievingly. "You are mad! How could what you described ever be enjoyable? You said he's going to . . . enter me."

I move my head from side to side. "That's part of the logistics, yes, but the entering bit can be a fun process if you both go about it the right way."

Bessie leans in as well now. "How do you mean?"

I rub my hands together, really hoping that I'm not making things worse. "Before we get into that, has there been anything you've liked doing with Richard so far? Has he kissed you yet?"

"Yes," she answers with a shy smile. "Three times."

"And how was it?" I ask.

She thinks about it a moment, and I'm beyond relieved that her smile stays in place. "I liked it. It was a bit wet at first, but then it was nice. The last time he kissed me, he held me close and squeezed against me while he did it, and it made my stomach feel strange, but a nice strange, if that makes sense."

Good for you, Richard. I knew I liked you.

"It makes perfect sense," I tell her. "What you were probably feeling then was desire and an attraction for Richard. That's normal and healthy and a positive sign."

Bessie nods, seeming grateful for the news.

"Some advice I would give you for tonight," I go on to tell her. "You might mention to Richard you want him to kiss you a lot—for a good long time. It will help your body to relax, and it will help get you ready for the next steps." I watch as her cheeks go red, no doubt remembering the "next steps" that I explained to her just a few minutes ago. "Of all the things I mentioned when I talked you through the process, was there anything that sounded interesting? Or like something you would like to try?"

Bessie pauses, her cheeks turning closer to maroon. "I suppose what you said about him touching me sounded all right. If he does it softly."

"Wonderful. So, you should tell him that you would enjoy some soft touching. And as you both explore a bit and you find out what you like, you can tell him to do it more."

Bessie sits back in her chair at my words. "I'm allowed to do that? My mother specifically told me to keep silent for the duration of it."

For a second, I start to feel annoyed with Bessie's mom, but then I remind myself that she was probably just passing on the same information that she was told for her own wedding night. In a time when nothing was more important than producing heirs, you would think that society would educate women to enjoy and crave sex as much as humanly possible. Instead, they keep cockblocking their own goal.

"I'm sure your mother did tell you that. Unfortunately, that might have been what she went through and what she was taught, but I've found that open communication is very important in the sexual process. If you tell Richard what you're responding to, he'll most likely continue to do it. A good husband will want to give you a nice experience, and I think that Richard wants to be a good husband to you."

Bessie takes a deep breath as she absorbs all the information. "And am I allowed to touch him, too?" she asks curiously.

Get it, Bess!

"Yes," I reply. "And just how you're going to tell Richard what you like, you can also ask him to tell you what he likes."

Bessie nods. "So . . . if he kisses me and we touch each other, will the entering part still hurt?"

I wait a moment, thinking of the best way to phrase my answer. "Honestly, it most likely will still hurt tonight, and it might continue to hurt for the first few times you and Richard are intimate. But the more comfortable you and he get with each other, the better it will be. In less than a month, I bet you'll love it."

"Do you love it?" she asks a few seconds later. "The bedding process?"

I let memories of Simon slip into my mind, pushing my legs together under the secrecy of my heavy gown. "Yes," I tell her with a small smile. "I love the bedding process."

Bessie looks astonished, but I shake my head and stand, prompting her to do the same. "Okay, this is your wedding day. We need to get out there and celebrate, and then we're going to the after-party."

"What's an after-party?" she asks.

I walk toward the door, smiling at her over my shoulder as I do. "You're going to find out . . ."

"What do you mean we flip the cup?" Lady Barrow asks from across the table. "The wine will splatter all over us."

The after-party is in full swing as I've assembled two solid teams in my inner receiving room. It's a bit overcrowded with Bessie's wedding guests, even though we only invited the courtiers we trust. We even coerced the guards into dispersing to the very outer doors in exchange for a substantial amount of wine, giving us relative freedom for the night.

"No, you drink the wine, then you flip the cup once it's empty," I explain. "It's a race, and whichever team finishes first wins."

"Do we all go at once?" Bessie asks.

"No, we go in a line. You go first and the last person is the anchor. Are we ready?"

Half the people say yes, the other half say no. Bessie, Elizabeth Norworth, and I are co-captains of our team, intermixed with other ladies-in-waiting and male courtiers. Lady Barrow and Lady Wessex are the co-captains of the opposing team. Richard is one of their number and is struggling to survive.

"Ready, set, go!" I yell.

Lady Barrow and I start drinking, and the Tudor crew picks up on the basics of flip-cup with surprising ease. Yelling and cheers erupt as the game progresses. Richard is the anchor of his team and victoriously flings his arms up in the air when he clinches the win at the very end. We take turns playing and rooting other players on until everyone in the room has had a chance. Then we're moving on to the next game.

"My turn," Bessie says through a laugh a while later. "Never have I ever said I was going to the chapel for confession but really I went swimming naked in the lake while on summer progress through Wiltshire."

Everyone oohs and aahs, except for Lady Wessex. She continues to pet Theo, who's in her lap, as she takes a drink from her cup. When she's done, a knowing smile spreads across her face. "Why, Bessie, you sneaky thing. Enjoy the show, did you?"

Bessie hides her smirk in Richard's shoulder as the room continues to laugh and drink. One of the courtiers stands up, taking a big gulp from his cup. "Someone else go now. And no more talk of getting your jollies off in the great hall. It was fun the first three times, but now it's just repetitive."

A half hour later, our group is well on our way to Tipsyville, if they're not residents there already. We're gearing up for a round of hide-and-spy, which is apparently what they call hide-and-seek here.

Lady Wessex rolls her eyes. "We are in a palace. This game could take hours, if not days."

"Don't go too far, then," I suggest. "And if you want to hide in pairs, you can." I give Bessie a pointed look. She nods in anticipation and grabs Richard's hand, pulling him off to "hide."

"The saltiest person is the one to count. That's you, Lady Wessex."

She half smiles, half hisses at me as she covers her eyes and starts to count. Everyone goes running from the room in opposite directions, most stumbling and laughing along the way. I take my time, walking down a hall as I look for a decent spot when a door I never noticed before opens beside me. I carefully steal a glance inside. The second I do, I'm pulled in all the way and the door shuts behind me. I'm about to start swinging when my abductor turns to lean back on the closed door—Simon.

"Barely any effort and you already happened upon my hiding space." His voice is playful, his eyes are smiling, but he looks tired, too.

I move closer to him and touch my cheek to his hand. "Hello," I say, feeling the beginning of scruff beneath my fingers.

"Hello," he answers softly.

I let my hand drop from his face and look behind me, seeing that we're actually at the top of a stairwell and not in a closet, as I assumed. It's a jarring realization. "Where are we?" I ask.

Simon walks up behind me, and I lean my head back on his shoulder as he wraps his arms around my waist. "It's a stairwell that leads to a lower room that has a hall leading to the kitchens. It's how the servants get up and down to deliver your meals without walking through the entire palace."

I slip out of his grip, moving to the top of the landing to peek down. It's quiet and dark. Probably out of bounds from hide-and-spy. I doubt anyone would be brave enough to look for us if we ventured down.

"Should we stay or go?" I ask.

Simon only pauses for a moment. "We should go."

I smile, awash with a pleasant kind of nerves as I head into the darkness and down the steps. I hear Simon behind me as we move farther and farther away from the party, until finally we're in an empty room with a long wooden table. The door is shut, and only faint moonlight is dripping in through the windows.

I walk around the rectangular table, moving my fingers along the surface, when Simon suddenly speaks.

"I'm to leave court. Tonight." My stomach drops, but I keep my features neutral as he goes on. "The king is sending me on an urgent errand to London. It shouldn't take more than a few days. I didn't want to leave without saying goodbye first."

I nod at the news. The table is between us, with Simon standing on the other side.

"That's too bad," I tell him. "I promised Bessie a party every night to celebrate her coming into womanhood. It's going to be fun."

"I'll be sorry to miss it." He starts to walk around the table, and I stay where I am.

"You should be. I'm going to introduce the court to the finer points of a game called beer pong, and it's a crowd favorite. It would have appealed to your competitive nature."

He's on my side of the table, taking slow but steady steps closer. "It's not the games that I'll miss," he says. We're only a couple of feet apart, and he takes my hand to interlock our fingers together. My stomach swirls, and I don't want to let go. I also don't want him to know how scared I am for him to leave.

I give his hand a reassuring squeeze. "At least we get to see each other now. For a while."

Simon nods. "It feels unfair. That all we have is a while." He looks down before going on. "I want you for longer than that."

His words strike a chord deep in my chest. "A while" might be all we'll ever have. Whether I stay or I get back home, he'll be out of reach for me, and the thought forms a painful lump in my throat.

I let go of his hand and turn to sit on the table, my feet dangling a foot above the stone floor. I turn to face him, catching his stormy, quiet eyes. "Tell me something about you that no one else knows."

He sits beside me and looks ahead. The room is deep in silence when he eventually says, "I'm a very good liar."

Something sinks in my middle at his words. His face is totally calm.

"What do you mean?" I ask.

His smile is soft as he gazes at me. "I've just always been good at lying." I don't know what to think, and he shakes his head at my nervousness. "The trick of it is, I never, ever lie unless it's massively important. I know people think that the more you lie, the better you get at it, but I find it to be the opposite."

My breathing levels at his lightened tone. My paranoid brain was ready to shoot me through the roof, but I should have known better. "And what have you ever lied about?"

Simon takes a dramatic breath. "I told my older sister that no man would marry her because she couldn't cook a meal. That wasn't the lie. She really hadn't cooked before. But then she tried to do it, so she could prove me wrong. And when I tasted the raspberry tart she made, I told her it was good, which was the biggest lie of my life."

It's annoying. And adorable.

"That's what was so massively important that you had to lie?"

"Well, she worked rather hard on it. I was only sick for a few days after, not that anyone was worried. Neville was still alive, so I was very much replaceable at that point."

"Hey," I tell him, stealing his hand back. "You're not replaceable."

He holds my hand tighter. "Now you tell me something that no one else knows about you."

If only he was aware of just how loaded that question is.

He's probably expecting a silly answer. Some mischievous little thing that I did and never told him or anyone about. But what I really want to tell him, what I'm tempted beyond all reason to tell him, is the truth. I want to tell him who I am.

But I can't.

Can I?

If I tell him the truth, that I'm not Catherine, what will he think? He'll think that I've had too much to drink. That I'm making things up for attention. Or he might believe me.

My mind is racing a million miles a second. Here in this time—here as Catherine Howard—I keep so much internalized. A world-changing, life-altering thing happened to me, and Matthias is the only person I can really talk to. Matthias, who barely lets me through his door. And then there's Francis, who would absolutely vampire-stab-me with a wooden stake through the heart if it would resurrect Catherine's soul.

I know that I have friends here, and I trust them, but I don't know if I can trust them with this. When I stop and think of the fact that I may be stuck here for an indefinite amount of time, I'm riddled with questions and plagued with anxiety. But when I'm with Simon, everything goes quiet. I can hear myself and I can hear him, and I trust him.

I take a steeling breath. "What if I told you that I'm not who you think I am?"

This is a mistake. I should stop. But I want him to know me. I *need* him to know me. Simon stays quiet, and I go on.

"You kept telling me that I was different that day I crashed into you in the hallway. That I changed from who I was before. What if there was a reason that I changed?"

His gaze clouds with worry as he inadvertently shifts closer to me. "Did someone hurt you? Did something happen?"

I shake my head and smooth my other hand over his. "Not like that. Something did happen, but I don't know how to explain it."

He goes quiet again, until he says, "Try."

This is it. Heaven help me.

"I'm not Catherine Howard." I blurt the words out, thinking the planet might explode once I say them. But nothing happens, and Simon keeps watching me. So, I go on. "My name is Lily Whitaker, and I was born in the 2000s in Santa Monica, California. That's in America. I lived with my mom and my grandma, but now I have my own place. I'm a PhD candidate in psychology. We have electricity. I drive a car and have a phone and I'm free to live my life the way I want to because that's how it is in the future. I'm from the future."

The words fall out of me in a dizzying tumble. I want to take them back, but I'm also absurdly glad that they're out. Adrenaline swirls in my gut, and it feels like I'm standing on the edge of a diving board as I wait for Simon to respond.

"You're from the future?" he asks lightly. He thinks I'm kidding. I still keep talking.

"I was visiting England with my friend Zoe, and we came to Hampton Court Palace. This place is more like a museum in my time. I don't think anyone even lives in it. I heard singing, I felt kind of sick, and then I'm pretty sure I fainted. When I woke up, I was here. In this body. In Catherine Howard's body. This isn't what I really look like. This isn't my voice. These aren't my hands or my face. None of it is me. And that's why I'm so different from the Catherine you originally met and remember. That's why I was so confused and running and trying to escape the day I bumped into you. It's why I asked you to call me Lily. It's because that's who I am—Lily. I'm Lily."

Simon stands up from the table. He's still looking at me and smiling, but it's falling little by little. "Is this another drinking game?"

I get up from the table, too. "It's not a game," I tell him. "I know what happens here, in history. I know that Henry will end up having six wives in total. I know that his daughter Elizabeth will be his longest-living heir. And I know that if the old version of history comes true now, then I'm eventually going to be executed for adultery. That's what happened when the real Catherine was here. It might happen to me unless I'm able to change it, but I don't think I'm doing a very good job."

My words sound like an ungraceful prophesy, and I see the shift in Simon's eyes—the echoes of concern. I don't know if he believes me, but I do know that he doesn't fully believe that I'm joking anymore either.

"It's the truth," I promise him. "Maybe I shouldn't have told you. Matthias, the king's astrologer, he knows, and he said I would mess up the timeline if I changed anything drastic. Maybe it was selfish of me to tell you, but I just . . . I want you to know the actual me."

Silence surrounds us, squeezing tight against our ribs until we hear voices near the door at the top of the stairwell. My heart is hammering at light speed. The air feels static and frail between us, like I could snap it in two if I reached out and grabbed it.

"We can't be found together," Simon says, urging me back toward the stairs. "Go up and tell them that you're alone. Say that you're tired of hiding and then everyone will follow you."

I latch onto the edge of his sleeves, unwilling to go. "What about everything I just said? Do you think I'm lying?"

He looks into my eyes, and I can see the chaos behind them, even as they never falter. "I don't think that you're lying."

I'm so stunned, I could fall over. "Why not?" I whisper. I might cry. The tears are there, but I don't let them loose. I need to focus on whatever it is that Simon is about to say.

"Because the one thing I believe in is you."

He believes me. The realization is mind-blowing, and I can't keep in my euphoric laugh as I kiss him. I don't mean to cry, but my cheeks are wet as I rest my forehead against his. "Thank you," I murmur. "I'll see you in a few days. When you get back."

He kisses me again, and I don't know how, but I step out of his arms and dash up the stairs. I want to stay with him so desperately that each step up and forward is physically painful. But even so, I feel a strength bursting through me so powerfully that I may come apart at the seams.

When I emerge out the door, I end up face-to-face with Lady Wessex. "Well, it took you long enough," I tell her with a smile, wiping under my eyes. "I was beginning to think you all went back to the party without me."

"If only we could," she says with her affectionate meanness.

We make our way back into my sitting room, where everyone is lounging and drinking once again. "What should we play next?" I ask.

Just then, Bessie and Richard stumble out from a side room, looking deliriously happy with their clothes noticeably off-center. Laughter and claps follow in their wake as they join us, but everything goes quiet when my sitting room doors suddenly burst open.

"His Majesty, the king!"

It's dead silent as Henry walks in. His limp is more dominant. His eyes are icy. When his gaze finds mine, it feels like the floor has fallen out from beneath me and my breath gets lodged in my throat.

"Hello, my love," he says through a smirk. "Have you missed me?"

Chapter Twenty

"I . . ." My voice stutters as Henry's eyes bore into mine. He's really here in this room, and his presence is nearly overpowering. "Yes, I've missed you very much."

He tilts his chin up, looking down his nose at me like he's humoring a child. "If you have, then come here and greet me."

I don't feel my feet moving, but I'm slowly approaching him. When I stand before him, he seems taller. It feels like his arms could reach each wall. I don't know if I'm doing the right thing when I go up on my toes and kiss his cheek. He takes my hand in return and kisses it, squeezing a little too hard before he lets it go.

I force myself to smile as I take a step back. He begins to slowly survey the room, walking the length of it and looking into the eyes of everyone who is here.

"I have heard many a tale of what has gone on at court in my absence," he says. "You have all been having quite the merry time, have you not?"

No one answers, and I don't blame them.

I wring my hands together, knowing that it's up to me to deal with my husband. "We tried to put on a brave face. But it wasn't the same without you."

Henry turns to look at me, and his eyes almost cut through me. The doting "lover" who cared for nothing so much as my happiness is long gone, and a stranger is here instead. Although this isn't really a stranger, is it? I'm simply meeting the real Henry.

"Really? I have been told otherwise." His words are still hanging in the air when Mistress Marshall enters the room. She smiles at me like a friend never would, and I blink against my rising panic.

I wait for her to speak, but nothing comes. What would be the point of it? Her entrance said it all.

Once Henry's taken stock of each guest in the room, he makes his way back toward the doors. "The day has come to an end," he says. "Let us all seek rest or prayer." He focuses his attention on me, and I don't know if I should smile or run. "After I talk a while with Mistress Marshall, I expect to see you in my chamber."

I nod and curtsy in response. Everyone files out of the room one by one, until only Mistress Marshall and I remain. She walks toward me with slow, delicate steps.

"Did I fail to mention that I have known the king since childhood? He trusts my judgment in many matters, as he knows I am his most loyal of subjects."

She's literally radiating an after-sex glow. That's how happy Mistress Marshall is right now.

"No, you never told me that," I murmur.

She tsks me under her breath. "How forgetful of me. In any case, I'm glad to be telling you now." She steps in close to me and takes my hands. "Consider it a peace offering."

An unforgiving chill settles through my fingers as I pull my hands away. Lady Rochford appears at the door, looking more than ready to pull Mistress Marshall out by her pointy gable hood.

"Take care, Your Majesty," the woman says quietly. "I will see to it that the king is illuminated to all your misdoings—*past* as well as present." She turns and leaves after that, and she and Lady Rochford bump shoulders in the process.

I say nothing when it's just the two of us left, and before I know what's happening, Lady Rochford places her hand on the small of my back and ushers me from the room.

Back in the privacy of my bedchamber, Lady Rochford is the first to speak. "Let us remain calm. That is the most important thing."

I snap out of my stupor, moving to my dressing table and grabbing three bottles of Bessie's sleeping draft that I hid away in a drawer.

"I have to kill him," I tell her, the bottles jingling in my shaking hands. "I have to kill him before he kills me."

Lady Rochford actually goes pale. "Mother Mary, I need to sit down." She moves to sit on the edge of my bed, rubbing her fingers into her forehead as Theo sniffs her waist.

"He knows." My voice is trembling, but I'm resolute. I have to do this. "Did you see how he was acting? There's no way that he doesn't know."

"Doesn't know what?" she asks, looking up. Then she shakes her head. "Don't answer that." She stands from the bed, following me as I begin pacing around the room. "He could be tired, Catherine. His leg could be ailing him, and his mood is foul."

I've never known Lady Rochford to be naïve. "There's more to it than that. And you heard Mistress Marshall, she's going to tell him everything." I'm still holding the bottles—so tightly that I'm a little nervous they could break.

"What will she tell him? As far as that witch knows, all you and we have been doing is drinking and dancing more than we should. That's poor decision-making, not a crime."

I stop pacing to face her with agitated eyes. "I'm pretty sure poor decision-making is a crime here."

There's a knock on the door, and Lady Rochford rips the bottles from my hands as the Dowager Duchess steps inside. "Good evening, Your Grace," she says, curtsying to the older woman.

The Dowager looks us over, taking both of us in before she speaks. "Well, I'm glad I won't be the one to ruin the evening. From the looks on your faces, it seems like it's already been lost to hellfire."

Her statement is ominous, but I don't know what could possibly be more ominous than my current situation.

"Why would you ruin the night?" I ask.

She closes the door behind her and pushes down on her cane as she walks farther into the room. "The letters that Dereham was after. The love letters where he wrote that you two were as good as married—they've been stolen from my rooms."

And my situation just got more ominous. I look to Lady Rochford, but she only shakes her head.

"It wasn't me," she says.

It feels like the room is tilting. My stomach lurches as I come to realize the truth. "It must have been Mistress Marshall." No one else says anything, and I go on, my voice surprisingly steady. "She told me that she knew about my past. She was so confident. And she's meeting with the king right now."

The room is quiet. No one tells me that I'm wrong. No one mentions an alternate possibility.

"I'm sorry, Catherine," the Dowager says. "I should have given them to you when I had the chance."

I swallow past the nerves in my throat as I look over at her. "It's all right. You couldn't have known."

Seconds tick by in silence until the Dowager speaks again. "From here on out, I will help you in any way I can, as will everyone at Lambeth." She makes her way to the door and is just beginning to leave when she turns and looks at me one more time. "Good luck, my girl."

She closes the door, and no sooner does the latch fall than it suddenly lifts and opens again. A royal messenger walks in, scanning the room until he sees me. "The king requires your presence immediately."

Lady Rochford moves toward him before I can even clock her location. "Enter this room without permission again, and I'll see you bound and beaten." She moves closer still, lowering her voice. "And not in the way that you like."

The messenger turns red and disappears out the door, though he ends up leaving it open. I follow after him and pause in front of Lady Rochford, carefully taking the sleeping drafts that she has hidden in her hands. She doesn't stop me. She lets me go. The king doesn't like to be kept waiting.

WHEN I ARRIVE in Henry's rooms, the bottles are stowed in my tight gown sleeve as I step farther inside. The space is still beautiful, but there's an oiliness to the air now. The crackling fire sounds sharp, and the meats on Henry's table smell like they're days too old.

"Hello, Catherine." My eyes track to find him, and he's unmoving in his chair near the fire.

"Hello, Henry," I answer.

He looks at the flames in the hearth as they snap and dance. I watch him as he sits, and his facial expressions have changed since the party. They're not pointy and shadowed. They're more reflective. Like he's somehow being pulled inward.

"Are you angry with me?" I ask, keeping my voice low. Repentant.

He finally cranes his neck to look in my direction. "Why would you think so?"

I shrug gently, my palms open. "You just seem different."

Henry turns back to the fire. "Perhaps my time away has altered your memory of me. Or perhaps you hit your head once more and forget yourself."

He sounds like a parent who's saying "I'm not mad. I'm disappointed." But I also see his right hand clenching into a fist against the armrest of his chair. The rage is in there, but it hasn't reached a boil yet. It's simmering for now.

"Tell me, how has your time been spent in my absence?" he goes on to ask. He's still not looking at me, and I step closer to him, trying to signify that I want to be near him. That I trust him. That he can trust me.

"I've embroidered mostly," I tell him. "I also made some changes to improve working conditions for the servants."

"Aren't you the perfect little queen?"

He isn't talking to me like I'm perfect. And when he turns to look at me, it isn't the look he gives. He continues to stare at me, saying nothing, and his hand is still balled into an unforgiving fist. My insides tighten as I reactively enter into fight or flight.

"Can I get you a glass of wine?"

Henry's smile is forced and barely existent. "How you spoil me," he says.

I take that as a yes and turn to walk over to the side table. I twist my wrist as I cross the room, letting the bottles in my sleeve loosen and slide into my palm. I don't want them to jingle, so I pour the wine slowly before I empty the contents of each bottle into the cup. My hands are shaking. My heart rate is in the stratosphere.

What the fuck am I doing? Am I actually going to kill the king of England?

I might hyperventilate. I steal a peek over my shoulder, but Henry is completely focused on the fire. I tell myself that it's him or me. I have to choose. But why does he look so sad?

No, this isn't just someone who's disappointed in their partner. Henry VIII is a murderer. He murdered Catherine. He murdered Anne Boleyn and countless others. And he'll probably murder me next.

And now I'm about to become a murderer, too.

I shake my head. It's not murder if he's planning to kill me. It's self-defense. I'd be doing the world a favor. I'd be saving others. I can't let history repeat itself. I think of Lady Barrow, and I remember what she said when she asked me for the wild carrot seed. If something is going to happen to me, I want it to be because of my choice, not because of my inaction.

I shove the empty bottles back into my sleeve and pick up the cup. It's him or me. And I choose me.

I turn and make my way back to his side, keeping the cup steady all the while. When I hand it over, he smiles as he takes it, and for a split second, he looks like he loves me as much as he ever had.

"I almost forgot how beautiful you are," he whispers.

My expression starts to soften, but then his free hand whips up, grabbing at my wrist and holding in a tight, angry grip. I'm certain that he's discovered the bottles or is about to. But that's my other hand, not the one he's now holding prisoner. He pulls my sleeve up, almost ripping it as he reveals my simple beaded bracelet. The bracelet that Simon gave me.

Henry touches the green and blue beads, poking and prodding at them like little bugs he's inspecting under a magnifying glass.

"Is this new?" he asks me. "Or have you had it all along?" His eyes are dark, and his voice has twisted back into ice.

"I don't remember," I hear myself answer, and he drops my wrist with a chuckle. He relaxes into his chair as I take an immediate step back. He gives the wine a sniff before bringing it to his mouth.

I don't breathe. I don't move. I don't know if I want to smack the cup from his hand or force the liquid down his throat. I don't do either as I stand and watch him. Henry's lips part to drink, but just before he does, he extends his arm and holds the cup out to his side.

He pours the wine onto the floor as his empty eyes burn into mine.

"Get. Out."

Static buzzes in my ears as the world stands still. I turn and leave before I can think of anything else. The door closes behind me, but I don't hear it. I'm moving through the corridor at light speed until I'm back in the alleged safety of my apartments. When I arrive, none of my usual ladies-in-waiting are there, except for Lady Rochford. And standing beside her is the Duke of Norfolk.

"Are you satisfied?" he asks, his voice filled with a quiet thunder.

I feel safer with Lady Rochford nearby, but panic continues to rise inside me. "Satisfied?" I ask him.

My uncle moves toward me. "The king received word that the palace has been a den of sin since the moment he left. You have been reveling, encouraging promiscuity among your women, and poisoning them to turn them barren."

I take in the claims, wondering if this is all of them, or if there's more. The duke is glowering down at me, but his petulance gives me an odd kind of steeliness. When I look up at him, I make sure my eyes are shocked.

"That is . . . absolutely not true. I can't believe that someone would make up such horrendous lies."

The duke leans back, his gaze faltering as he looks at me. "You deny it, then?"

"I vigorously deny it."

He steps away from me, clearly surprised by my response. "So, you never attained and distributed herbs to your ladies? Herbs that would render them and their wombs useless? And you never consumed them yourself?"

I take my anger and channel it into righteous shock. "That is a horrifying accusation." I throw in a rushed sign of the cross for some extra spice.

"And what of their lewd behavior? As queen, you are meant to exemplify piety and dignity, and instead you made a mockery of this court in front of the Italian ambassador. This very evening, you allowed men into your rooms."

"There were dozens of people in my rooms tonight," I clarify. "We were playing a game."

"*None* of this is a game!" he shouts. He crosses the length of the room to confront me but does so in a deadly calm. "It is also rumored that you show particular favor to Simon Gainsford. Did you allow the Gainsford boy to take liberties with you?"

I'm more grateful than ever that Simon is gone, hopefully safe in London, where the dangers here haven't touched him yet. They're officially starting—the rumors that lead to Catherine's downfall. To *my* potential downfall. Still, I look at my uncle with unflinching certainty. "I would never betray the king."

His eyes flash with indecision before he turns his hardened gaze to Lady Rochford. "You," he hisses. "You were meant to watch her. How far must our family fall until you have had your fill?"

She steps forward, moving directly beside me. "My loyalty is to the queen."

"Your loyalty is to me!" the duke bellows.

Lady Rochford doesn't answer. She doesn't cower. She stares him dead in the face and my uncle turns first, dragging a hand through his hair and beginning to pace.

"Should I go speak to Henry again?" I ask.

He doesn't stop walking the room. I can tell he's trying to formulate a plan, but he doesn't know which route to take. "The king has no desire to see or speak with you. A violent temper has consumed him, and you're better off out of his sight until these rumors pass—*if* they pass." His countenance brightens then as he suddenly turns to face me.

"Are you with child?" he asks, sounding hopeful. "If you are, it would change everything."

I subconsciously put a hand to my stomach. I think about telling him I just felt a kick to fuck with him but then decide against it. "No," I tell him. "I am not with child."

He looks at me with all the nothingness that I'm sure consumes his very being. "Then what good are you to anyone?" He walks off without another word, only stopping just before he reaches the door as he turns to look at me. "Ask nothing of me on your account. If the king is done with you, so am I."

I take a slow step toward him, my hands falling to my sides. "Oh, you think so?" He continues to watch me as I go on. "You see, as it happens, you aren't done with me. Because *you* are the one who put me in this position. *You* brought me to court. *You* encouraged the marriage to the king. And I'm sure *you* assured Henry of what a wonderful, fruitful wife I'd be."

I'm close to him now, so close that I can feel the rage vibrating off him, as well as the realization that I'm right. "You better get your shit together," I tell him, "because if I go down, I'm going to make damn sure that you go down with me. Howards stick together."

I don't know if I've ever seen him so angry, and the sight fills me up with joy.

He swings the door open and walks out, slamming it shut behind him. Lady Rochford and I stay where we are, and the lingering silence feels like a third person in the room, breathing and living beside us. I'm the first to speak a few seconds later.

"What a charming family we have."

Lady Rochford looks at me, for the first time seeming unsure of herself. "You shouldn't have baited him like that," she says.

I walk deeper inside the room, stopping to stand in front of the mirror. "He's the least of my worries."

Lady Rochford's reflection shakes her head. "He shouldn't be. I've seen firsthand what he can do. And he is ruthless when it comes to his own survival."

I'm sure that she's right. She often is. But the only way out of this is through it, and I have to keep pushing until the end.

"You also mustn't underestimate the king," she goes on. "You have yet to fully see his fangs, but I assure you that they bite."

"I know," I answer, turning around to catch her gaze. "But my fangs can bite, too."

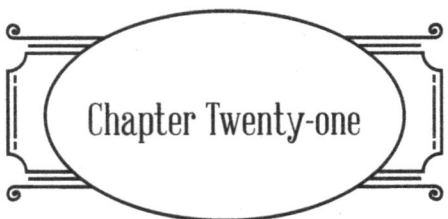

Chapter Twenty-one

The following morning, I'm sitting in my audience chamber, which I've had set up so that there's a table in the middle of the room. I'm at the head, and around me are Lady Rochford, Bessie, Cecily, Bartholomew, William, Lady Barrow, and Lady Wessex. Everyone is tense, sporadically squirming in their seats. The wheels of gossip are always in motion at the palace, and I'm sure the news of the king's irate early arrival has spread like wildfire.

"Thank you all for being here," I say, making my voice loud enough to be heard by everyone present. "Now, please raise your hand if you have ever been personally victimized by Henry VIII."

I raise my own hand up in the air, and slowly but surely, so does everyone. I let them linger there for a moment until I fold my hands onto the table, taking a cleansing breath.

"I've gathered us together today because out of everyone here at court, you seven are who I trust the most. You're my friends and confidants... and now you're my privy council."

Glances shift around at my words. Lady Barrow inches a little closer to the table. "Your Majesty, queens don't have privy councils."

"Well, they should." She sits back at my response, her face disguising a little smile as I go on. "I'm going to speak honestly. Now that the king is back at court, it's safe to say that he's very unhappy with me."

"How unhappy?" Lady Barrow asks, leaning forward. "Lovers'-quarrel unhappy or getting-sent-to-the-Tower unhappy?"

I take a beat. "Probably closer to the Tower one."

Lady Wessex rubs her face with her hands. "So this isn't so much a privy council as it is a death council."

"I don't see it that way," I tell her. "I asked you all to come here because I want to know what you think."

"What does it matter what we think?" she counters.

My shoulders slump a degree as I look back at her. "Do you hear yourself right now? You are smart, you are mean, and you are undeniably fun. Do you honestly believe that what you think doesn't matter?"

She goes to pour herself a glass of wine from the center of the table, but Lady Barrow stays her hand.

"What exactly do you anticipate the charges to be?" Bessie asks. Her eyes hold the same focus as when she's trying to solve a medical issue. Clear, methodical, unafraid.

"All I know at this point is that the king is highly displeased with me. He doesn't approve of how I've conducted myself while he's been away. He believes my ladies-in-waiting and I have been promiscuous and that I've taken measures to stop you all from having children."

Lady Wessex and Lady Barrow catch each other's eyes, and I keep speaking so no one notices it. "There's also a strong possibility of an adultery charge."

"Obviously," Bartholomew replies.

"Was it that obvious?" I ask.

His expression hovers between yes and no. "Well, it's more obvious now that you somewhat just confirmed it. Who was it? Was it Culpepper?"

"That's who I'd pick," Cecily adds.

William nods. "I would initially resist but ultimately pick him as well."

"Isn't it irritating how deeply attractive people are drawn to each other?" Lady Wessex asks. "It's gluttonous, if you think about it."

Lady Barrow claps her hands to get everyone's attention before turning to me. "We're going off topic. What physical proof do they have against you?"

There's the million-dollar question.

"There's the possibility of written evidence from someone I was with before I even met the king, but all I know for sure right now is Mistress Marshall's testimony."

Lady Wessex jeers as she slouches back in her chair. "Didn't I always say that woman was Satan's sister?"

"If that's the case," Bessie interjects, "then it's just her word against yours. We can all deny her claims. We'll tell the inquisitors that we've never served a queen kinder and more virtuous than Catherine Howard."

I start to smile while also shaking my head. "I don't want any of you to lie for me. Don't risk yourselves for my sake."

"It's not a lie," Cecily says. "It's the truth. You saw all of us, including me and my family, as people when no one else did."

William's mouth curves as he catches my eye. "I'm quite certain we're the first musicians to sit on a privy council."

I grin back at him, and Bessie places her hand over mine. "You're my dearest friend," she adds.

I try to answer her, but my throat is tight. I look at Lady Wessex with waterlogged eyes, but she only crosses her arms. "Skip me," she mutters.

I can't help but laugh, and when I turn to Lady Rochford, she takes a painful breath as she refuses to make eye contact.

"I would like to embroider with you at some point in time," she begrudgingly admits. "One-on-one."

A keener victory was never felt. When I look to Lady Barrow, she's as serene as ever. "You risked plenty for us as well, Catherine. If we wish to do the same, then let us."

I nod and glance down at the table, finding words hard to come by. Luckily, Lady Rochford doesn't.

"When the king's inquisitors come," she begins, "they are going to question all of us on the doings of the queen. What her character is, what her hobbies are. Have you seen her behaving in ways unbecoming of a queen? Has she given you medical advice, given you aid, have you heard any talk of possible indiscretions? And we will tell them our truth: we have simply spent our days praying and embroidering with her. They will latch on to any and every bit of information you give them, and they will use it to break you." Then: "But they can't break us all, can they?"

A warm silence spreads between us, only broken when Lady Wessex speaks. "And if all else fails, I'll kill Mistress Marshall in her sleep. I'm rather skilled in making deaths look accidental."

Another silence spreads, this one not as wholesome and fuzzy.

"Have you killed many people?" Cecily asks.

Lady Wessex looks down to inspect her fingernails. "The only true mastery can come with repetition."

Okay, then.

I place my palms down on the table with a gentle tap. "Well, hopefully it doesn't come to that, but thank you for your willingness."

"What now?" William asks.

Everyone turns to me for an answer, and I give it to them with confidence. "Now, we rewrite history."

FRANCIS IS STANDING across from me in a deserted hallway that Lady Rochford brought us to, giving us complete privacy. "I want you to leave court," I tell him plainly.

He looks back at me with a sullen frown. "Is my presence that disgusting to you?"

I go to answer, but Lady Rochford beats me to it. "The queen is soon to be investigated. A team of inquisitors will seek to uncover every scandalous aspect of her past, and the most scandalous aspect that exists is you."

Francis looks between us in surprise, which soon gives way to defiance. "I'm not afraid of being questioned," he tells Lady Rochford.

"You will be by the time they're done with you." Francis remains unflinching, and Lady Rochford tilts her head off to the side. "Do you think that you won't be punished for having carnal knowledge of the queen before she was married? They are going to tear you apart, Francis. Slowly. Limb from limb."

My stunned eyes shoot over to her. She has to be exaggerating. I hope to God she is. I start to feel queasy as the gravity of the situation sinks in a little further.

"They can't fault Catherine for what she did before she wed the king," Francis answers.

Lady Rochford folds her arms across her chest. "They can do whatever they please."

Francis looks to me, his eyes sunken and his face pale. "What do you say to all of this?"

I swallow down my growing fear, speaking to him honestly. "I don't want them to hurt you." Then I add, "You can come back after some time has passed. To check on things."

To check if it's Catherine who's here, or me. I don't say it, but Francis's small nod tells me that he understands.

I think he's going to push me for more, but he instead turns to Lady Rochford. "Will they look for me?"

"I'm sure that they will. If there is somewhere far off for you to hide, that's where you should go."

I watch as sadness crosses Francis's face, but there's a steadfast determination in his eyes as well. He hasn't given up hope. A few moments later, he gathers my hand in his and places a kiss to the backs of my knuckles.

"Goodbye, then," he murmurs against my skin. "I will come back once it's safe." I say nothing when he walks quietly from the hallway, and Lady Rochford moves to my side once he's gone.

"Ready for the next one?" she asks.

A few minutes later, Lady Rochford returns to the hallway, this time with Thomas Culpepper trailing behind her.

He smiles mischievously as soon as he sees me. "A clandestine meeting," he teases. "To what do I owe the pleasure?"

I glance over to Lady Rochford, and she disappears out of view down the hallway. I lean back against the wall, and Thomas does the same beside me.

"I need to know exactly what happened between you and me before I fell and hit my head." He lifts up a questioning brow, and I shift my body along the wall to face him. "Everyone seems to think that we were close, but no one knows how close. And I need to know the truth."

"The fact that you don't remember is quite a blow to my ego."

His demeanor is still light. I don't buy it. "You say that with a smile, but I wonder if it actually hurts." I need to show him that I see him. The actual him and not the performance.

He twists over to face me as well, his smile thinly falling. "I don't get hurt," he tells me.

I let my eyes soften as I watch him. "Everyone gets hurt sometimes."

He chuckles and turns back to look at the parallel wall, and I just keep watching him. "All we ever did was talk," he eventually tells me. "When we met, you were beautiful, and obviously I wanted you at first, but my desire to talk to you became stronger than my desire to seduce you. It was very unusual for me."

Thomas pushes his shoulders back after he answers. I'm making him uncomfortable and I'm glad. Sometimes you can only truly know someone by walking side by side with them through discomfort.

"Why was it so unusual?" I ask him. "Don't you like getting to know people?"

"Of course not," he answers.

"But how can that be true when so many people at court like you? Anyone I mention you to is drawn to you, and none of them know why."

"It's because I'm handsome," he says, tucking his hands behind his back against the stone wall. "I'm sure they secretly hate me. Or they would if they got to know me. You got to know me, and you still liked me. You were different."

"I'm sure other people would connect with you if you would give them a chance."

Thomas lets out a quiet sigh, still not turning to look at me. "People are more trouble than they're worth."

I let that sit for a moment before I speak again. "*You're* not," I end up telling him. "You're not more trouble than you're worth."

Thomas turns to me, and for a brief second, I see the man behind the legendary charm. "I think instead of building walls to protect yourself, you built a stage instead. And rather than making friends, you began to collect admirers. For whatever reason, you didn't deem anyone safe enough . . . until me."

Thomas remains perfectly still, with only his eyes moving. I begin to worry that I might have given the psychologist in me too much freedom with that one, so I relax my face and shrug. "But what do I know?" I end up saying. "I'm just telling you what I think."

Thomas pushes off the wall to stand across from me. His posture isn't very guarded, but he isn't at ease either. "Can I tell you what I am thinking?" he asks.

I nod and he looks down the hallway before glancing back at me. "I'm thinking that I'd like to show you something." He reaches inside his doublet packet, pulling out a small, compressed pile of papers that I know I've seen before.

Those are Francis's letters.

My breath catches as I look at them. I'm afraid to move or speak too loud. "Where did you get those?" I ask him.

He casually tosses them in the air and catches them, reverting back to his autopilot playfulness. "I stole them. How else would they come into my possession?"

He tucks them under his arm and I swallow hard while trying not to focus on them too anxiously.

"And what are you planning to do with them?"

He leans back on the wall as he looks at me with a considering gaze. "I could use them against you. I was meant to be the king's watchdog while he was away, and we aren't as close as we used to be. If I give them to him, he would forgive me for my poor performance and reward me for my loyalty."

"I'm sure he would," I reply quietly.

"But that would be rather boring, wouldn't it?" He grabs the letters from under his arm and tosses them over to me with an arcing throw. I catch them like my life depends on it, which might actually be the case. I look down at the papers in my hands, filled with so much relief and hope that I barely know what to think.

"Why are you giving these to me?" I hear myself ask.

Thomas takes a small step closer to me. "Because I protect the people I love."

His L-bomb shakes me to my core, but I'm still so distracted by the letters that I don't respond to him until he's halfway down the hall.

"I love you, too, Thomas! In a friendship way!" My voice reaches him in the distance, prompting him to stop and turn back to me with a playful tilt to his mouth.

"No, you don't," he says. "But you did before you hit your head. And hopefully you will again someday. Let me know if you require any further assistance."

Ummmm...

That's as far as my brain takes me until I sense Lady Rochford beside me a minute later.

"Should I inform him of the plan?" she asks. I frantically nod while I hold up the letters between us. "Inform him," I tell her. "I'm going to get rid of these."

"Do it now. The rooms in this hall keep embers burning all day, and the ashes will be gone in hours."

She sets off after Thomas, and I dart into the room closest to me. I fall to my knees in front of the hearth, unfolding each letter with shaking hands. They're all letters from Francis, written in the same handwriting until I get to the last page.

There it is. Catherine's story. It's folded up more than the other papers and is written in decidedly feminine script. I can barely understand a word of it, but at the bottom, it's signed *Catherine*.

A bit of her soul. This is what Matthias needs to send me home!

I throw Francis's letters into the fire, making sure that they're burned beyond recognition before I take off running. I run and I run. Down and down. Through the corridors, through the servants' hall, until I'm just outside Matthias's door. I don't bother to knock, instead just flinging it open as I hold Catherine's story up over my head.

"Matthias, I have it!" My jubilant yell turns to nothing as I focus on the room around me. It's empty. Eerily, entirely empty.

I walk farther inside, and nothing remains. No mean bird. No mountain of books. No Matthias. The only evidence that he was ever here are the stag antlers over the fireplace. I guess he wasn't able to hide it this time.

I hear footsteps in the hallway behind me, and I rush out to see who they belong to. A servant is passing by with a tray of bread.

"Excuse me," I call out.

The man turns and moves toward me, and I step back inside the room. Once he joins me, his gaze jolts open in shock. He bows so low that he nearly drops his bread to the floor. "Forgive me, Your Majesty. I didn't recognize you."

"Don't worry about it," I assure him. "I'm sorry to bother you, but do you know what happened to the man who used to live here?"

He looks inside the room, still startled but growing calmer. "You mean Matthias? Creditors came looking for him this morning and he snuck off through a back stairwell. Said you could have his stag antlers."

No. Please, please no.

"He did?" I ask softly.

The man nods. "Beg your pardon, Your Majesty, but if you don't want them, I'd be glad to take them off you. That bollocks of an astrologer owed me three shillings."

He walks off after another bow. I turn to look back in the room, holding Catherine's story tight in my fingers before I gracelessly shove it into my sleeve.

Matthias is gone, and I'm well and truly on my own. No magical ritual is going to send me home. Not even a charismatic, semi-drunk astrologer is here to help me. History is out for blood and my head, and if our plan doesn't work, then I might already be too late.

When I get back to my rooms, I'm optimistic that I can keep my spirits up, until I see the nervous look on Lady Rochford's waiting face.

"What's the matter?" I ask her.

"There's something I need to tell you, Catherine." She takes a tentative step toward me, then stops herself. "I sent a messenger to London to make contact with Simon this morning, but it seems that he never arrived."

I look at her blankly. I try to tilt my head in question, but I'm suddenly unable to move. "What do you mean?"

She clasps her hands together in front of her, never veering from my gaze. "I mean that Simon is missing."

Chapter Twenty-two

Lady Rochford suggested that I sleep in her room tonight. She could feel my anxiety surging and thought I could do with the company. She wasn't wrong.

Sitting on her bed now as she walks Theo, I find myself in a constant state of waiting. Waiting to see if Henry comes to find me. Waiting to hear the sound of armed men coming to drag me away. Waiting to hear news that Simon is dead or imprisoned or that he fled the country after I told him who I really was.

The waiting game is a strange sport. I'm in control of my own mind but not my fate, and it's such a hard truth to reconcile. I try to concentrate on my breathing instead. In for four, hold for seven, out for eight, over and over and over.

My knees are hunched to my chest as I sit in the middle of the bed when the bedchamber door creaks open. I turn my head to look, expecting to see Lady Rochford, but Simon walks in instead.

But it can't really be him, can it? My imagination is playing tricks on me.

"Simon?" I whisper.

He locks the door behind him and slowly begins to cross the room. I get up from the bed in an instant, walking barefoot across the floor to meet him halfway. I can see him and smell him and feel him, placing my hand on his chest.

"What are you doing here? No one knew where you were."

"Lady Rochford invited me in. Do you mind it?"

I nervously shake my head. "No. But why did you come back?"

"I wanted to see you."

"But Henry—I think he knows about us. He looked at my bracelet like he knew. What if he comes looking for you?"

"No one knows that I came back. No one knows where I am, actually."

He brings his hand up to cover mine, and I feel the thrumming of his heart beneath the pads of my fingers.

"I thought with what I told you before you left, and with Henry coming home, you'd want to be as far away from me as you could get. I wouldn't blame you if you did."

Simon smiles peacefully. "Why would I ever want to leave where you are?"

His words wrap around me like the fuzziest sweater after being out in the cold. I wonder how much he knows about what's going on now. If he has any idea of what might be waiting for us.

"How much did Lady Rochford tell you?" I ask him.

He holds my hand tighter against him. "She told me everything, including the king's suspicions of me."

"How can you be here if you know? Why don't you hate me? Didn't she tell you that I ruined your life?" I try to pull my hand away from him, but he won't let go. "What if I was supposed to save Catherine? What if I was supposed to save everyone and I failed? What if I didn't change anything?"

"You changed everything for me."

I pull again, but to no avail. My hand stays pinned to his chest. I never should have let this happen. I was too comfortable. Too confident. With our every conversation, every touch, every kiss, I endangered him. I knew from the beginning that Catherine's life could be cut short, and I took Simon along for the ride. I should have stayed away from him. If I really cared about him, I would have. Now *this* is where we are.

"They're going to question you," I tell him.

He's still so calm. My stark opposite. "I know."

"They could arrest you."

"I'll lie my way out of it. I'm good at that, remember?" I wonder if he actually believes that, or he's just saying it for my benefit.

I shake my head, wishing his words were true but knowing that they're not. "Not out of this you won't."

He finally lets my hand go and cups my cheeks in both his palms, keeping my gaze locked with his. He's purposefully giving me tunnel vision—trying to stop me from seeing anything but him. He doesn't know it's unnecessary. All I see is him regardless.

"I don't want to think about that now," he says. "I just want to think about you."

I don't understand why he's doing this. He shouldn't be thinking about me. He should be thinking of how he can escape. He should be on a horse right now, getting as far away from here as he possibly can.

"You can still leave," I tell him. "You can go and hide and make a new life somewhere. You need to go while you still can."

Simon drops his hands to my hips, casually holding me like we're debating what movie to watch in bed rather than saving his life.

"I'm a creature of habit. I like it here. Plus, I want to hear what life is like in the future."

"How are you so calm?" I demand, gripping his arms. "Don't you understand what's going to happen?"

"I understand. I also understand that no matter where I go, I'll be hunted. And I would much rather stay with you in the meantime."

His eyes are filled with resolve. He isn't going anywhere, despite my wishing that he would. I try to wrap my brain around it, to accept it, but I keep finding myself at blame's doorstep.

I move my hands up to stroke along the sides of his neck, needing to feel the warmth of his skin. "I'm sorry I wasn't more careful. Now you're trapped here."

"I'm not trapped, Lily. I'm exactly where I want to be."

I shake my head. "You wouldn't think that if you knew what I knew. About the future. About what happens."

"You know what happens to me, then? At the end of all this?"

I nod, even though I didn't really know about him in the future. In the future, it was supposed to be Thomas. But I guess that's the one thing I changed. I saved Thomas and condemned Simon. He wasn't supposed to be here, but he is now. And it's no one's fault but mine.

"So, all this doesn't end well?" he asks, not seeming overly bothered either way.

"I'm pretty sure it doesn't."

Just saying it out loud—it feels like I'm being torn apart at the seams. Simon only smiles at me, and I don't know how it's possible. How can he smile through this?

"If that is true," he says, "then I want what is left of my life to be right and good. And the only way to do that is to spend it with you."

I let out a tearful, broken laugh. He can't know what he's saying.

He tilts my face up to look at him. "No matter the danger. No matter what happens. Be here with me."

I move my hand up to his cheek, and he kisses my wrist. I drink in the feel of his mouth along my vein. I want that feeling everywhere.

He smiles at my audible intake of breath and begins walking me backward. "I can't decide if you are more beautiful in the moonlight or in the sun."

"I like you in the sun," I tell him. I picture him back with me in California. He could have lived on the sea breeze. Golden and happy. We would drink together on the beach and tease each other in the waves. "I wish I could show you where I'm from."

I feel myself hit the edge of the bed, and Simon brings his body flush against mine.

"Tell me," he says.

I try to focus, but the sensation of his hard muscles against my chest doesn't make it easy. "I'd take you straight to the beach. I know you have beaches in England, but California is different. It's much warmer there; the water is, too. I think you would lay in the sun for hours."

He traces his hands up my arms and down my back, and my nightgown bunches and spills everywhere he goes. "What else?" he asks me.

"I'd teach you how to surf. That's where you stand on a board and ride the waves. You wouldn't be good at it at first, but you'd learn quick. You'd want to go back every day. It's addictive like that. Sort of like riding a horse."

He pushes my hair behind my shoulders, baring my neck to him. My skin is tingling, and my blood is humming.

"I'd take you for tacos at my favorite spot. I'd buy you sunglasses and a T-shirt. Maybe a hat to wear backward. You'd be classic California."

I can't stop touching him. His broad shoulders. The strong column of his throat. Having him in my grasp here but envisioning him in the future is a heady combination.

"Then what?" he asks, kissing the hollow dip of my collarbone.

Breathing is so much harder with him doing that. "Then we'd go back to my apartment—where I live. It's small, but it's cozy. I think you'd be happy there."

He pulls back to look at me, a soft storm of emotions etched across his moonlit face. "I would be there with you?" The question comes out more like a declaration. Like there's no other possibility other than the two of us being together.

"Of course," I answer.

"Then I know that I would be happy." His hands drift to my waist again, and he lifts me up to sit on the edge of the mattress, looking down at me and cradling the back of my neck. "Would you be happy there with me?" he asks.

I'm almost happy now, and here we're standing on the brink of our world collapsing. If this is how I feel in his arms now, I can hardly imagine how I'd feel tucked away with him in my safe, quiet life.

"I'd be the happiest I've ever been." I say it without a hint of doubt because I have none.

I picture what we could have again, and I've never wanted anything more. It isn't fair. None of this is. Simon and I should have nothing but time in front of us. Instead, it's slipping away faster than we can fathom.

"Stay." He pulls me tighter against him, sensing or seeing my fear. "Stay with me."

My mind is reeling, and Simon must know that there's only

one way to stop it. He dips down and pulls me up with a frantic tug. Our lips meet and everything goes quiet. I can stay with him here. Not in the palace, but in this place that only exists when we're together—a state of want and need. Acceptance and escape.

His mouth parts as he takes in a labored breath, but it's like he's stealing mine. I tilt my chin up, giving him a slow kiss before easing away to slide back toward the center of the mattress. I stay sitting up as I move, and he crawls over me, following my path. My arms are straining as I lean my weight backward, and Simon keeps moving over me, enveloping my body in his until I drop down. He pushes up on his arms as he hovers over me, holding my gaze like we're the only two people on earth.

"It doesn't matter how long we have," he says, his voice achingly low. "It always would have seemed short. No matter how long we were together."

My arms reach around his neck. I try to pull him down to me, but he doesn't move. I watch as a primal kind of hunger fills his eyes.

"Tell me that you're mine." His hips bear down on me at his words, and I automatically rub against him in return.

"I'm yours," I whisper, trying and failing again to bring him closer. "And you're mine."

He smirks at the possessiveness in my voice. "Yours," he tells me, finally letting me feel the weight of him. "Ours. This could only be ours."

When we kiss this time, it's not tender or slow. This kiss is a clash of fire and fear, and we stoke the flames as high as they can go. His tongue delves into my mouth in a consuming sweep, and I'm there to meet it with mine. I knot my fingers into his hair and my hips never stop moving, jolting upward to grind against him. He feels impossibly hard, and we're not even undressed yet.

He pulls back to bring his lips to my neck. Mouthing it and grazing it with his teeth. In my fevered state, I almost want him to bite down. I wrap my legs around his waist and pin my body to his, rolling my hips as I draw my fingers down his back through the thin layer of his shirt.

"Greedy," he chuckles into my ear. "Whatever you want, it's yours."

I wish I could return his smile, but I can't. All I can think about is how this might be our last time. The last time I can be with him like this. When I speak, my voice is cracked, and my hands are shaking as I pull him closer. "I just want you. Please."

Simon looks down at me in a breathless kind of awe. I watch as the playfulness dissipates from his gaze, and he seems like he wants to say something but can't. It's all right. He doesn't have to.

He ducks down and kisses me, and this is what it's supposed to be like. This feeling of utter rightness. My fingers reach down to grab the bottom of his shirt, and he leans back so I can pull it over his head. When he moves close again, the hard ridges of his chest brush against me. I want to tell him more, show him more, but words don't seem good enough. Instead, I tuck my hands and push at him, urging him to roll over and lay flat on the mattress.

He lets me lead with the smallest question in his eyes, which gives way to a hazy hunger as I climb on top of him, straddling his waist. My nightgown bunches up beside me, and on my part, there's nothing between us when I roll against his pants-covered cock.

He hisses out an indistinguishable curse as I draw my center back and forth, and he tilts his head back into the pillow. Moving in near slow motion, I reach down and draw my nightgown up, dropping it onto the mattress beside us and baring myself to him completely. He seems in a trance as he drinks me in, his hands drifting to my hips so he can anchor me to him. I start to tremble—not from the night air roving over me but from his penetrating gaze. I lean down to kiss him, and he wraps his arms around me like I'm something so precious, he would protect me from anything.

I lean up a little and my nipples rub against his torso as I hold myself just above him. He brings a hand between us to rub a hardened peak, and a whimper slips from my lips. The sound sends a noticeable tremor through Simon's body, and he reaches lower to pull at the fastenings of his pants. I sit back to help him, tugging at the strings and adjusting my stance to pull the fabric down his legs. He's as bare as I am now, but I hardly get to take in the tantalizing sight before he draws me against him as I was before, settling me in his lap and pulling me down by the back of my neck to kiss me hard and wild.

Simon's hands move to grip the fullness of my ass as he urges me forward and back, moving his hips against me. I can feel the wet warmth of his cock sliding against my stomach, and I reach down to spread the moisture along his throbbing length. A moan rumbles out from his throat, and I pump my hand around him to coax even more sounds out of him.

Lifting myself up, I position him just outside my dripping entrance. One sway of my hips is all it would take. "Do you want me to stop?" I ask coyly.

He shakes his head and squeezes my ass harder. "No," he answers. "I want to die like this."

I can't hold out anymore. I lower myself onto him, groaning loud when he's in so deep that my muscles lock in a pleasure-filled spasm. I look down at Simon, his eyes closed and his jaw slack. He looks lost in an ocean of sensation. I could almost get off on the fact that I sent him there, but I need to make this last. I can't ever let it stop.

I roll my hips with deliberate slowness, my hands bracing on his chest. I lift myself up to the point that he almost slips out before I drop down so he can fill me again. Over and over. Up and down. Sweat is beading down my chest, glistening in the firelight, when I feel my pussy starting to shiver. I'm getting close, but I strain against it, holding it at bay even though it hurts.

Simon must feel the precarious pleasure coursing through me because he suddenly sits up, keeping himself locked inside me as he slides in even farther. My head falls back in silent bliss.

I eventually look back down as he keeps rocking against me. His hands shift to my hips to lift and drop me onto his cock at an unrelenting pace. Heat is pounding through every inch of my body and I'm close to seeing stars.

He dips his head to suck my nipple into his mouth, and I grab onto his hair so tight that it has to hurt. He shifts to swipe his tongue over and around the other peak, doing it again and again until I let out a helpless cry at how unimaginably good it feels.

Simon sits back, still thrusting with and into me as he holds my barely focusing gaze. "Stop fighting," he tells me, leaning in to kiss me with parted lips. "Let go for me, Lily."

Something coils inside me at his command, and my folds squeeze down around him as I shudder and scream. I muffle the sound against his shoulder, but he yanks my head back and crashes his mouth to mine. I swallow his roar as I feel him explode inside me, and I want to stay in this lust-drunk moment until the world stops.

Time feels nonlinear as we pant together in the aftermath. Simon falls backward, keeping me tucked into his chest as we rest against each other. Eventually, I shift over so that he slips out of me, and I smile against the subtle soreness between my legs. We lie there for a while, trading gentle touches between us as we come back to reality.

"Tell me more about what you are like in the future," Simon urges a minute later, his fingers running up and down my back. I settle more comfortably against him, oddly realizing that I now have to strain a bit to remember what I looked like before.

"I have red hair," I say against his chest. "And freckles. I got seventeen stitches just under my chin when I was little, so I have a big scar. You can't see it unless I lift my chin all the way up, but I think it gives me character."

He runs his finger under the unmarred skin of Catherine's chin, seeming like he's looking for it. "And you are not married where you're from?"

I smile at his question. "I'm definitely not married. I'm only twenty-four."

"I'm twenty-four," he says, "and my father says I am halfway through life."

I lean up to look at him, bracing my weight on my elbows. "That's not what it's like in the future. In my time, people live well into their nineties if they're healthy and lucky. And most people don't even get engaged to be married until they're in their late twenties."

"What activities fill your days?" he asks.

"I study and I work. I'm going for my PhD in psychology, which is the scientific study of how people think, feel, and act. I love my job so much."

"What do you love about it?"

I fold my arms across his chest and lower my chin to rest on them. "I love developing meaningful relationships with people who don't necessarily have the support or a support system in place that they can trust. I love giving my patients the tools they need to work through whatever it is that they're struggling with. When I took an intro to psychology class in college my junior year, I knew it was all I wanted to do."

Simon runs his fingers through my hair, tucking it behind my ear on one side. "Was I the first person you met when you came here?"

His chest rises beneath me as he breathes, and I have the inexplicable need to get closer. I sneak one arm under him and pull with the other, rolling a bit to pull him on top of me. He's the weighted blanket I never knew I needed. Simon smirks at our new position. "Yes, you were the very first person I met."

"What did you think of me then?" he questions, pushing up on his arms but letting his bottom half rest against me.

"At first, I thought all of this was some kind of a show, and everyone was pretending. When I saw you, I thought you were handsome, and a good actor, and tall."

"I am rather tall," he agrees. My knees bend up at his waist of their own accord. The closer he is, the more comfortable I am. He slowly starts lowering himself down, sliding his hands under the pillow behind me and bringing us chest to chest. "And what do you think of me now?"

I look inward and ask the same question to myself, and I give him the unedited, honest answer that comes to mind. "I think that I've never felt this close to anyone before."

"Not even in your time?"

I shake my head and wrap my arms around him. "No. Not even then."

A pleased kind of tenderness overtakes his features, and he steals down to kiss me. I kiss him back and close my eyes, foolishly hoping that if we get lost enough in each other, then maybe no one will find us.

I WAKE UP to a gentle shaking feeling, and as my eyes flutter open, I find Lady Rochford standing at the foot of the bed.

"Catherine, he has to leave now. It's almost morning."

I turn my neck and see Simon is already awake beside me, his gaze much more serious than it was a few hours ago. We silently sit up, looking at Lady Rochford and then at each other.

"He has to leave," she says again. "I will watch the door." She crosses the room and exits, and Simon and I remain in painful limbo.

I swallow past the lump forming in my throat. "This is it, then."

"No," Simon replies determinedly, twisting to face me and taking my hand. "This isn't it. Your plan is going to work."

In only a minute or two, he'll be gone, and I smile against the pain that builds deep inside my chest. "You're right," I tell him. "Our plan is going to work."

Except for the fact that it might not. But I'm not going to tell him that. Instead, I slip out of bed, and he does the same.

"You know things. You've done things differently." He picks his clothes up from the floor and starts hastily pulling them on. "Events are not destined to end the same. What happened between us couldn't have happened if Catherine was here. I know this wouldn't have happened."

"History says otherwise," I tell him. "It wouldn't have been you, but it would have been someone."

"History can be wrong." He strides around the bed until he's standing in front of me, clasping my hips. "You're going to prove it wrong." I don't answer right away, and Simon goes on. "Lily, whatever force it was that brought you here, it wouldn't have done it without a reason."

"I hope so," I tell him. "But I need you to listen to me. You have to promise that if you're questioned, you'll swear you don't care about me, and nothing ever happened between us. Don't admit to anything. Do whatever you have to do to meet me on the other side of this. Promise me."

Simon's fingers dig into my waist, but it doesn't hurt. I put my hands over his. He brings his face down to mine, his breath warm against my cheeks. "I promise," he says. "I won't let anyone hurt you."

I pull his head down and kiss him. It's tender and a little shattered, like it's possible that it might be the last time. When I lean back, his eyes are still closed. "Go," I whisper.

His eyes flash open, and he takes the smallest step back. "You are going to win," he says.

I know he won't go unless I agree. "I'm going to win," I assure him.

He stays where he is, and I commit his image to memory before he turns and leaves. I'm left alone, blinking my eyes against the encroaching fear. Fear doesn't control me. I control me.

I can do this. Not just for me, but for Catherine, too. Maybe no one fought for her in her time, but I'm going to do it now. I'm going to fight for her, for me, and all of us, and I am going to fight dirty.

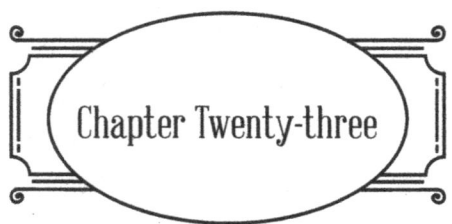

Chapter Twenty-three

When Lady Rochford and I return to my rooms an hour later, my ladies-in-waiting and maids of honor are noticeably absent. Time stretches, another hour passes, and they never arrive as they do every morning. When Lady Rochford eventually goes to look out in the hall, her face is serious but composed when she returns.

She sits down in the chair beside me. "There's a wall of guards outside the doors. They said no one is permitted in, and we are not permitted to leave."

I nod my head. I'm not entirely surprised.

"Is this what happened the last time?" I ask her. "Did he do this to your sister-in-law, Anne?"

"Yes," Lady Rochford answers. "The king has a flair for the dramatic."

A few moments pass in silence until I speak again. "You'd think he'd try to be original this time around."

Lady Rochford shrugs. "You'd think so, wouldn't you? It's terribly dull to do the same thing every few years." Then she adds, "Between me and you, the king was never the sharpest chisel in the carpenter's tool chest."

"I believe that," I tell her. "So, what happens next?"

"Well, in a short while, one of the king's councillors will arrive, and he'll tell you that you are confined to your rooms. We'll stay here for a few days or weeks as they investigate your charges or make up ones that strike their fancy."

I make a *meh* face as I look over at her. "That's kind of predictable."

"Quite so," she agrees. "Very predictable."

An hour or so later, it's the Archbishop of Canterbury, Thomas Cranmer, who eventually enters my bedchamber, with two royal guards in tow. When he speaks, he doesn't gloat or try to scare us. He's indifferent. It's just another day at the office.

He tells us that I'm confined to my rooms with Lady Rochford and that I will remain here for however long is necessary for my investigation to complete. I've been informally charged with treason, adultery, and various other crimes against the crown. If I'm found guilty, I'll be brought to the Tower of London. If I'm not . . . well, he doesn't really mention what will happen if I'm not guilty.

When the archbishop leaves and the guards stay at their posts, Lady Rochford places her hand over mine. It feels like I just received a loving embrace from my black cat, who only ever scratched at me, and it's a nice distraction from the possible fate that could await me.

When I twist my neck to glance over at her, her eyes are unusually vacant. "What's it like to be going through this again? After what happened to Anne."

Lady Rochford lets go of my wrist and stands, suddenly moving around the room as she looks for a task. "I loved my sister-in-law," she says after a while. "And my husband, George. I know that's not what the court gossips choose to believe, but it's true. I was happy with my life and happy with my family. But when Anne failed to give the king a son, the tides began to turn. We could feel ourselves slipping from the king's favor, and Anne set a dangerous precedent by getting the king to divorce Catherine of Aragon. Through doing that, queens became disposable, and then she was disposable, too."

She picks up a book, opening and shutting it before looking back at me. "And then she was imprisoned. They did it before the investigation was complete. The trial was hardly a trial at all. It was a farce, at best. Our uncle, the Duke of Norfolk, oversaw all of it. I didn't know at the time, but I was his puppet. And because of him, I lost everything I loved the most."

"What did he do?" I ask.

Lady Rochford moves to the window, opening it a crack to gaze out. "Our uncle told me that if I spoke against Anne and George during their investigations, I could save them. That if they then confessed it as well, they would be spared. I had no idea that he had already condemned them in his own mind and in the minds of others. He used me to make his plans a reality."

Placid as she may be, I can hear the shame in her voice. "If he used you, it wasn't your fault," I say reassuringly.

Lady Rochford keeps her eyes trained out the window until she turns back to me. "I was foolish and weak. I should have stood against him and the disgusting lies he contrived about my husband and sister. Instead, I cowered when they questioned me. I panicked. I betrayed two people I held dear. I can't undo what I did to them, but I made a vow after their deaths. Whosoever was true and put their trust in me, I would not fail again. I served Anne of Cleves faithfully, and now I serve you. And I will not let us fail."

I walk over to her and take her hands, and she shockingly doesn't pull them away. "I believe you," I tell her. "We're going to get out of this."

"One way or another," she says quietly.
I take a deep breath and nod. "One way or another."

WE STAY SHUT up in my rooms for over a week. We're given three meals a day. Water and ale, and little else. I end up thinking of Simon most days. I hope he did as I asked. I hope that he's staying safe. He should be if things go according to plan. But it's so easy for my mind to slip into dark crevasses now, being isolated like I am. When I give in to those moments, I imagine Simon being tortured into a confession or being starved to death in jail. It's strange to think it, but I'm at the point where I actually want to be interrogated.

On day nine, we hear footsteps approaching, and it's the letdown of a lifetime when the Duke of Norfolk joins us in the sitting room. He arrives with a team of guards, and I start to think that maybe isolation wasn't so bad.

"Take Lady Rochford to another room," he tells them. "I need to speak privately with the queen."

Her body tenses beside me. I know she doesn't want to leave, but the three guards who yank her up and across the room don't seem to overly care about what we want.

"She can walk on her own! You don't have to pull her like that." I'm not sure if the guards hear me through the clatter of their heavy footsteps, but Lady Rochford looks at me over her shoulder, and I know that at least she heard me.

"Have a seat, niece," the duke says. He gestures to a chair a few feet off, and I slowly move to do as he bids. He sits down across from me and stretches out in his chair, taking up all the space he can.

"Have you been well?" he asks.

I place my hands on the two armrests. "I've been better." I tilt my head to look at him, but I can't quite gauge his mood. "Where is my dog, Theo? A servant took him out for a walk a few days ago and never brought him back."

The duke smirks. "Bad queens don't get puppies." I seriously consider lunging at him, but he speaks again before I get the chance. "I believe the king gave the animal to a woman named Catherine Parr. She's a lady-in-waiting to his daughter Princess Mary."

I disappointed him and so he takes away my dog. Henry is a heartless prick.

"And how is the king?" I ask.

"He is heartbroken, of course."

"Of course," I reply, maybe a bit too sarcastically.

The duke straightens his posture at my tone, pushing his shoulders back into the chair. "Perhaps you do not adequately understand the depth of His Majesty's love for you, Catherine. Or the *former* depth, as it now stands. Mistress Marshall's testimony was damning, to say the least."

"Unfortunately, Mistress Marshall has had a personal vendetta against me since I fell in love with the king. It is my belief that *she* is in love with the king herself and contrived these lies in the hope of gaining his favor and his heart."

That's our story and we're all sticking to it. At least, that's part of it.

My uncle's jaw hardens. He strums his fingers down against his knee, looking over at me like I'm a hand of cards he's deciding how to play.

"You have always been a little mystery to me, you know," he

says steadily. "When the king first took an interest in you, I was certain he was to make you his mistress. Yet he did not. Instead, he made you his queen, and I was certain then that it must have been because you were with child. Yet you were not. Still, the king was so besotted with you. For a while, I was sure he must somehow love you for yourself alone. Maybe the power of love exists after all. But then you had to go and ruin everything. Do you know how the king suffers?"

"How does he suffer?" I ask.

"Since hearing news of your alleged treachery, his temper flares without restraint. He cannot sleep. He eats only four full meals a day. The pain in his leg torments him worse than it ever has. Yet when he speaks of you, I still detect a hint of warmth in him. Somehow, he has not yet forgotten you. Why is that, Catherine?"

I wait a beat, then discover that he is actually waiting for me to answer.

"Because true love conquers all?" I venture.

A rigid coldness glazes over the duke's eyes. "You will admit that you bewitched the king. You poured potions down his throat to make him love you."

It's really hard to gasp instead of laugh. "You think that I'm a witch?"

"I think you fed the king potions without his knowledge."

That's up for interpretation. "I would never, ever have any form of contact with a potion. I don't even know what potions are."

The duke sits back once more. "So you never knowingly distributed ingredients to your women to make them barren? And you never drank them yourself to remain infertile?"

I let my jaw drop. "All I want, all any of us women want, is to be fruitful for our husbands. It is my greatest dream to give His Majesty a son."

My uncle isn't buying it. I keep my eyes downcast, remaining firmly in character as a crestfallen queen with baby fever.

"Did you use any of your potions on Simon Gainsford? He is your current lover, is he not?"

Hearing him say Simon's name hurts more than I anticipated. For his own safety, I reveal nothing in my features, remaining completely blank. "The only words I ever exchanged with Simon Gainsford were of the love I bear to my husband, the king."

The duke takes a close look at me. I wonder if, deep down, he knows that no one actually loves the king. "And Gainsford is not the first, is he? There was also Francis Dereham before him."

"I have no idea who that is," I tell him. "Wait, wasn't he the Dowager Duchess's secretary at Lambeth?"

"He was," the duke answers. "I was at Lambeth just a few days ago and spoke to my stepmother. She didn't recall ever having seen you in company with Dereham."

The Dowager Duchess said she'd help me. It seems she's making good on her promise.

"That's because I never was." I keep my expression saturated in naïve honesty, and the duke rests one of his ankles on a knee.

"I interviewed her staff as well, and every one of them went on to say what a modest, sweet girl you were. Indeed, you dedicated your days to embroidering and praying to God."

"The two most important things," I agree.

For a second, the duke looks as though he's actually trying to subdue a smile. "Then we searched the residence. Mistress Marshall mentioned letters that might be hidden, detailing the depths of your former relationship."

"More lies on her part. Such letters don't exist." And this time, I'm being truthful. They don't exist anymore.

"Nothing of note was discovered," the duke admits. "And on top of that, Francis Dereham has mysteriously vanished from court and has yet to be found. Which is remarkable since he was here but days before your investigation began."

"I hope that he's all right," I reply. "Though as I said, I didn't really know him."

"Indeed," the duke commiserates. "From Lambeth, we then went on to question your ladies-in-waiting and maids of honor here at the palace. All of them spoke at great length of your piety, generosity, and infallible purity."

I love my Tudor girl squad. Just saying.

"One lady-in-waiting, Joan Harrington, stated that it was through your unending dedication to the king that she learned to be a more obedient wife and that she will name her next-born daughter Catherine."

Hope swells in my chest. Our plan is working. We're changing the narrative.

"Joan is a fine woman. I'm glad I was able to inspire her."

"And another lady-in-waiting, Lady Wessex, says that thanks to your dedication to the church, she now attends mass four times a day. She even briefly considered entering a nunnery so that she could serve the Lord as faithfully as you do."

I bite the inside of my cheek. "I've prayed long and hard for Lady Wessex. I'm honored that I could lead her back into the light."

The duke continues to watch me, but I only grow more confident under his stare. "A number of inquisitors have been at work within the palace, but no matter who we ask—servants, cooks, musicians, scullery maids—they all speak of the love and admiration they bear to you. One redheaded flutist went so far as to refer you as the most noble and loyal queen to have ever lived."

Oh, William. It's always the quiet ones who make the most convincing liars.

"If I've pleased the people, it is only because I've followed the example of the king, who they love above all others."

My uncle doesn't try to hide his smile now. "You're very good," he says quietly. "You're a Howard through and through, aren't you?"

He bops me on the nose with his index finger, and I'm very tempted to bite it off.

"All right then, my interrogation is complete. I'm sure Lady Rochford is parroting the same pretty words in the next room. You ladies have done a good job for yourselves."

He gets up from his chair and heads to the door. And I jump up before I know what I'm doing.

"Wait," I call after him. "Where are you going?"

"I'm off to relay the details of our conversation to the privy council. You wouldn't believe the amount of paperwork that goes into deposing a queen."

Shocking. I never knew that state-sanctioned murder was such a tedious task.

"Where does that leave me?" I ask. And I hate the fact that this horrendous man knows my fate and I don't.

"That's up to the king," he says after a pause. "If you have any witchcraft left in you, you best prepare to summon it."

He moves closer to the door, and I step after him. "Why would you even suggest that?"

His eyes are coy as he turns to face me. "Because the king wishes to see you. You can expect him within the hour."

I go immobile at his words, knowing that this isn't part of Henry's typical game. He cut all contact with Catherine of Aragon once he wanted her gone, and he never spoke to Anne Boleyn again after her imprisonment.

I want to ask the duke more questions, but he's gone before I can utter another word.

He closes the door behind him, and I listen as the guard locks it from the outside. I need to think. I need to get ready. If Henry is coming to see me, then our plan must be working. He's going off script, and it's a welcomed change. The most important thing is that I play this right. And I need to play Henry if I'm going to survive.

Two hours later, the door opens again. Henry walks inside, with his classic puffy sleeves and his too-tight hose. Then I hear the key being turned in the lock, and it's just the two of us now. The room feels smaller with him in here with me. Not just because of his stature, but because he seems to drink up all the energy and air wherever he goes, leaving nothing for anyone else. I stand from my chair, clasping my hands together over my skirt.

"Hello, Henry."

His eyes flash with rage. "You dare speak my name after what you have done to me?" He steps farther into the room, his limp more noticeable than ever.

Gone are his love-bombing, mirroring ways from the beginning of our relationship. We've now advanced to the blaming stage. The part where he devalues and discards and seeks revenge. He's angry and assessing, and I'm not at all surprised by his shift.

Henry is a shining example of narcissistic personality disorder. All the traits are there: the unquenchable thirst for admiration, the constant feelings of self-importance, and the almost complete lack of empathy for others.

Without a detailed social history, I can't give a definite assessment, but I'm sure both medical and environmental factors are at play. Henry and the rest of the world see him as handpicked by God to rule England and now the church—and anyone who wouldn't display at least some degree of narcissism in his position would be a rare find. I'm also pretty sure his traumatic injury in the joust must have affected him. From what I gathered, his mental health went into decline almost immediately after, and I'd be shocked if the two weren't connected.

But Henry takes his narcissism to a different level—a decidedly murderous one. This is especially true in the arena of love, or what he perceives to be love. He puts women on a pedestal only to shoot them down. Affection is performance based. If I'm not giving him the self-affirming fuel that he needs, then I'm a mistake that needs to be punished.

"I'm so pleased to see you," I tell him.

He shakes his head and turns away, walking past me to stand nearer to the hearth. "Every word from your mouth is steeped with lies. You have made a fool of me!"

I stay calm. I need to be calm if I'm going to do what I need to do. "No one could ever make a fool of you."

"You tricked me into marrying you," he accuses. "You used dark magic to enchant me and then took poison to keep me from giving you children."

This would be the ideal moment to mention that we've never actually had sex, but unfortunately, I have to keep the words bolted down. Instead, I go with "Is that what you believe?"

His eyes flash brighter. He's looking for a fight. "It is what I know to be true. *You* pursued *me*! Every look you gave, every word you spoke, told me that you loved me."

In true narcissist fashion, he's making himself the victim. Placing the blame solely with me rather than taking responsibility for his own actions. He literally has had me locked in a room for over a week, and he wants me to believe that he's the one being treated unfairly.

"And what is love to you?" I ask, slowly stepping toward him.

His eyebrows go up in surprise at my approach. "Do not speak to me as if you are my equal. You are being held prisoner for your deceitfulness and betrayal. And should I so choose, you could rot in the tower for the rest of your life. If I am merciful, I will grant you a quick death."

He doesn't like my questions. He wants me to remember who's in control. Message received.

"I'm sorry, Your Majesty. I only ask you questions because I'm so relieved and overjoyed to see you. These past days without you have been the most painful of my life."

His eyes soften a degree then. He's happy that I'm suffering.

When dealing with a narcissist, confronting them head-on will only make matters worse. I have to feed his ego. I need to convince him to be the savior that he believes himself to be. And I need to do it now.

Slipping into damsel-in-distress mode, I inhale a quivering breath. "Your Majesty, husband, you are more important to me than anything in this world. I'm sorry that I disappointed you. I'm sorry that you are unhappy and that I'm the cause of it. And I'm so sorry that I'm not the wife you rightfully deserve."

He pauses, my honey-sweet repentant tone once again capturing his attention. "I know well why you are undeserving of me. But I would hear it from your own lips."

"Because," I tell him, "I cannot give you a son."

Henry turns to face me, his eyes totally transfixed. "How do you know that?"

I go over the script we came up with in my privy council meeting. "The day you left on your travels, I prayed and prayed that we conceived on our wedding night. But when my monthlies began a few days later, I knew that we didn't. And that's how I know that God couldn't have blessed our union. He didn't bless it because I'm not worthy of you. All the blame lies with me. And I know that I can't remain married to you because of it, despite the fact that my heart yearns for you with every single beat."

Flattery. Validation. Remorse. Acquiescence.

"I'm consumed with shame for the pain I caused you. All I ever wanted was to prove my love for you, but I know that I hurt you in unimaginable ways."

Henry sits down in one of the chairs, eating up each of my words like delicious morsels.

"You *have* hurt me, Catherine. You have hurt me more than you could ever comprehend."

It's time to go all in now, and I kneel down by the side of Henry's chair. "I know that," I tell him. "You were and are everything a husband should be. It was me who failed. Only me."

He hunches over the table, bringing himself close to me and trying to read my gaze. If he could see what was really in there, he would read the words: *fuck you.* He sits back with a sigh.

"My astrologer told me as much."

Shock thunders through me as I rock back on my heels. "What?"

"My astrologer, Matthias, came to see me a week ago, before he fled the palace. It was early morning, still dark. He told me that he was studying the star charts from the day you were born, and he had a prophecy that you would bear me no heirs. He said a thick mist covered your womb, whatever that means."

I stare wide-eyed at Henry. I don't know if I should laugh or cry.

"A mist?" I ask, making sure I heard the king correctly.

Henry only nods. "He claimed it was through no fault of your own and that God had grander plans for me. He believed that if I spared you, an army of sons would follow with my next wife."

Matthias, you beautiful bastard. He didn't abandon me. At least, not without corroborating my story first, which I absolutely never told him. I must have the mist to thank for that.

The king turns to me then, gauging my reaction before he goes on. "I have also been told by many that everyone at court knows of Mistress Marshall's love of me. And that is what led to her coming forward against you."

Holy shit. Our story has traction. The king has heard it.

"It's not her fault. No one can help their love for you. I couldn't, even when I knew you should marry someone far above me."

Flattery. Validation. Remorse. Acquiescence.

Henry places his hand on mine as it grips the armrest. "Are you afraid?" he asks carefully. He really is enjoying this.

"Yes," I answer.

"Do you wish for me to show you mercy?"

It's now or never. I need to make him want to rescue me at this crucial moment, even though he's the one who put me here. It really is do-or-die.

"I wish for your mercy, but I seek your forgiveness above all other things. The world knows that you're a just and honorable king, with unparalleled strength and wisdom. I pray that you can show compassion to a scared young girl who loves you, so that all can see you as the righteous, merciful ruler that you are. Only you can save me."

Try as I might to be mentally strong, I'm only human, and I'm not immune to the potential horrors of my situation. I don't want to be imprisoned here forever. I don't want to be executed. I don't want them to touch Simon. I let my genuine fear of death flood my senses, squeezing me tight and bearing down on me. My breath turns heavy as tears flurry in my eyes.

"The world could have been yours," Henry says, pushing himself up to stand. "You could have had all of it. Now, you shall have none."

He turns and makes his way to the door, and I jolt upright, pushing past the emotion in my throat to speak once more.

"Your Majesty," I say softly to his withdrawing form. He stops walking and turns back. "I hope that you find happiness someday. And the love that you seek."

He stares at me for several seconds before he leaves, the door slamming shut behind him. I don't know what he's thinking, and it's terrifying to know that he holds my fate in his hands. I've played the game the best I could, and now I have to wait to see the outcome.

I also wait for Lady Rochford to return, but she never does.

I'm alone again.

In time. In this room. And the truth of it is, I might not ever get out.

Chapter Twenty-four

It's a strange sensation when you realize that you might die. Standing at the window, watching guards amass in the courtyard, I wonder if they're gearing up to take me to the Tower. At any moment, they could enter my room and carry me off. My uncle could walk in to laugh in my face and say goodbye. Henry gets to decide if my life is finished or not, and I go back and forth between feeling intense hurricanes of emotions to feeling nothing at all.

I've been kept in total isolation for the past fifteen days without Lady Rochford. A guard comes in and brings me food, but that's the extent of my human interaction. He refuses to speak to me, no matter what I try. Maybe my impending execution is the reason for the silence. Why should I be allowed visitors or conversation when soon enough I won't be allowed to live?

I've read Catherine's story more times than I can count, even though I can only decipher every other word. The paper is worn and crinkled, the ink is smudged, and her handwriting is very elaborate. Every letter curls. But what I can read of the story is good. She could have had a future. I had one of those once, too. I'm holding the story even now since I don't have anything else to do with myself.

I had a laughing fit last night. I'm sure that will be a fun tale for the guards to pass down to their kids someday. The hysterical queen giggling in her apartments as she was under investigation. For a few brief minutes, I couldn't help but find the humor in my situation. Before Zoe and I decided on visiting England, I pitched the idea of Cabo. If we went with my suggestion, we could have been drinking mojitos on a sandy beach. Instead, I'm back hundreds of years in time and I'm probably about to be beheaded in a public square.

This would only ever happen to me.

I'm convinced our plan didn't work. We tried our best. The plan was good. But it was also a long shot. There's nothing else I can do. Nothing I can say. My life isn't mine anymore, and soon it will cease to exist all together. I might throw up. My heart is hammering, my palms are sweaty, and when the door to my room opens, I consider fighting whoever walks in. Why shouldn't I? I fold up the story and shove it back into my sleeve. I'm preparing to ruthlessly pounce on my jailer, but when Lady Rochford is the one who enters, I freeze in place instead.

"Lady Rochford?" I ask, wondering if I'm having a stress-induced hallucination.

A little smile appears on her face. Bessie comes running in next, flinging herself directly into my arms and almost knocking me over.

"Catherine! Catherine, are you all right? Are you well?"

I'm so entirely stunned that I wonder if I can even speak. "I'm fine," I somehow mumble out. "What are you doing here? What's going on?"

Bessie leans back, almost breathless, with her hands still locked on my shoulders. "The king has annulled your marriage. He stated that a doctor examined you and found you to be infertile, so the church issued your marriage null and void."

It worked. Holy fuck, our plan actually worked.

"Are you sure?" I ask Lady Rochford.

"I'm sure," she answers. "I doubt that I would be alive to tell you otherwise."

I hold my breath as I wait for someone to say something else, but both women are waiting on me. "Now what?" is all I can think to ask, my voice and body shaking. Lady Rochford moves closer.

"You will be stripped of your title as queen. If you agree to only ever speak highly of the king and say nothing of your marriage, you will be granted a hunting lodge in Lincolnshire where you may reside with a threadbare allowance. You will retain no household staff, apart from whoever wishes to go with you freely. In short, you will live, but you will live your life away from court and in disgrace."

"In disgrace?" I whisper.

"In disgrace," Lady Rochester echoes.

We say nothing else, until she and Bessie and I scream and hug in utter joy.

"I'm going to live in disgrace!" Happy tears stream down my cheeks, and I feel like I'm in a hopeful state of denial. How can this be true?

"There is something else," Lady Rochford says. "You are not permitted to remarry. Ever. Should you attempt to do so, you will be forcibly sent to a nunnery."

There you are, Henry. I love how he just had to sprinkle his assholish tendencies into my sentence, just on the off chance I forgot. He craves control, and he found a way to keep it, even while letting me live.

"That's okay," I reply, still in disbelief. "Marriage is the last thing on my mind right now."

Bessie hugs me again and I squeeze her tight with all the

relief pulsating through me. When we step back, tears are in her eyes.

"I honestly thought it was over for me," I say. "I can't believe we all made it out of this alive. Did they station all those guards out in the courtyard to scare me?"

I look between them as neither Bessie nor Lady Rochford answers. Instead, they go quiet and catch each other's gaze.

"What is it?" I ask.

They remain silent, and the longer they do, the more afraid I become. A million different scenarios pass through my mind until one word—a name—sounds out like a siren.

"Where is Simon?" I ask.

Bessie wipes at a tear falling from the corner of her eye as Lady Rochford takes a fortifying breath and speaks.

"Simon confessed that he tried to seduce you on multiple occasions. He swore that you continually refused him each time, always professing your love and loyalty to the king."

No. No. No. No. No. No. No.

"It is treason to admit to lewd thoughts about the queen," Lady Rochford continues, "let alone to admit that you actively tried to seduce her."

I step backward and shake my head. Everything is spinning. There has to be a way out of this.

"Where is he? What can we do?" It feels like my heart is twisting in a sick, snapping motion. My airways are closing. This can't be real, and I need to find him.

Lady Rochford moves closer to me, trying to calm a spooked horse. "Simon knew that the king needed to have someone's blood. He didn't want it to be yours."

I hear drums in the distance, or maybe it's just the sound of pounding in my head. "Where is he?" I demand again. "Tell me where he is!"

Lady Rochford stays quiet, and I turn to Bessie. Her face is tense and indecisive. I stand in front of her and take her hands in a desperate grip. "Bessie, please. What if it was Richard?"

Her gaze falters. She doesn't look at Lady Rochford. She keeps looking at me, and I tug her hands forward, trying to pull the answer out of her.

"He was placed under arrest and is being taken to the Tower. The king is at chapel, and they'll journey past him as they take Simon out."

Chapel. Simon is near the chapel.

I take off in a run before either of them can stop me.

"Catherine, don't!" Lady Rochford's voice tries to reach me, but I'm already gone. Flying past the startled guards at my door and down the sparsely populated corridor.

I can figure this out. I can stop them. I just need to run faster. I need to get to the chapel. Simon's life depends on it.

Onlookers move to the side as I storm past, watching me with curious, wide eyes. No one bows or curtsies anymore. Just sympathetic frowns and bewildered stares.

When I get to the gallery outside the chapel, I stop in my tracks. Sweat is dripping down my neck. My insides are burning. Looking at the surrounding crowd, it reminds me of a small-scale spectacle. The walls are lined with noblemen and ladies, looking forward with jeering gazes.

I stare down the center of the gallery to where the guards are a few yards in front of me. I can distinguish Simon's silhouette mixed in beside the silver armor. He's barely on his feet, being dragged by the guards holding him under his arms. He's in a white shirt that's stained with old and new blood. God knows what he's endured already. Bile swirls in my throat, and it feels like the floor is opening underneath me.

"Simon!" His name rips out from my throat, and everyone turns to look at me. The guards turn, too. And I'm able to see Simon's face. Our eyes lock, and time stands still. I'm terrified but elated to see him, and he grants me the smallest smile. It's soft and outlined with relief. He almost seems happy. I smile back, even as tears stream down my face. I wonder if they'll ever stop falling.

I feel arms and hands latching onto me then, around my shoulders and my midsection. Guards are trying to restrain me, but Lady Rochford and Bessie push them off. The guards holding Simon start walking again, continuing to pull him down the gallery and away from me.

"Don't!" I scream at the top of my voice. "Let him go!"

"You cannot yell, Catherine! You mustn't draw attention to yourself." It's Bessie's voice in my ear, but I don't listen. I keep clawing the hands off me. Somehow managing to break free, I start sprinting down the gallery again. I have to get to Simon.

My feet are pounding against the floor. The guards aren't too far off—they're just about to pass the chapel doors. I've almost closed the distance between us when Catherine's letter starts burning against my wrist inside my sleeve. It feels like my arm is being split open, my skin being charred off layer by layer. But I can't stop. I keep reaching for Simon. My chest constricts as music begins to play in my ears. "Pastime with Good Company."

I hate that fucking song.

My legs don't work anymore, and my vision blurs. Someone must strike at me because suddenly I'm tumbling backward. The base of my skull smashes into the floor with a crack, and I try to breathe but can't. A wave of heat surges around me until it turns to absolute cold. Then the world goes blissfully dark.

I MIGHT HAVE died. I can't be sure. Maybe a guard stabbed me as I ran for Simon in the gallery. Maybe Henry stabbed me. I wouldn't put it past him.

If I am dead, I'm very comfortable. It feels like one of the mornings when I've woken up, but it's a dark rainy day and my bed is so cozy. I snuggle deeper into the blankets. It's bad out there but safe in here. Just a few minutes longer.

"It is a nice world we've found, is it not?"

I open my eyes and realize that I'm standing. At least, I think I'm standing. It's hard to tell through the thick fog. I could be outside. The fog or the air around me is sweet-smelling and calming. I wouldn't mind staying longer.

Maybe I'm lost in Matthias's mist? No, his mist would be more erratic than this. This place is just for me. I can tell.

"It took me a while to get my bearings when I arrived as well."

I try to stay focused on the voice this time, a voice that sounds so familiar. Is it mine? No, not mine, but almost.

I look deeper into the fog, and a shape starts to appear. It's hard to decipher, but then it's crystal clear.

"Catherine," I say steadily. And it's my voice this time. Not hers. Mine.

"Hello, Lily," she answers. "I started to wonder if you would ever arrive."

Her smile is teasing, and she looks so happy, like she just woke up from a much-needed rest. She's wearing a gown of shimmering gold but no crown. Flowers are braided through her free-falling hair. I'm glad to see it. Crowns are overrated.

I look down to see what I'm wearing, and it's a sleeveless white nightgown, cut just below the knees. It's definitely not a Tudor nightgown, but it's not obviously modern either, seemingly stuck somewhere in between.

"How long have you been here?" I ask.

Catherine tilts her head, daintily clasping her hands in front of her. "As long as you've been where you were. I have quite enjoyed my time away. No one to grab at me or steer me where they please. I almost forgot what it felt like." She waits a moment before adding, "Thank you for stepping in for me. I knew I had chosen well."

Her words give me pause. I stepped in for her. She chose well. I blink my eyes as I try to absorb the information. "You were the one who sent me back here?"

Catherine nods and gives me another smile.

"But why? Why did you do that?"

She thinks a moment before responding. "I liked what you called the king when you looked at his portrait. After you heard what he had done to me. You said he was a hat made of an ass."

My eyebrows slant up in a question. "You mean when I called him an asshat?"

"Yes, just that," she says with a grin.

"And *that's* why you sent me back?" I ask, with a mix of horror and wonder.

Catherine shrugs at my question. "You defended me. No one else did that—at least not while I was alive." She waits a moment before speaking again. "Looking back now, I don't know that I really meant for you to take my place. I saw you, and I was thinking of how brave you must be after what you said. How you probably would have done everything differently if you were me. And then I found myself here. Perhaps rather than my choosing you, we chose each other."

Her words are a lot to unpack, and I'm not sure where to start.

"Do you see everyone who visits the palace? Have you been there since your death?"

"I only see people on certain days," she answers. "Usually when I walk the gallery and sing."

When she sings . . .

"You know, I'm pretty sure people can hear you sometimes," I tell her. "They say that you're a ghost and that your spirit is screaming and wailing as you run outside the chapel."

Catherine leans back with an affronted glare. "That is quite rude. My singing voice is lovely."

"I know it is," I assure her. "It's not necessarily a bad thing that people can hear you. It sort of made you famous."

Her indignation gives way to intrigue. "Really?" she asks. "Am I truly famous?"

I let out a bemused chuckle. It's good to know there's still laughter here. In limbo? The afterlife? I still don't know where we are. My brain jumps back to where I was all this time as I look quizzically over at Catherine.

"Did you see what I was doing as you? Back in your time?"

"Not until today," she answers. "Up until then, it felt like I was in a very pleasant dream, and then all of a sudden I was standing here with you, and the memories were in my mind."

I can't help the disappointment I feel. On some level, I was hoping that she would have all the answers. I want to understand why and how this happened. "Did I do what I was supposed to do?" I ask her, still yearning for any kind of clarity.

She thinks about it but seems unsure. "What do you think you were meant to do?"

"I don't know." I look around the fog. For what, I don't really know. "Maybe I was supposed to save you?"

An innocent smile crosses her face. "You did save me. And others, from what I see."

"I didn't save Simon."

She smiles wider, and I don't smile at all. "I think he would say you did."

I can't help the hopeful surge in my chest as I look around into the fog once again. "Is Simon here, too? Can I talk to him?"

Catherine looks at me sympathetically. "I am afraid not. It is just you and me."

I should have guessed that, but it doesn't make it hurt any less. "What do we do now?" I ask.

She pulls a flower from her hair and walks up to me before tucking it into mine. "I think it is time for us to go home."

She steps back, and my eyes whip up to meet her gaze. "You mean *home* home?"

She nods and excitedly bounces on the balls of her feet. "I believe so. I get to live my own life now. Without my uncle, the king, or anyone telling me what to do."

She looks thrilled, and honestly? Good for her. For my part, I can't believe I'm finally going back to where I belong. But something still feels off.

"Thank you for all you have done for me, Lily. I promise I won't forget it." Catherine begins to fade into the fog, her appearance turning blurry. Panic fires through me, and something inside screams that this can't be it.

"Wait!" I call. She shifts back into focus, though she seems confused as she does. I'm speaking before I've decided what to say. "After what I did for you, shouldn't I get something in return?" She steps closer to me in question, and I take a determined breath. "I want you to bring Simon back. You need to bring him back."

Catherine averts her gaze with an understanding sigh. "What is done cannot be undone, Lily."

I shake my head. "Are you kidding me? I literally just undid your murder."

"It isn't in my power to bring people back," she says. "I told you, I don't even know how you or I got here. I still don't know how we are here now."

"You have to try," I tell her, my firm voice tinged with desperation. "He doesn't deserve to die, just like you didn't deserve it. You have to save him."

Catherine only looks at me, seeing that I won't back down. "I will try, though I doubt it will do any good." I'm ready to push her further, but the fog begins to thicken between us. "I have to go, Lily."

She's all but lost in the mist, and I can barely see her now. "Wait! Promise me that you'll save him!"

Her image is gone, but I hear her voice in my head, one last time: "I have to go now. And so do you."

I try to speak, but the breath is squeezed out from my lungs then forced back in. A razor sharpness slashes through my mind as a heavy weight covers me, digging me into the fog. I go down and down, deeper and deeper, until I plummet into a sea of emptiness.

It's dark. So dark, until I open my eyes.

"Lily?"

Chapter Twenty-five

"Lily? Are you okay?"

My vision slowly comes into focus as I see Zoe standing in front of me. She's staring at me with worried eyes, and her hand is on my shoulder. My heart is beating in a strange rhythm as I look at her, and there's a quiet buzzing in my ear. I turn my gaze further to see where we are, and I'm standing just outside the chapel, next to the open door. This evil, cursed chapel. I look inside, and there are red velvet ropes all along the interior, and people taking pictures with their cell phones.

Oh my god. I made it back. I actually made it back.

Zoe is holding both my shoulders now, her expression filled with concern as the soft buzzing begins to fade. I feel immobile as my feet stay planted just outside the chapel doors.

"You look like you've seen a ghost," she says.

Oh, if she had any fucking idea.

I reach a hand up to feel hers on my shoulder, needing physical evidence that she's real. "You're really standing here, right? And you see me?"

"Of course I see you. Are you sure you're okay?"

She takes hold of my hand and lowers it between us. I look down at the contact, still bewildered and in a daze. The fingers I'm moving seem the right size. They have the right feel. These are my hands. These are my actual hands.

I use my other hand to reach up and grab the tips of my hair. My distinguishably red hair.

"Take out your phone," I suddenly tell Zoe. "Take out your phone and pull up your camera. I need to see what I look like."

"What's going on?"

"Zoe, please!" I shout.

"Okay, okay!" She fumbles as she pulls her phone out and quickly switches it into camera mode. She hands it to me, and I reverse the angle to see myself. I look for a very long time.

I'm me.

I'm me.

I'm me.

I stare and stare, and I start to cry. I drop her phone to the wooden floor and squat down, covering *my* face in *my* hands and cry until it feels like I'm going to burst.

I'm home. I'm here. No one is trying to kill me. No one is trying to marry me. No one is coming to lock me away. Because I am Lily Whitaker. Lily Whitaker.

I feel Zoe crouching next to me, rubbing my back even though she has no idea what's wrong with me. She wouldn't be able to guess it in a million years even if she tried.

"It's all right," she tells me in a soothing voice. "Everything's fine. You're fine."

Her comforting words pull me deeper into the present moment. I'm home. I'm here. I'm safe. I'm finally safe.

But what about everyone else? Catherine? Simon? Lady Rochford?

Taking a breath, I pull my face out of my hands and rub underneath my eyes.

"What happened to her?" I ask.

Zoe seems puzzled, leaning back a bit to look at me. "What happened to who?"

"To Catherine Howard," I clarify. "Did you see anything about her? What does it say about her now that I'm back?"

I push myself into a standing position and start walking briskly down the hall. I scan the walls as fast I can, looking for any evidence of her. This is the Haunted Gallery. Is it still the Haunted Gallery? Where was the sign I saw when I first came here with Zoe? I run to the end of the hall where I remember it was. The sign isn't there anymore. Spinning around, I leave the gallery and set off down the wide set of stone steps through the corridor.

"Lily! Wait up!" I hear Zoe, but I can't stop. I need to find Catherine. I have to find out what happened to her. Reaching the landing, I set off down another hallway, and I spot an employee standing along the wall.

"Can you tell me about Catherine Howard? Queen Catherine Howard. Was she killed? Did he kill her?" I'm panicked and breathing unevenly, but I don't care. This is more important than breathing. Zoe appears at my side, also huffing and puffing from her run.

The employee looks blank for a moment before he quickly stands up straight. "Yes, I'm sorry. This is my first day. Catherine Howard. I remember memorizing her part from the packet they gave me."

I continue to stare at him like all our lives depend on his next words, and he takes a nervous breath. I'm about to start shaking him when he finally speaks.

"Little is known of the one-month queen, Catherine Howard. After her brief marriage to Henry VIII was annulled, the king ordered all records of her destroyed. Not a single portrait of her was ever found, and much of her story remains a mystery. Some say that she lured the king into marriage with her youthful beauty and charm; some even claim witchcraft. Today, nearly all scholars agree that the young girl was an unwilling participant in the dangerous games at court and was unjustly abused by those around her, including her uncle, the disgraced Duke of Norfolk."

My throat catches. History remembers Catherine and remembers her as they should. Despite Henry doing what he could to hide her story, the world knows the truth now.

"It is believed that Catherine Howard lived out her days peacefully in the country, along with a small group of her former ladies, one being Lady Jane Rochford, the once sister-in-law of Queen Anne Boleyn. Some historians believe that Catherine went on to write and publish several chivalric tales under a secret name, but the claims were never substantiated."

I wait for him to say more but nothing comes, and we end up staring at each other for several seconds. "Is that it?" I ask.

"That's what I've memorized, yes."

Okay, all that is good. Catherine was safe. She lived in peace. Lady Rochford was with her. "Do you know anything about Simon Gainsford?" I try next.

His gaze turns blank again. "I'm sorry, I don't know him yet. Like I said, it's my first day, and I really better be going." He walks off, and I can feel my heart beginning to race.

"Zoe, I need your phone again. Please, I need it."

She immediately hands it over to me, and I see it's scuffed from where I dropped it a minute ago. I know her code, and so I move my fingers across the screen and go straight to the first search engine I see, typing in Simon's name. I skim the results and find him mentioned in a few variations of Tudor-dedicated websites. The second option seems the most legit, so I click on it with shaking hands and read the small paragraph it directs me to.

> Simon Gainsford was an English courtier of Henry VIII. Gainsford was believed to be a favorite of the king and was said to be a "handsome youth." Simon fell from the king's favor and was executed in the Tower of London in 1540 after he was found guilty of unknown charges. Many believe his downfall was linked to the enigmatic one-month queen, Catherine Howard.

He was executed. Catherine didn't save him. I didn't save him.

I frantically check the rest of the links, hoping to find something else, anything else, besides what I've read already, but everything is the same.

He was a favorite of Henry's. He was handsome. And he died.

My chest feels hollow, and my legs feel weak. Everyone made it, except for him. Why not him? He deserved to live. We all did.

I morbidly start to wonder where he was buried and foolishly hope it was near a tree. He would have liked that. My eyes once again fill with tears, but I hold them back. I need to see. I switch my internet search of Simon over to the images section, hoping to catch a glimpse of him.

He isn't there.

Of course Henry would have had his portraits destroyed as well. My hatred for that man is fucking boundless.

"Lily? I think that we should leave now."

I look at Zoe, who is watching me with growing worry. She wants to leave Hampton Court. It's all I've wanted for these past weeks, too. I would have done anything to leave this palatial prison. To get as far away as possible. But now that I'm ready and able, I can't even comprehend it.

"I don't think I can go," I tell her, my voice cracking. "I don't know what to do."

"Just walk with me," she says calmingly. "The bad vibes of this place are getting to you."

I look around the audience chamber we're still standing in. Everything seems so old and patched up now. I saw it in its glory, but even then, its beauty was carved with cruelty. A sparkling house of horrors.

I let Zoe take the phone from my hand, and once she tucks it away, we start to walk. We walk and walk until we're outside the palace. Until we're at the Hampton Court railway station. Until we're on the streets of London. Until we're back in our hotel room.

Zoe orders room service, and I go to the bathroom and lock the door. There's a shower and a sink and a toilet. They seem so luxurious to me now. I strip out of my modern clothes and turn the shower to hot before stepping inside. I stay in for an outrageously long time. The water hits me like a baptism. Like a rebirth. I know that whatever I experienced is over now and there's no going back. Not that I would ever want to, but I think it's possible to still grieve for something you hated.

But there were lots of parts that I didn't hate—people I didn't hate. Bessie. Lady Rochford. Cecily. Bartholomew. William.

Simon.

I turn my face to the hot, still-running water and hold my breath under the almost burning spray.

They weren't all just a dream. I know they couldn't have been. They were real. As real as anything.

I imagine what it would be like if they were here with me now at the hotel. At any moment, Bessie would burst through the door, dying to tell me something or conducting an exam to see if I'm concussed. Lady Rochford would be sitting back on the bed, scowling at the two of us as she tried out the TV, but she'd be smiling on the inside. Bartholomew would be scrolling TikTok.

And Simon . . . Simon would wait for me on the balcony. When I went out to join him, he'd touch my cheeks and kiss me, not caring in the least who saw us. We wouldn't have to hide anymore.

Each one of my friends is there with me in my mind's eye, so vibrant and real and free. But then I return to reality, and I know they're lost to me. Irrevocably, heartbreakingly lost.

Chapter Twenty-six

"I know this is a stupid question, but you have our passports, right?"

"Huh?" I look at Zoe, still feeling completely out of it, even now that I'm inside my own body. I barely slept more than a few minutes last night. When I was back in time, I always thought that I would have the sleep of my life if I was able to sleep on a real mattress again. But every time I closed my eyes, all I could see was them.

My former friends. My former life. All my mistakes. All my triumphs. The girl I saved. The man I lost.

I can't stop thinking of them now.

"Lily? The passports?"

I look over at Zoe and try to manage a smile for her. I'm able to do it, but it's half-hearted.

"Yeah, I have them." I pat at the hidden passport carrier I'm back to wearing again, and it feels like nothing now that I'm accustomed to layers upon layers of garments and pins covering every inch of my body. I catch myself reaching up to adjust the French hood that I'm definitely not sporting anymore and opt to tuck my hair behind my ears instead.

Even after half a day, I still feel out of joint in my own skin. I can't stop fidgeting as Zoe and I stand at the tube station, still deciding where to go.

"I heard Winston Churchill's war rooms are interesting. Or

we could go see Big Ben one last time. Which are you in the mood for?"

I know she's talking to me, but it's so hard to hear her when my mind is filled with Simon. Simon smiling. Simon playing with Theo. Simon holding me when the whole world was going to hell around us.

I rub my eyes, still feeling half asleep as Zoe waits for my answer. "Yeah. Whichever one you pick will be great."

The train rumbles into the station, sending a breeze whirling past us as it comes to a gradual stop. Zoe is still looking in one of her guidebooks as the doors open and we step aboard. I catch a glimpse of my reflection in one of the long windows, and before I can stop myself, I imagine Simon's reflection beside me. I picture his small smile. I picture his hand resting over mine on the pole I'm holding on to. I force a blink, fighting the sting in my eyes, and when I look at the window again, it's just my reflection alone. But I start to feel an undeniable pulling inside me.

I need to get off this train.

I look at Zoe and she's still reading. She might kill me, but I know that this is right. I know I have to do this.

"I'll meet you back at the hotel tonight," I tell her.

Her eyes dart up from the book. "What?"

I jump off the train just before the doors close, and Zoe moves to the glass as I stand breathing hard on the platform. "I love you!" I call to her. "I'll see you tonight!"

I dart off as the train pulls away with Zoe still at the window. I run the stairs two at a time until I'm aboveground again. It takes me less than a minute to hail a cab, and when I get inside, I tell the driver to take me to Hampton Court Palace.

Eighty pounds later, I'm back at the palace, power walking through the main entrance. It's hard to see it now, after having seen it as I did before. But I'm a woman on a mission, even though I don't know what my mission is.

When I pay my fee and get inside, I begin to do a fast-paced version of the tour from yesterday (or was it weeks ago?). I stride through the great hall, the watching chamber, the guard chamber, and the kitchens. Then I go to the bane of my existence, the chapel. I end up back in the no-longer-haunted gallery, and it's empty except for a few meandering tourists.

What am I doing here? What am I even looking for? I feel more lost and confused than ever, and I know that I can't spend my life squatting in this palace.

Rushing back here like I did is beyond mentally unhealthy. I'm never going to get the closure that I'm yearning for, and maybe I need to accept that. No matter how much it hurts. No matter how wrong it feels. Simon isn't here. Catherine isn't here. And I shouldn't be here either.

I begin to make my way out of the gallery and head toward the nearest set of steps. I'm reaching into my bag to find my phone, planning to text Zoe with some excuse for running off, when I suddenly hear a loud voice from the floor below me. I stop walking as I listen.

"How many times must I tell you? I don't know what an admission ticket is, nor do I need one since I live here at the palace." The echoing words reach me from my place at the landing and I think I'm hallucinating again.

I slowly start to descend the stairs as a much calmer voice speaks.

"Sir, you need an admission ticket if you are visiting the palace, and you are certainly not permitted to enter the premises in costume. I don't know how you were allowed inside in the first place."

"As I told you, I wasn't allowed in. I *live* here."

I keep descending the steps, and I have to be dreaming. That's why I'm hearing the voice that I am. It's my own grief speaking—not Simon.

But as I carefully make my way down, the man whose back is facing me is certainly similar to Simon's. Then there's his broad shoulders. And his chestnut hair. Even his shirt is the same—billowing white and stained with blood. Maybe I'm having a flashback. This person is obviously jittery, beginning to walk away and then returning as he stays in conversation with the employee.

The middle-aged male rubs his eyes, appearing drained and nearing his wit's end. "As I explained to you, sir, as *all* of us explained, there are no horses for us to give you nor is there a messenger for you to send."

"And as *I* explained, I am a gentleman of the king's privy council, and if you would unlock that door there and give me access, I could prove it to you. I need to see the queen."

I look at the door that my hallucination is trying to get to, and I immediately recognize it as being an alternate entrance that eventually leads to the queen's audience chamber.

I keep descending the stairs, now nearing the bottom.

"If you don't leave now, I'm going to call the authorities." The employee notices me approaching and holds his hand up to stop me. "Miss, for your own safety, I'm going to ask that you please return upstairs and use an alternate exit."

IN MY TUDOR ERA

The man he's talking to turns to look at me, and I fall down the last step.

Holy fucking shit!

"Simon?" I semi-shout. This isn't happening. I know that it's not, but . . ."Simon," I say again. He turns around fully, and his startled green eyes land on mine. Searching them. He takes in the rest of my appearance, especially my red hair.

"Lily?"

I barely hear it, but I hear it.

"Are you Lily?" he asks, moving toward me.

I have a clear view of him now, and I see every familiar feature. But I still need to make sure. "What did you take me to see on our walk that you swore you never took anyone to see before?"

A hopeful smile forms on his face. "I took you to see my tree." He hesitates as his expression then turns momentarily guarded. "What were we doing that night when we sat with Theo in the garden?"

Oh my god. Oh my god. Oh my god.

"You were teaching me how to calm him." I think I might be having a heart attack. "Where were we when I recommended bird watching as a hobby instead of jousting?"

"In the servants' hall. I was there because Charlie loves a kitchen maid and he helped me with training."

This is real.

This is real. This is real. This is real.

He walks toward me again, and he doesn't stop until he's standing directly in front of me. "What did you promise to teach me in California?" he asks. He smells the same. He's breathing the same. Everything about him is the same because this is really him.

"I said that I'd teach you how to surf. Then we'd eat tacos, and then we'd go home." I reach out to place my hand on his chest, and he feels the same, too.

"How did you get here?" I ask quietly.

Simon shakes his head. "The last thing I remember is I was being pulled away from you, down the gallery. I thought a guard must have struck me from behind because it felt like I was falling to the floor, but when I opened my eyes, I was here. Everyone was staring at me and asking what part I was meant to be playing."

He lifts a hand, stroking my cheek like he used to, and I close my eyes against the sensation. When I open them, I try to look for signs that I'm making this up. But he's so remarkably real. He dips his thumb to rub under my chin, and he smiles at the feel of it. "The scar is smaller than you made it seem."

This is wild. This is impossible. And I don't care.

"I can't believe it's really you," I say, leaning into his palm. "It said online that you were killed, but the king must have lied about it."

Jealous. Delusional. Petty. All very on brand for Henry.

Simon's eyes never leave mine as he continues to touch my face. "You can keep asking me questions if it makes you feel better. It seems we have plenty of time to spare."

God, I hope that's true. I take a breath and really try to think of something only he would have the answer to. A second later, I know exactly what to ask. "When did you first tell me that you loved me?" It's a trick question, but his small smile makes it clear that he's aware of that fact.

"I haven't told you yet," he answers. "But you know that I do."

My heart might actually implode inside my chest.

When Simon leans down to kiss me, I don't mean to close my eyes. I want to keep looking at him. Reassuring myself over and over that he's here. His mouth moves against mine, and I pull him so close with no intention of ever letting go.

But when the employee clears his throat beside us a few seconds later, I do loosen my hold a little. Simon and I look at him, still in a daze.

"I'm sorry," the older man says firmly, "but I'm going to have to ask you both to leave."

I blink as I gaze over at him, letting my arms fall from around Simon's shoulders. I go to bring them to my side, but Simon catches one of my hands, weaving his fingers through mine.

My stomach flips. How can this be real life?

"Sorry. Yes, we'll leave now," I tell him. I start to move, but then decide against it. I turn back to the man one more time. "Before we go, I just want to double-check, you do see this person with me, don't you?"

The employee looks Simon up and down. "You mean the young man wearing a bloody shirt and tights? Yes, I see him. Quite tall, isn't he?"

My heart soars, and I squeeze Simon's hand tighter. "He really is," I agree. "Thank you so much."

I'm on a cloud as we make our way to the palace exit. Catherine did it. She saved him. Everyone always underestimates her, but Catherine Howard was killed, refused to go to the afterlife, manifested me back in time, and then lived out her life in simple splendor as a secret author, single and free from her toxic royal ex. If that's not boss energy, I don't know what is.

I think of her as Simon and I walk out of Hampton Court Palace hand in hand. There's an undeniable giddiness in my step. We're together. We're breathing. There are so many things I want to show him, and I immediately start drafting a mental list.

But as our feet touch the cobblestones of the now tourist-inhabited courtyard, I glance over at Simon and realize that I *am* going to somewhat miss seeing him dressed in his loose white shirt and britches. Maybe we'll keep the outfit—for birthdays and anniversaries. Because while maybe not all the time, sometimes, it can be fun to embrace your Tudor era.

Acknowledgments

Thank you to my wonderful literary agent, Kevan Lyon, for continuing to believe in me (even when I might not).

Thank you to Dr. Megan Piesman for your amazing and thoughtful insight into the world of psychology.

Mary, thank you for reading this a million times with me. Can you just read it one more time?

And Mom, thank you for sharing in every moment, every update, and every step of this process with me. The best part of getting good news is sharing it with you.

About the Author

Kate Bromley is a romance author, part-time preschool teacher, and full-time book lover. She writes funny, heartfelt love stories filled with sharp banter and happily ever afters. She lives in New York City with her husband and sons.

www.ingramcontent.com/pod-product-compliance
Ingram Content Group UK Ltd.
Pitfield, Milton Keynes, MK11 3LW, UK
UKHW040237250426
12048UKWH00043B/1568